The Negritude Poets

An Anthology of Translations from the French

Edited and with an Introduction by Ellen Conroy Kennedy

A Richard Seaver Book

The Negritude Poets

The Viking Press   New York

Library of Congress Cataloging in Publication Data
Main entry under title:
The Negritude poets.
  "A Richard Seaver book."
  Bibliography: p.
  1. French poetry—Negro authors—Translations into
English.   2. English poetry—Translations from French.
3. French poetry—20th century—Translations into Eng-
lish.   I. Kennedy, Ellen Conroy.
PQ3986.Z5E55   841   72–78987
ISBN 0–670–50579–X

Acknowledgments

For permission to translate "Trahison," "Sacrifice," "Cannibale," "Vaudou," and "Hérédités" from *Musique nègre*, © 1931 Léon Laleau, the editor is grateful to Léon Laleau, rue Grégoire, Pétionville, Haiti; for portions of "Bois d'ébène," "Sales nègres," and "Nouveau sermon nègre" from *La Montagne ensorcelée* by Jacques Roumain, © 1972 Editeurs Français réunis, to Editeurs Français réunis, Paris; for "Ma Grand-mère," "L'Aurore au fond du cirque," "Le Fromager," "Tourbillons," "Le Feu de brousse," "La Rencontre du 'Bida,'" and "Comme d'une fleur" by Fily-Dabo Sissoko from his *Poèmes de l'Afrique noire*, © 1963 by Les Nouvelles Editions Debresse, to Les Nouvelles Editions Debresse, Paris; to M. Flavien Ranaivo, Directeur de l'information et de la radio-télévision Tananarive, Madagascar, for his poems, "Vieux thème mérine," "Vulgaire chanson d'amant," "Emportez-moi," "Le Zébu," "Choix," and "Détresse"; to Editions Gallimard, Paris, for "First Problem" by Aimé Césaire from *Les Armes miraculeuses*, © 1946 by Gallimard; to M. Césaire personally and to The Third Press for several poems from *Cadastre* and *Ferrements*, © 1961 and 1960 by Les Editions du Seuil; to Editions Pierre Jean Oswald, Paris, for extracts from *Feu de Brousse*, © 1957, 1970 by Pierre Jean Oswald, *Le Mauvais sang*, © 1955, 1970 by Pierre Jean Oswald, *Epitome* © 1962, 1970 by Pierre Jean Oswald, and *Arc musical*, © 1970 by Pierre Jean Oswald, all by Tchicaya U Tam'si; to Editions Seghers, Paris, for "Je vous remercie mon dieu," "Souviens-toi," "Le Monde que nait," "Ode à l'Afrique," and "Couronne à l'Afrique," poems by Bernard Dadié from *Légendes et poèmes*, © 1966 by Editions Seghers; and for "Aux Festins de la terre" and "Préceptes congolais" from *Premier Chant du depart* by Martial Sinda, © 1955 by Editions Seghers. For permission to translate poems of J. J. Rabéarivelo, the editor has addressed Les Amis de Rabéarivelo, Tananarive, Madagascar.

For permission to reprint the following copyrighted translations, the editor is most appreciative: Carolyn Kizer's translation, "Seven Sides and Seven Syllables" of Edouard Maunick's "Sept Versants, Sept Syllabes," which first appeared in *Poetry* magazine, July 1968; Teo Savory's translation, "This Strange Calculation of Roots" of Edouard Maunick's "Cet Etrange calcul de racines," which appeared in the *Unicorn Journal*, Spring 1968. Langston Hughes's translations of "Guinea" and "When the Tom-tom Beats" by Jacques Roumain, and John Peale Bishop's translation of "The Peasant Declares His Love" by Emile Roumer appeared in *An Anthology of Contemporary Latin-American Poetry*, edited by Dudley Fitts, © 1942 by New Directions Publishing Corporation, and are reprinted by permission of New Directions Publishing Corporation. "Oblivion," Jessie Redmond Fauset's translation of the poem by Massillon Coicou, is from James Weldon Johnson's *The Book of American Negro Poetry*, © 1922, 1959 by Mrs. Grace Nail Johnson. Edna Worthley Underwood's translation of "Country Graveyard"

114916

by Charles Pressoir is from her *Poets of Haiti,* Mosher Press, Portland, Maine, 1934. The editor is grateful to Clayton Eshleman and Denis Kelly for translation of poems by Aimé Césaire that appeared in slightly different version in a Caterpillar booklet, *State of the Union,* Bloomington, Indiana, 1966.

All other translations of poems appearing in this volume are the editor's, although some in the Africa section benefited from Paulette J. Trout's first drafts. Translations of eight of the eleven poems by David Diop in this volume first appeared in *Journal of the New African Literature and the Arts.* The translations of "French Garden," "Three Nocturnes," and "To New York" by Léopold Senghor were first published in *Sample Copy,* University of North Carolina, Chapel Hill. The translations of sixteen poems by Léon Damas, together with an article on his work, previously appeared in *Black World.*

For permission to translate the following poems the editor is grateful to *Présence Africaine,* Paris: "Bonguemba," "Dans une tempête," and "Esanzo" from Antoine-Roger Bolamba's *Esanzo,* © 1955 by Présence Africaine; Aimé Césaire's *Cahier d'un retour au pays natal,* © 1956 by Présence Africaine; "Ils sont venus ce soir," "Obsession," "Il est des nuits," "Position," "Hoquet," "Solde," "Limbé," "La Complainte du nègre," "Si souvent," "Nuit blanche," "Blanchi," "Pareille à la légende," "Shine," "Réalité," "Ils ont," and "Et Cetera" from *Pigments* by Léon G. Damas, © 1962 by Présence Africaine; "Minerai noir" from *Minerai noir,* © 1956 by Présence Africaine, and "Romancero d'une petite lampe" and "Epiphanies des dieux de vaudou" from *Un Arc-en-ciel pour l'occident chrétien,* © 1967 by René Depestre; "Animism," "Kassak," "Viatique," "Désert," "Diptyque," "Souffles," and "Présage" from Birago Diop's *Leurres et Lueurs,* © 1967 by Editions Présence Africaines; "Les Vautours," "Ecoutez, Camarades," "Défi," "Le Temps du Martyr," "A un enfant noir," "A ma mère," "Les heures," "Nègre clochard," "Afrique," "Rama Kam," and "Auprès de toi" from David Diop's *Coups de pilon,* © 1956 by Présence Africaine; "Pays chauds" and "Silence" from René Maran's *Le Livre du souvenir,* © 1958 by Présence Africaine; passages from Edouard Maunick's "Jusqu'en terra Yoruba," from *Présence Africaine,* no. 54, 1965; "A mon mari" by Yambo Ouologuem, from *Présence Africaine,* no. 57, 1966; an abridged version of Jacques Rabémananjara's *Antsa,* © 1962 by Présence Africaine, also an extract from *Lamba,* © 1961 by Présence Africaine, and the poem "Complainte" from *Antidote,* © 1961 by Présence Africaine; "Black Beauty," "Marie Galante," "Prière d'un petit enfant nègre," and "Ghetto" from Guy Tirolien's *Balles d'or,* © 1961 by Présence Africaine; "Mon Pays," "Berceuse," "A Toi," "Amour," and "Femme" from Elolongue Epanya Yondo's *Kamerun! Kamerun!,* © 1960 by Présence Africaine.

The editor thanks Editions du Seuil, Paris, France, for permission to translate parts IL, L, LI, and LII of "Les Indes" by Edouard Glissant, from his *Poèmes,* © 1965 by Editions du Seuil, and for permission to translate selections from *Poèmes* by Léopold Sédar Senghor, © 1964 by Editions du Seuil. From that latter volume the following poems are reprinted by permission of Georges Borchardt, Inc.: "Jardin de France," "Joal," "Masque nègre," and "Je ne sais en quel temps c'était." It should be noted that the following poems from the same volume, printed here in the editor's translations, are not available for reprint and appear by special permission of Atheneum Publishers: "Night of Sine," "Prayer to the Masks," "The Totem," "Ode for Three Kôras and Balaphong," "Return of the Prodigal Son," "Prayer for Peace," "New York," "Midnight Elegy," and the excerpts from "Songs of Signare" which begin: "Long, long you have held between your hands," and "And we shall bathe, my dear, in an ambience of Africa." Readers are referred to the volume entitled *Selected Poems* by Léopold Sédar

Senghor published by Atheneum Publishers, in translations by John Reed and Clive Wake.

Special thanks, too, to The Third Press for permission to use the editor's own translations of the two "Songs for Signare," beginning "I walked you to the village . . ." and "Your face, the beauty . . . ," and "Song of the Initiate," all from *Nocturnes*. The reader is referred to the Third Press edition of *Nocturnes* translated by John Reed and Clive Wake. The editor also wishes to thank The Third Press for allowing her to use the translations by Clayton Eshleman and Denis Kelly of Aimé Césaire's "Magic," "Missisippi," and "The Wheel," all from *Cadastre*, and of the same poet's "Beat it, Night Dog" and "On the State of the Union," from *Ferrements*. Readers are referred to The Third Press's edition of both works, in translations by Emile Snyder and Sanford Upson.

Finally, for permission to reprint Sangodare Akanji's translation of "Brushfire" from Tchicaya U Tam'si's book of the same name, thanks to the Mbari Society at Ibadan, Nigeria.

For Pat
and our children,
Oliver and Erin,
and for
two other mentors,
Saunders and Germaine

Acknowledgments

The editor hereby gratefully acknowledges those other readers, historians, critics, interpreters, anthologists, and translators of black French-language writings, without whom her own work would have been impossible: Lilyan Kesteloot, Armand Guibert, Gerald Moore, Ulli Beier, Janheinz Jahn, Abiola Irele, Clive Wake, Léopold Sédar Senghor. She wishes particularly to thank Paulette J. Trout for earlier, joint endeavors on African poetry in French, on which portions of the present volume have inevitably drawn.

This anthology owes much as well to friends and colleagues thirteen years of exploring black literatures have brought: Samuel W. Allen; Wilfred Cartey; Mercer Cook; Marietta and Léon G. Damas; Christiane and Alioune Diop, and their daughter, Marie-Aida Diop Bah; James Farrell; Judith Gleason; Helen Kitchen; Carolyn Kizer; Charles R. Larson; Taban Lo Liyong; Maurice Lubin; Edouard Maunick; and Dorothy Porter.

Melissa T. Jones, Reather Kelly, Olwen Price, and Katherine Litzau were more than generous in helping complete the manuscript and caring about its contents. Alice Jugie in Paris was tirelessly resourceful at tracking down photos and recalcitrant permissions.

But most of all I owe thanks to Germaine Brée, for many years of encouragement; to J. Saunders Redding, for the original invitation to undertake this book; and to Jeannette and Richard Seaver, my editors. Padraic Kennedy knows my gratitude for many more elusive forms of sustenance.

All translations in *The Negritude Poets* not specifically credited to other translators are the editor's own.

Contents

Caribbean Poets in French

African Poets in French

Indian Ocean Poets in French

Introduction

Poetry has been the single most important artistic manifestation of the black-world cultural and intellectual movement which, since the close of World War II, has come to be known as "negritude." This anthology traces its development by gathering, translating, and commenting on key texts of black poetry in French since 1900, and by situating the men who wrote them. In all, twenty-seven poets are represented by approximately 170 poems. These poems, together with the commentaries, offer a broad perspective of the poetry of black self-awareness in French, a body of work still neglected and too little understood in the English-speaking world.

Until very recently, most of the poets included in the present volume were relatively unknown in America. Aimé Césaire's long poem *Cahier d'un retour au pays natal* (*Notes on a Return to the Native Land*), which coined the word "negritude," was published in 1944 in France, with a preface by André Breton, and enthusiastically received. Three years later, a French-English edition of *Notes,* still the "lyrical monument" of this group literature, was published in New York by Brentano's, in a translation by Lionel Abel and Ivan Goll under the title *Memorandum on My Martinique.* Despite Breton's laudatory preface, the American edition of the work seems to have vanished virtually without leaving a trace. By 1947 and 1948 the negritude poets were already making their mark in France, in anthologies edited respectively by Léon Damas and Léopold Sédar Senghor. Another ten years were to pass, however, before black poets in French would begin to make any impact on English-language readers.

In April 1959 a special Africa issue of the *Atlantic Monthly,* illustrated with photographs of African sculpture, offered translations of short poems by David Diop, Léopold Senghor, and Tchicaya U Tam'si, along with three African folk songs transcribed by Léon Damas. In the early

1960s translations of the same poets, plus two others—Birago Diop and Jean-Joseph Rabéarivelo—appeared occasionally in little magazines (notably the Nigeria-based *Black Orpheus*), and in a few African, British, and American anthologies devoted to Africa. In 1964 a first volume of poems by Léopold Senghor, selected and translated by two British scholars, John Reed and Clive Wake, was published in England and reprinted in New York the following year.

The American public had little or no notion that the new African poetry in French was closely related *not* to the African poetry of English-speaking neighboring lands, which blossomed later under different influences, but to the work of contemporary black West Indians. Aimé Césaire, Léon Damas, and Jacques Roumain, poets from the French Caribbean, shared with the French West Africans the international racial awareness summarized by "negritude"; indeed, the two groups of writers had created it together during their student years in Paris on the eve of World War II; they were soon joined by the Madagascan writer Jacques Rabémananjara. If the importance of the Caribbean poets was mentioned, they were carefully set aside and dismissed by anthologists of the Africans as a separate group. Despite their growing interest in continental Africa, British and American scholars also ignored the fact that both these groups of poets had been strongly influenced, thematically and stylistically, by American poets of the Harlem Renaissance.

During their student days in France in the 1930s, many young African and West Indian poets-to-be read Langston Hughes, Countee Cullen, James Weldon Johnson, Claude McKay, Jean Toomer, and Sterling Brown, both in English and in French translations, and were deeply struck by their ideas and their approach to literature. The Africans and West Indians even came to know several of the black American writers personally on the latters' visits to Europe. Revolutionary in its day, Hughes's declaration of the 1920s, "We younger Negro artists who create now intend to express our individual dark-skinned selves without fear or shame," became one of their rallying cries. The carefree spontaneity of ethnic life in Claude McKay's novel, *Banjo,* became another romantic ideal for the Senghor-Damas-Césaire generation.

In the early 1960s the American civil-rights movement was forcing reforms that had a great impact on American society. The new black self-awareness was also giving birth to a new generation of black American poets: LeRoi Jones, Donn L. Lee, Nikki Giovanni, Sonia Sanchez, and others. They rarely knew or read French, and generally had little more than a nodding acquaintance with the black French-language poets whose work has such strong thematic and stylistic parallels with their own. As late as the fall of 1969, Julius Lester, surveying the black literary scene in *The New York Times Book Review,* decried the absence of English-language editions of the uniquely important black French-language writer, Aimé Césaire. At the start of the 1970s, it was still only Africa, the black poets of Africa, and writings on African themes that were thought to be of interest to the American reading public, and only these had been published.

Senghor's subtle response to racism, the carefully mastered anger, for example, in many of his World War II poems, *Hosties noires (Black Host),** was overlooked. David Diop's "Africa!" "Vultures," or "A Time of Martyrdom" were sometimes included by anthologists who noticed the younger Senegalese was violently anticolonial, but no one translated his poem on Emmett Till, whose more universal protest against racial injustice strikes closer to home. Bernard Dadié's moving "I Thank You, Lord, for Having Made Me Black" was likewise omitted from English-language anthologies of this era.

Also unknown in America—on the grounds that he was a Caribbean (and therefore automatically a "marginal" poet)—was Léon Damas, who in 1937 had stung the French, in his volume entitled *Pigments,* with lines like these:

> . . . I always feel about
> to foam with rage
> against what surrounds me
> against what prevents me
> ever from being a man

and the Haitian Jacques Roumain, whose *Bois d'ebène (Ebony Wood),* poems published in 1944 after his untimely death, included:

> We're simply
> done
> in Africa
> in America
> with being
> your negroes

* The title's double allusion is to African soldiers who were both "black victims" and sometimes, by sacrificing their lives, a "black host" or offering, in the Eucharistic sense.

> your niggers
> your dirty niggers
> we won't take it any more . . .

Until now, except for a few American black poets and intellectuals—notably Langston Hughes, Samuel Allen, Mercer Cook, and the Trinidad-born Wilfred Cartey—and a few white academics, the work of Aimé Césaire and other French Antillean poets remained virtually unknown in the United States, and unpublished. During the early 1950s when he lived in Paris, Samuel Allen recalls, he fruitlessly sent dozens of letters, articles, and poems he had translated to numerous American literary magazines on behalf of the editors of *Présence Africaine.* It was fifteen or twenty years too soon, he concluded, for this literature or its ideas to make their mark in America.

Jean-Paul Sartre's essay "Black Orpheus," however, published as a preface to Senghor's anthology in 1948, had even then called attention to the racial themes in both the new West Indian and, to a lesser extent, the African poetry in French. In addition to Sartre's essay, there were, by the late 1950s, Samuel Allen's valuable article "The Black Poet's Search for Identity," and *Muntu,* by Janheinz Jahn, the German popularizer of African culture. There were also the literary articles and poems regularly appearing in *Présence Africaine,* and the limited editions of many individual poets it published. A few African and West Indian writers—Senghor, Césaire, Glissant, Dadié—were published by the large French houses. By 1962 the first literary history and criticism of the negritude poets was published by the Belgian scholar Lilyan Kesteloot.* Her short study of Césaire in the popular *Poètes d'aujourd'hui* series appeared shortly thereafter, as did Armand Guibert's volume on Senghor. Robert Boudry's little-known but valuable booklet on the Madagascan poet Rabéarivelo was published by *Présence Africaine* in 1958. These were among the indispensable sources on which foreign scholars could rely for a guide to the new black writers, for essential background and bibliographic information.

Even during the 1960s "negritude" was touchy, vague, mystical—a much-misunderstood affair. Certain of Senghor's early statements seemed to suggest that there were genetic rather than cultural differences of sensibility between blacks and whites. These were anathema to English-speaking black writers such as Ezekiel Mphalele, a self-exiled victim of

---

* Published in English as *Black Writers in French: A Literary History of Negritude* (Philadelphia: Temple University Press, 1974).

apartheid South Africa. The young Nigerian Wole Soyinka made fun of them with his witticism on tigers and "tigritude." A similar skepticism toward negritude has affected the newer generation of English-speaking writers who emerged in the late 1960s from East Africa: the Ugandan Taban Lo Liyong and the Kenyan James Ngugi. Like Mphalele and the Nigerian poets and novelists, they wish to create and be judged by universal standards of art, to draw freely on whatever inspiration and models they choose. To them negritude has suggested a romanticization of Africa, an aesthetic restriction to some doubtful "universal black style," an emphasis on traditional African literary forms; in short a limitation of the artistic vision to that which flatters, that which protests, that which has social or political usefulness, rather than to an individual search for truth.

To some of these writers of various nationalities "negritude," "black culture," or "negro-ness" has often looked like the sterile rhetoric of some new form of segregation rather than of pan-ethnic liberation.

It is perhaps significant that the young Nigerian poets nurtured at Ibadan in the late 1950s and early 1960s found formal and stylistic inspiration in such Americans as Ezra Pound and T. S. Eliot, but not at all in black American poets—unlike their French-language counterparts. The decade of the '60s appears to have had a similar effect on most Ghanaian and Sierra Leonean intellectuals as well. More pressing needs and preoccupations in those years took precedence over an exploration of their potential relationship to the rest of the black world. Soyinka's sarcastic attitude toward negritude can perhaps best be understood as a rejection of any overly simplistic view of universal black solidarity—literary or otherwise.

On the black American scene "negritude" has had its difficulties, too. Asserting that "very few American Negroes are of pure African blood," Ralph Ellison has commented at length on the "Americanness" of black American experience:

> . . . The American Negro people is North American in origin and has evolved under specifically American conditions; climatic, nutritional, historical, political and social. It takes its character from the experience of American slavery and the struggle for, and the achievement of, emancipation; from the dynamics of American race and caste discrimination, and from living in a highly industrialized and highly mobile society possessing a relatively high standard of living and an explicitly stated equalitarian concept of freedom. Its spiritual outlook is basically Protestant, its system of kinship is Western, its time and historical sense are American (United

States), and its secular values are those professed, ideally at least, by all of the people of the United States.

Culturally this people represents one of the many sub-cultures which make up that great amalgam of European and native American cultures which is the culture of the United States. This "American Negro Culture" is expressed in a body of folklore, in the musical forms of the spirituals, the blues and jazz; an idiomatic version of American speech (especially in the Southern United States); a cuisine, a body of dance forms and even a dramaturgy which is generally unrecognized as such because still tied to the more folkish Negro churches.*

"It is not culture which binds the peoples who are of partially African origin now scattered throughout the world," Ellison continues, "but an identity of passions. We share a hatred for the alienation forced upon us by Europeans during the process of colonization and empire, and we are bound by our common suffering more than by our pigmentation. But even this identification," Ellison maintains, "is shared by most non-white peoples, and while it has political value of great potency, its cultural value is almost nil."†

In *Notes of a Native Son*, James Baldwin writes of the ten years he spent as a young man in Paris, "involved, in another language, in the same old battle; the battle for his identity." Baldwin describes his reaction to meeting French-speaking black students from Africa:

> . . . there begins to race within him, like the despised beat of the tom-tom, echoes of a past he has not yet been able to utilize, intimations of a responsibility he has not yet been able to face. . . .
>
> They face each other, the [American] Negro and the African, over a gulf of three hundred years—an alienation too vast to be conquered in an evening's good will, too heavy and too double-edged ever to be trapped in speech.‡

In *Nobody Knows My Name*, Baldwin asks, and answers, the question, "Do the earth's black populations [have] anything that can legitimately be called a culture?" His response is close in spirit to Ellison's. After brilliantly characterizing the widely disparate personalities and viewpoints of the delegates, and reacting strongly himself as an American, Baldwin concludes:

* *Shadow and Act* (New York: Random House, 1964)
† *Ibid.*
‡ New York: Dial Publishing Co., 1964

. . . there *was* something which all black men held in common, some-
thing which cut across opposing points of view, and placed in the same
context their widely dissimilar experience. *What they held in common
was their precarious, their unutterably painful relation to the white world.
What they held in common was the necessity to remake the world and no
longer be controlled by the vision of the world and of themselves held by
other people.* What, in sum, black men held in common was their ache
to come into the world as men. And this ache united people who might
otherwise have been divided as to what a man should be.*

"An identity of passions" that black men held in common (Ellison's
phrase) is precisely the theme that emerges most forcefully from the
pages of this anthology. It runs through Césaire's *Notes,* from the first
evocation of the imprisoned Toussaint Louverture to the final picture of
the poet himself atop the mountain on his island. The image recurs in a
dozen powerful variations in the poems of Roumain, Dadié, David Diop,
U Tam'si, Maunick, and in Depestre's "Ballad of a Little Lamp." The
reverse images also abound, particularly in the poems of Damas, in
Césaire's *Notes* and in Glissant's *The Indies*—the sensations of choking
oppression, of human beings denied their integrity.

The ultimate effect of this poetry is supremely ethnic, but also more
than ethnic. As Sartre put it twenty-five years ago, "This poetry, which
at first appears so racial, is ultimately the song of every one of us and for
every one of us."

Throughout human history, art and literature have given the most
illuminating and enduring record of peoples and civilizations. One may,
like Ellison, have serious reservations about whether there is some uni-
versal African-derived common-denominator culture of black peoples.
One may share Baldwin's uncertainty about "the despised beat of the tom-
tom," the implications of an African past one "has not yet been able to
utilize." Where literature is concerned, one can at least postulate that
identities of passion have produced, and will continue to produce, writ-
ings from the Negro diaspora that will be significantly related in theme,
in subject matter, and perhaps as well in style. But the question cannot
even be intelligently discussed without careful comparative studies of
these contemporary literatures, which exist in poems, plays, novels, short
stories, and essays by peoples of African descent in Africa and the rest of
the Western world.

* New York: Dell Publishing Co., 1961. (Italics added)

114916

The First World Festival of Negro Art held at Dakar in 1966 was based on the assumption that there was such an international relationship in all the arts. Whether or not one subscribes to this assumption, one has to admit that the Festival called well-deserved attention to many artists and art forms still known only locally, highlighting their relationship to one another by genre, subject matter, style, and language. The literary awards given at the Festival constituted the first critical survey of black literature on an international basis.* Virtually ignored at the time in the United States, the English-language literary prizes honored several Americans, including Kenneth Clark for his sociological study *Dark Ghetto,* and LeRoi Jones for his one-act plays. Robert Hayden, who won the Grand Prize for poetry, was scarcely known in the United States at the time, but has since published two volumes of poetry and begun to earn the reputation he deserves. The greatest contribution of the Dakar literary awards, however, was to underscore the fact that black literatures are thriving, that they have an international past, present, and future deserving not only an international readership but the continuing evaluation and attention of informed observers.

There already exists a small but growing international community of scholars devoting their careers to the study and teaching of black literature. It is they, and their students, who will be the translators, critics, anthologists, biographers, historians, editors, teachers, and interpreters of these writings throughout the world in years to come.

To accept the concept of an international black literature as valid and useful is by no means to suggest that writers of African descent can be viewed or judged only on an ethnic basis. Langston Hughes, for example, is indisputably an American writer, whose work is part of the mainstream of twentieth-century American literature. Yet, as a black writer expressing a particular personal and group sensibility, Hughes's work has had, and will doubtless continue to have, an impact on writers in lands as far-flung as South Africa, Haiti, and Senegal. Similarly, while Aimé Césaire of Martinique is a poet, essayist, and playwright intimately connected with French culture, French surrealism, and the French literary heritage, it is above all as a black man that he addresses the world and his people. "We reclaim ourselves with precocious insanity, with blazing madness, with tenacious cannibalism. Accommodate yourselves to me. I do not accom-

---

* For a more detailed account see Ellen Conroy Kennedy, "A Literary Postscript on the Dakar Festival," *African Forum,* Summer, 1967, pp. 54–58.

modate myself to you!" he cried by way of literary manifesto many years ago in his magazine *Tropiques*.

There is a character in Genet's *The Blacks* who declares, "Make poetry, since that's the only domain in which we're allowed to operate." From the mid-1930s until the eve of African independence, direct political action was in general immediately and forcefully repressed in the French colonial empire. Poetry, rather than the essay or any of the more extended literary forms, became for black French-language intellectuals a powerful emotional and aesthetic outlet.

That the negritude movement has produced so many artists of the first rank is, on one level, a tribute to the French culture they both acquired and transformed. On another level, making, reading, absorbing, and responding to negritude poetry became a form of "consciousness-raising," through which one participated in forging a new vision of self and group. Negritude poets have often addressed their poems to one another like open letters. A poem is sometimes one half of a dialogue in which ideas and feelings are exchanged. The "Introductory Poem" of Senghor's World War II book *Black Host,* for example, is dedicated to Léon Damas, and constitutes Senghor's reply to the final sardonic call to action in Damas's *Pigments*.

Similarly, David Diop and Francesco Ndintsouna salute Damas's "They Came That Night" with their own imitations of his signature poem about the European violation of Africa. The dedication makes their borrowings an explicit homage. Jacques Roumain's and Senghor's debts to James Weldon Johnson, and David Diop's often subtler debt to Roumain and Césaire are remarked on later in this volume.

By 1950 the work of the elder generation of black poets was having great impact on a new generation of students from the colonies. Thanks to *Présence Africaine* and the activities of S.A.C. (The Society of African Culture), postwar black students knew and read their elders and followed their debates, both poetic and ideological. Many tried their hands at poetry themselves, publishing their verse in often short-lived student magazines, in privately printed vanity editions, or even in the pages of *Présence Africaine*.

By the 1960s the best of this new black literature, not only poetry but folk tales, stories, novels, plays, and essays, was being included in school and college programs in French West Africa, Africanizing a curriculum that had long focused on French culture alone. In the present decade the same literature may well find a place in American college and school curricula that have too long emphasized the cultures of Western Europe alone.

Since the 1930s black French-language, or "negritude," poets have reflected not only an awareness of their ethnic past but a sensitivity to current events. Damas in *Pigments,* published in 1937, was even then aware of the horror of Nazi racism toward the Jews and its threatening implications for the black man. Poems of Roumain in the early 1940s, of Césaire and David Diop in the late 1950s, react to incidents of racial injustice in America as well as those in the French colonies and South Africa. Maunick's "Seven Sides and Seven Syllables" projects images of the racial incidents in Birmingham, Alabama, in the early 1960s and of his visit to Nigerian shrines later in the decade. In his newest, untranslated book of poems *Fusillez-Moi!* (*Shoot Me!*), Maunick responds to the tragic Biafra–Nigeria War. U Tam'si's poems reflect the bitter experience of the Congo in the '60s, of his friend Lumumba's death as well as the more hermetic record of his personal life. Depestre's *Arc-en-ciel pour l'occident chrétien* (*Rainbow for the Christian West*) protests the American involvement in the Bay of Pigs, while his most recent work, *Cantate d'octobre* (*October Cantata*), is inspired by the death of Che Guevara.

Living amid the ferment of four generations of twentieth-century life, many of the poets in this volume, whether West Indian, African, or Indian Ocean islanders, have played a significant role in politics. Two paid for their political beliefs with their lives, meeting death at the hands of their own countrymen: Massillon Coicou of Haiti in 1908, and Fily-Dabo Sissoko of Mali in 1964. Others, such as Bernard Dadié of the Ivory Coast or Jacques Rabémananjara of Madagascar, knew the grim walls of French colonial prisons in the 1940s and 1950s. Some, such as René Depestre or Edouard Maunick, still live in exile from their native lands whether by choice or by necessity. From the lifelong deeply religious conservatism of Léopold Sédar Senghor of Senegal, moreover, to the equally lifelong revolutionary communism of the Haitian René Depestre, these poets represent every shade of political opinion.

From a literary viewpoint, they present a similar range, from the personally accented classical verse of Durand, Coicou, Laleau, and Maran of the "tracing-paper poet" generation to all the idiosyncratic variations of free verse style of the negritude group: the hallucinatory fantasy world of a Rabéarivelo; the ironic, staccato malaise of a Léon Damas; the pounding militant vision of a David Diop or a Jacques Roumain; the nostalgic evocations of the Senegalese past of a Senghor or a Birago Diop; the lost Africa depicted by a Paul Niger, a Guy Tirolien; the powerful voodoo exorcism of a Depestre; the great dramatic sweep of an Aimé Césaire; the dazzling self-deprecatory irony of Tchicaya U Tam'si or Léon Damas; the simple lyricism of Sissoko, Yondo, or Bernard Dadié.

Because the emphasis of this anthology has been not only literary but also historical and social, literary criteria have obviously not been the sole factor in determining its contents. The object has been to present a representative spectrum of black poets from the former French colonial empire. The twenty-seven poets were born and raised in six nations of West and Central Africa; on islands in the seas of two hemispheres, the Caribbean, and the Indian Ocean. They come from vastly different points on the globe; they come from all sorts of family backgrounds and economic levels. They are city, country, and village people, with varying educations, who have made their living in many different callings. Sometimes they are widely traveled, with the unsettling experience of living in other cultures for extended periods of time—like Senghor, Tchicaya U Tam'si, and Edouard Maunick. Sometimes, like the extraordinary Rabéarivelo of Madagascar, they lived their entire lives within a few hundred miles of the place of their birth. Most grew up in intimate contact with either Christianity—usually Roman Catholicism—or Islam, and often with some form of African animist tradition as well. Many emerge from traditional African cultures, or, like Depestre, from a Haitian culture close to its African roots, and their poetry bears these rich traces.

However different the background—geographical, economic, educational—of the twenty-seven poets whose works are presented in these pages, they speak to us with beauty, humor, eloquence—and often anger— that transcends the barriers of race and language. In projecting their private visions, fears, and frustrations, they allow us to see and feel what they have felt and seen, and to discover anew the bonds that unite us all in brotherhood.

E. C. K.
Columbia, Maryland

Chronology

1885–1900	New universal non-patriotic racial themes in poetry of Oswald Durand and Massillon Coicou of Haiti.
1903	W. E. B. DuBois's *Souls of Black Folk* (U.S.A.).
1921	René Maran's *Batouala: véritable roman nègre* is published in Paris and receives Goncourt Prize. DuBois and NAACP convene Pan African Congress in London, Brussels, and Paris.
1922–1930	The Harlem Renaissance. Claude McKay, James Weldon Johnson, Jean Toomer, Countee Cullen, Langston Hughes, Sterling Brown are publishing separately. Considered as a group in Alain Locke's anthology *The New Negro,* 1925 (U.S.A.).
1927	*La Revue indigène,* influenced by the thought of Jean Price Mars, is founded in Haiti by Jacques Roumain, Emile Roumer, and others.
1928	Jean Price Mars's *Ainsi parla l'oncle* is published in Haiti. French translation of McKay's *Banjo* is published in Paris.
1930–1934	*La Revue du monde noir* is published in Paris; editor, Mlle. Paulette Nardal, has salon where black American, West Indian, and African writers meet.
1932	The single issue of *Légitime Défense* appears in Paris, and is suppressed.
1934	*L'Etudiant noir* is founded by Léon Damas, Léopold Senghor, and Aimé Césaire.
1937	J. J. Rabéarivelo commits suicide in Madagascar. Léon Damas publishes *Pigments* in Paris.
1939	Aimé Césaire publishes parts of *Cahier d'un retour au pays natal* in French magazine *Volontés.*
1941–1943	*Tropiques,* a magazine edited by Aimé and Suzanne

Césaire, appears in Martinique. Discovery of Aimé Césaire by André Breton.

1945 Jacques Roumain's *Bois d'ebène* published in Port-au-Prince.

1946 French Union is created; Césaire, Damas, Senghor, Rabémananjara, Tchicaya (*père*), Sissoko, and other colonials are elected to French National Assembly. Césaire's *Les Armes miraculeuses* is published in Paris.

1947 Malagasy Rebellion; Rabémananjara, in prison, writes *Song*. Complete *Cahier* is published in Paris with preface by Breton; a bilingual French-English edition appears simultaneously in New York. Senghor's *Chants d'ombre* and Damas's anthology *Poètes d'expression française d'outremer* appear in Paris.

1948 Richard Wright moves to Paris. Senghor's *Hosties noires* and his *Anthologie de la nouvelle poésie nègre et malgache*, with preface by Jean-Paul Sartre, "*Orphée noir*," are published. Founding of *Présence Africaine*, Alioune Diop, editor.

1952 Frantz Fanon's *Peau noire, masques blancs* is published in Paris.

1954 U.S. Supreme Court declares public school segregation unconstitutional.

1955 U.S. Supreme Court orders public school desegregation "with all deliberate speed." Emmet Till is murdered in Money, Mississippi.

1956 First Congress of Negro Artists and Writers is held in Paris. Martin Luther King, Jr., leads bus boycott in Montgomery, Alabama. David Diop's *Coups de pilon* is published in Paris. School desegregation incidents in U.S.

1957 Ghana gains independence. First Federal Civil Rights law since Reconstruction creates Civil Rights Division in Justice Department.

1958 Second Congress of Negro Artists and Writers held in Rome. Guinea becomes independent of France.

1960 Senegal, Ivory Coast, Mali, Cameroon, Congo/Brazzaville, and other African nations granted independence from France. Civil war in (formerly Belgian) Congo/Léopoldville. Lumumba dies.

1961   Frantz Fanon's *Les Damnés de la terre* published in Paris.
       Fanon dies in U.S. Freedom Rides in United States.
1962   Tchicaya U Tam'si's *Epitomé* published in Paris. Algerian
       independence after five-year revolution. 1000 jailed in civil
       rights demonstrations in Albany, Georgia.
1963   Martin Luther King, Jr., leads demonstrations in Birming-
       ham, Alabama. The March on Washington.
1964   Senghor's *Poèmes* collected in single volume. Maunick's
       Les Manèges de la mer published in Paris. Civil Rights Act
       —strongest in U.S. history—prohibits racial discrimination
       in public places, bars poll taxes.
1965   Malcolm X assassinated. Voting Rights Act outlaws literacy
       tests in U.S.
1966   First World Festival of Negro Arts held in Dakar, Senegal.
       Prizes for Black Literature in English and French. Concept
       of "Black Power" first articulated in U.S.A. Fanon's
       Wretched of the Earth published in New York.
1967   Summer of black riots in 100 American cities. Fanon's
       Black Skin, White Masks published in New York. Biafra
       secedes from Nigeria to begin 20-month Civil War. De-
       pestre publishes *Un Arc-en-ciel pour l'occident chrétien.*
1968   Martin Luther King, Jr., assassinated. Rioting in 125
       American cities. Student strikes. June, Robert F. Kennedy
       assassinated. August, violence erupts in Chicago at Demo-
       cratic National Convention. November, Nixon elected.
1969   Black studies requested by students at 140 American uni-
       versities; Ford Foundation grants $1 million to help develop
       programs.
1970   New editions of Césaire's poems appear in France, London,
       Mexico City. Damas moves to U.S.A. Maunick publishes
       Fusillez-Moi! U Tam'si's *Selected Poems* appear in Eng-
       lish.
1972   Damas's *Pigments and Névralgies* reprinted in Paris.
1973   *Présence Africaine* enters twenty-fifth consecutive year of
       publication.
1975   Second World Festival of Negro Arts held in Lagos,
       Nigeria.

Caribbean Poets in French

 Durand

 Coicou

Maran

Laleau

Roumain

Roumer

Pressoir

Tirolien

Niger

Damas

Césaire

Glissant

Depestre

HAITI *(1840–1906)*

Oswald Durand

OSWALD DURAND, PLAYWRIGHT, ESSAYIST, AND POET, noted for his "merry and tempestuous living," is the grand old man of Haitian letters. If most of his patriotic eulogies and sentimental love poems—written in the style of such popular nineteenth-century French poets as Victor Hugo—are of little interest today, there is, nonetheless, a quality in much of Durand's work that proves, as a recent Haitian critic maintains, that he was "the first . . . to capture nuances of the real Haitian world."

"Francie-the-Possessed," composed not in Creole but in French, describes a voodoo ceremony Durand himself must have witnessed. Such religious rites, closely related to those of West African tribes from which the original population of Haiti is descended, survive almost intact in rural Haiti to this day.

Among Durand's conventional French poems there are verses addressed to a host of young ladies—Leilas, Idalinas, Mariannes—aristocrats and simple country girls. "The Black Man's Son" records the sting of prejudices still not rare a hundred years after this poem was written.

Francie-the-Possessed

See her there, Francie-the-Mad
   entering the circle.
She's possessed, she flies
   —Gaze upon her face!

She prays and falls upon her
   knees before the crowd.
Her rolling eyes are wild.

She motions for a knife,
her almond eyes
    fixed on the unknown.

Between her hands the weapon
    glints like flame.
She leaps, she calls upon her
    dreadful God, on Legba.

The drums are thundering,
    the hands clap time,
the joyous crowd takes up
    the long refrain.

There she is, the black girl, Francie,
    whirling,
the spirit is within her, thirsting
    —Look upon her face!

Silence now, the sybil speaks.
The crowd, long motionless, draws near.

The spirit murmurs mystic words
    of blood, of life and death,
and as in ancient times
    the oracle emerges.

It is that Legba, awesome god,
    requires blood,
and stalks among the fearful band
    in search of it.

Hear the drum thunder,
    the hands clapping.
The crowd grows anxious,
    listening to the dark refrain.

See her there, lightfooted Francie,
    entering the circle.
The deadly god, his law, hold her in trance
    —Gaze upon her face.

So tiny that she scarcely treads
    the gleaming ground.

Her skin's as black as ebony
    without the slightest wrinkle.

Before her now a pure white lamb is led,
his head with lace and ribbons decked.

They dance around the victim,
    chorusing the chant,
awaiting the ecstatic moment,
    the instant of the blow.

The rumbling drum,
    the clapping hands,
monotonously beat
    the long refrain.

See her there, the lovely Francie
    whirling.
She turns and takes the bleating lamb
    —Gaze upon her face!

The time is near, the moment
    close at hand.
Preparing for the sacrifice,
    Francie takes the knife.

The weapon in her hands
    shoots fire.
The sybil bows, calls out to Legba!

The priestess, eyes ablaze,
    strikes twice.
The lamb falls, and the crowd
    acclaims the Voodoo god.

The drum roars, thundering
    like cannon,
Ending now the long refrain,
    The long and toneless chant.

The Black Man's Son

At twenty, I loved Lise. She was frail and white.
While I, child of the sun, alas! too dark for her
Won scarce a glance from those bright eyes.

Yet my mother was as white as Lise.
She too had shining eyes of blue;
And when she blushed in fear or in delight
Pomegranates seemed to bloom.

Her hair was blond as well, and in the breeze
Veiled a face grown pale with grief.
My father was more black than I.
But church had joined their colors in a sacred knot.

And then on her fair breast one saw the sweet antithesis
—a babe as brown and golden as the maize,
As ardent as our tropic sun is, always.

Orphaned, I saw Lise and loved her.
Her face grew pale such trembling words to hear
The black man's son struck fear
                    in the white folks' daughter.

Ϻᴀssіⅼⅼοη Ϲοіϲου

LIKE DURAND, HIS MUCH YOUNGER CONTEMPORARY Massillon Coicou belonged to a privileged elite whose cultural orientation was entirely toward the French. Durand and Coicou were cultivated, well-educated Haitians who held many government posts at home and abroad, devoting themselves to literary pursuits in their spare time. Their prime importance lies in those themes in their work that anticipate the Haitian Renaissance of the 1920s: the emphasis on authentic folk sources related to the African past and the life of the common people.

With Coicou there was an additional humanitarian concern: his keen sense of social injustice. The Haitian critic Ghislain Gouraige writes that Coicou's historical dramas on Haitian themes, his social satires and poetry were often a "condemnation of his time, the poverty of the peasants, the exile of the better classes [to Europe] and the blind exercise of criminal power."

Just a few years after his *Liberté* (*Liberty*) had been performed in Paris in honor of the centennial of Haitian independence, during one of those periodic political upheavals for which Haiti is notorious, the forty-three-year-old Coicou perished before a firing squad, for alleged political crimes. This sincerely religious man, a professor of philosophy who put his convictions to work in such projects as teaching the illiterate of Port-au-Prince to read, paid dearly for being so outspoken.

Of the three Coicou poems presented here, two have been chosen mainly for thematic and documentary reasons. "The Lord's Prayer" attests to Coicou's compassion for the poor and hungry. And, as Mercer Cook has recently pointed out, the before-and-after of negritude can be seen by contrasting the posture of Coicou's "The Slave's Lament," written about 1900 ("Why am I a Negro? Oh, why am I black?"), with the African Bernard Dadié's poem ("I Thank You, Lord, for Having Made Me Black") written some fifty years later. The third and perhaps best of

7

Coicou's poems is "Oblivion," translated by the late Jessie Redmond Fauset.

The Lord's Prayer

The mother said: Come now, say your prayers.
Don't fall asleep. You can't leave praying
                              till tomorrow.
Smiling, then, the child began: "Our Father
Who art in heaven, hallowed by Thy name.
Thy kingdom come. Thy will be done on earth
As it is in heaven. Give us this day our
                              daily bread . . ."
Stopping here, the boy fell silent
Beneath the weight of sobs he tried to choke
                              in vain.
But why did the childish eyes
Fill suddenly with tears as he knelt
Before his mother, praying to our Lord?
—It was night. Everywhere the lights
                              were going out.
Once more overwhelmed with heavy cares
His father had brought them home no bread.
                    The child had no more faith.

The Slave's Lament

1

Why am I a Negro? Oh, why am I black?
When God cast me in my mother's womb
Why did watchful Death not rush her to the tomb?

I would not have known this awful pain,
And drop by drop would not have drunk this gall,

This sense of utter nothingness. . . .
But God condemned me, destiny pursues me,
Intoxicated by my blood, my tears!

2

Why am I a Negro? Oh, why am I black?
When God cast me in my mother's womb,
Why did watchful Death not rush her to the tomb?

The bird is free to soar and freely sings,
The wind is free to blow where e'er it will,
The limpid waters, too, can flow through fields of green.
Such happiness, such joy are not for me:
                    I am a slave
With nowhere to find rest except the grave.

3

Why am I a Negro? Oh, why am I black?
When God cast me in my mother's womb
Why did watchful Death not rush her to the tomb?

The master's voice grows heavy,
The lash unfurls upon my back,
If I dare to tremble
The whip sings till I bleed.
When I cry for mercy,
It's not laughter that I need.

4

Why am I a Negro? Oh, why am I black?
When God cast me in my mother's womb,
Why did watchful Death not rush her to the tomb?

Last night I dreamt of Liberty,
Of freedom from this endless toil.
Joyously I roamed, no longer slave,
Through spaces, places that were mine!
But no, God made me black.

5

Why am I a Negro? Oh, why am I black?
When God cast me in my mother's womb,
Why did watchful Death not rush her to the tomb?

Where are you, Lord? When a soul that prays
From here below is suffering and true,
I'm told his prayers rise straight to You.
                    But You do not hear!
Have Negro prayers no weight against this awful fate?

6

If You hear me You can see me, too.
If I curse, alas! You see that I am weeping.
All-knowing, You must know my endless pain!
My silent suffering, Lord, has been so long and great
You must forgive me, if I've learned to hate!

Oblivion

I hope when I am dead that I shall lie
In some deserted grave—I cannot tell you why,
But I should like to sleep in some neglected spot,
Unknown to everyone, by everyone forgot.

Lying there, I should taste with my dead breath
The utter lack of life, the fullest sense of death;
And never hear the note of jealousy or hate,
The tribute paid by passers-by to tombs of state.

To me would never penetrate the prayers and tears
That futilely bring torture to dead and dying ears;
There I should lie annihilate and my dead heart would bless
Oblivion—the shroud and envelope of happiness.

—*Translated by Jessie Redmond Fauset*

FRENCH GUIANA/ MARTINIQUE ❀ *(1887–1960)*

René Maran

RENÉ MARAN WAS NOT PRIMARILY A POET BUT A FINE novelist, storyteller, and biographer who occasionally expressed himself in verse. His importance as a twentieth-century black literary and intellectual figure, however, is such that no anthology of this scope would be complete without him.

Though he was born in 1887 in Martinique, where his father held a minor governmental post, René Maran's parents were from French Guiana. When he was eight, Maran was taken to France by his parents and left at a boarding school in Bordeaux. For his parents it was a necessary but painful sacrifice, the only way their child could be assured a first-class education. Maran grew up, then, cut off from his family, his roots, his homeland, a colonial child "set out to Racinate among the Latins." This invented word was Maran's pun, combining an allusion to Racine with the French verb *raciner,* meaning to set something out to root. The loneliness of this childhood is recorded in poems he wrote many years later. Though they may have been carefully composed in the neutral third person, they are very intimate. The two Maran poems presented here are from his *Le Livre du souvenir (The Book of Memories).* The last poem, "Silence," is a testimony to the hard-won tranquillity of Maran's later years in Paris, the almost religious asceticism of his life of reading, thinking, writing, lived at a remove from worldly struggles. Other psychological aspects of Maran's situation as a black Frenchman are dealt with in two semiautobiographical novels of his mature years, *Un Homme pareil aux autres (A Man Like Any Other),* a story of interracial love; and *Le Coeur serré (The Constricted Heart),* which have never been translated but are discussed at some length in Frantz Fanon's *Black Skin, White Masks.*

Maran paid a stiff price for his courage in the public arena. Like

11

other educated black Antilleans of his generation, and like his own father, Maran served in Africa with the French colonial administration. It was his ten years in French Equatorial Africa that inspired Maran's first and most famous work, *Batouala*, which won the coveted Goncourt Prize in 1921. In spite of its success, *Batouala* provoked a scandal that almost ruined Maran's government career. His great sin was to have presented Africans and African life through African eyes—humorously, sympathetically, but objectively. *Batouala* also presented a new picture of Europeans, with all the excesses and abuses of their colonial administration. Maran's candor was taken as an indictment of much in the French colonial system, as indeed it was.

Other books with African settings followed: *Djouma, chien de brousse* (*Djouma, Dog of the Bush*) in 1927; *Le Livre de la brousse* (*The Jungle Book*) in 1934; and *Bêtes de la brousse* (*Animals of the Bush*) in 1941. Maran greatly admired certain pioneers of the colonial era in Africa—Stanley, Livingston, Savorgnon, and Felix Eboué—whom he studied and wrote about in later historical essays and biographies. Mercer Cook calls attention as well to Maran's many sensitive articles on race relations, particularly one on America's Little Rock school desegregation (see *Afrique et le monde*, October 3, 1957), written when Maran was in his seventies.

This courageous, independent writer, an intensely private man aligned with no political group, is admired today for the scope, perception, and objectivity of his prose—both fiction and nonfiction. René Maran was one of the first witnesses to black solidarity, and in that sense a precursor of negritude.

TWO POEMS FROM *The Book of Memories*

"*Tropicals*"

One finds in every boarding school,
Set out to Racinate among the Latins,
A few of those children whose eyes
Hint at distant tropic skies.

Popular with classmates,
They wish they could flee

For islands and byways
They remember only dimly.

They keep their distance
In a world of laughing,
Teasing schoolboys, who do not have
This resonance, or this inward searching.

Sometimes, when a foggy, cloistered twilight
Rouses who knows what secret doubt
                    in their great eyes,
They'll gaze at their thin hands,
Then at the homework to be done
And yield to memories
That make them live—in dreams.

Silence

My relatives are dead. As for my friends,
My childhood friends, where are they?
Life has scattered them;
Scattered them like seeds blown by the wind.

I am alone. Noises rising from the city,
Its useless agitation, do not disturb me.
Easygoing, free and proud, I live in peace,
Protected from the world and all its struggles.

The season of blossoms and the season of apples
Unreel their gorgeous games before these eyes in vain;
I consider life and mankind in the mind;
My only intimates are books.

But now and then realities intrude,
Despite my taste for solitude.
Suddenly I feel my senses wake,
A great uneasiness invades.

Calling forth the times of doubt
When mind and flesh come face to face,
I make the choice. And afterward, in pain
I feel the silent pounding of this solitary heart.

HAITI ❈ *(1892–   )*

Léon Laleau

BEFORE RETIRING TO A TRANQUIL OLD AGE IN HAITI, Léon Laleau led a long "double life" as writer and diplomat in Paris, Rome, Peru, Chile, and London. As a young man, he was close friends with several important figures of the French literary world, the poets Jules Supervielle and Anna de Noailles, and the novelist Paul Morand.

Between 1916 and 1932 Laleau published more than a dozen novels, stories, plays, and collections of poems. Of the poems, *Musique nègre* (*Black Music*), published in 1931, is Laleau's best-known work, partly because Senghor included several selections from it in his history-making 1948 anthology.

Though Laleau was sensitive to the cultural originality of the West Indies, he tended to remain bound to a very classical and European "discipline of the beautiful." In rhythm, style, vocabulary, and rhyme schemes, Laleau's poetry followed the French Parnassian models. But where subject matter was concerned, as Senghor wrote in 1948, "Beneath the classical form the green shoots of Negro themes peep through. The black man presents himself here, it is true, with his most primitive instincts, in a kind of stylization that betrays him. [Laleau's] aim is to make his difference felt, and perhaps it was not a bad idea to do so by means of a rather raw outburst of feeling."

It might be interesting to compare the poems from *Black Music* presented on the following pages with two early and rather "Laleauesque" poems by Senghor, "Totem" and "In a French Garden."

FIVE POEMS FROM *Black Music*

Betrayal

This haunted heart that doesn't fit
My language or the clothes I wear
Chafes within the grip of
Borrowed feelings, European ways.
Do you feel my pain,
This anguish like none other
From taming with the words of France
This heart that came to me from Senegal?

Cannibal

This savage wish on certain days
To mingle blows and blood
With lover's motions,
To feel beneath the bites
That make the kisses last,
The sobbing of the loved one, and her pain:
    O fierce unquenched desires
        Of my dark forebears
            Who partook of human flesh!

Legacies

On certain nights I hear within the screeching of the horn
    that called my forebears to the mountain long ago.
I see them there, limbs streaming, knives gleaming,
    with murder in their eyes and blood upon their clothes.

But all at once amid the cries of hate and war
    I seem to hear a slow air by Rameau—
Woodwinds mingling with the Negro shouts,
    Fine dancing pumps with common worn-out shoes.

Sacrifice

Beneath the sky, the cone-shaped drum is rumbling
    —the black man's very soul.
The heavy spasms of his body, the loved one's
    sticky sobs offend the evening calm.

At the corners of the clearing
    There are torches set like lowered stars.
The darkness reeks of lemon balm
    Dried in beds of acajou.

From the guardian spirit,
    Rising in the incense now and then,
Comes the bleating of the goat, who, in the breeze,
    Detects the odor of his blood at hand.

Voodoo

Time has wrinkled your face,
It is stippled with a pink stigmata,
Love, and your nose, my dear,
Has swelled like a tomato.

Your husband, Gideon,
Having drunk his evening punch,
Takes up his old accordion
And settles in his rocker.

Then come the voodoo tunes,
Evocative of nights when you,
As priestess, were possessed
By some demented god within your flesh.

You danced, danced ardently,
With eager loins, ecstatic eyes,
And the wild call of a lover
Yelping toward you from the trees.

Swifter than a flight of doves,
Carida, has this time gone by—
And its music in the night,
How difficult to hear it now.

Jacques Roumain

BEFORE HE WAS TWENTY, THE TALENTED, HANDSOME, aristocratic Jacques Roumain had been in school in England, France, Switzerland, and Spain, and was fluent in several languages. Returning home to a Haiti suffering the indignity of American occupation, he became, in 1927, one of the founders of *La Revue indigène* (*The Native Review*), a small literary magazine through which a group of young Haitian intellectuals set out to explore the Haitian present and its living African heritage. These writers were discovering that they were not French, and would no longer look exclusively to Europe for their cultural models.

This was a significant departure. The young people of the period had been very much impressed by the ideas of a professor-diplomat some years their elder, a physician named Jean Price Mars (1876–1969), who had recently returned from a long stay in Europe. Dr. Price Mars had studied under the pioneering French and German anthropologists whose researches in Africa were leading to a new evaluation of those peoples and civilizations so long dismissed as "savage." In his personal contacts with the *Revue indigène* group, and in *Ainsi parla l'Oncle* (*Thus Spake Our Uncle*), the key work he published in Haiti in 1928, Price Mars described the cultural riches of African civilizations, stressed their obvious continuities in native Haitian folklore and religion, and urged his countrymen not to turn their backs any longer in shame on a unique heritage.

"Our only chance to be ourselves is to repudiate no part of the ancestral heritage. Well, for eight-tenths of us this heritage is the gift of Africa," he wrote in *Thus Spake Our Uncle.* "Accept the ancestral patrimony, therefore, as a bloc. Turn it around, weigh it, examine it with intelligence and circumspection, and you will see that it reflects as in a broken mirror the condensed image of all humanity."

Two of Jacques Roumain's most memorable poems date from this early Africanist period, when he was in his early twenties. They were discovered in *La Revue indigène* by Langston Hughes, who translated them for the NAACP magazine, *The Crisis*. "Guinea" depicts the beauty Roumain saw in the Haitian peasant's vision of heaven as the distant half-remembered Africa from which his forebears had been uprooted, while "When the Tom-Tom Beats," with its final line dismissing "the white that made [him] a mulatto" as mere "spit upon the shore," evokes the light-skinned Roumain's fascination with his black ancestral heritage. In the poems of Roumain, as in the lyric verses of Nicolás Guillén and Regino Pedroso, two Cuban writers Hughes also translated at that time, the American was struck by the candid and sympathetic treatment of "the African strain in the New World," by the efforts of these French- and Spanish-language black poets to free the poetry of their islands from "outworn foreign patterns," and also by their implicit moral concern for "the problems of the darker peoples."

Jacques Roumain pursued these ideals with such vigor and such great personal magnetism that he soon became the "uncontested leader" of his generation of Haitian intellectuals. As the American historian of Haitian literature, Naomi Garret, has noted, Roumain "turned his back upon a life of luxury to become a social menace to his class and a spokesman for the inarticulate masses."* Despite the vicissitudes of his career and his frequent absences from Haiti, Roumain retained a leadership role until his untimely death in 1944, at the age of thirty-seven, while on a diplomatic mission to Mexico.

From the late 1920s, Roumain was composing poetry and fiction rooted in the peasant life and rural landscape of his homeland. His long poem, *Appel,* was published in Port-au-Prince in 1928; a volume of short stories, *Les Fantouches (The Puppets),* in 1930; and the novels *La Proie et l'ombre (The Victims and the Shadow)* and *La Montagne ensorcelée (The Enchanted Mountain)* in 1931. *Gouverneurs de la rosée* (translated by Mercer Cook and Langston Hughes as *Masters of the Dew*), published in 1944, the year of his death, is a moving short novel still considered Roumain's finest work. It concerns a young Haitian farmer who returns to his village after several years abroad, and his efforts to find a new source of water to save the village from certain ruin. The tale is well told, laced with the heady romance of two young people, with the

---

* *The Renaissance of Haitian Poetry, Presénce Africaine,* Paris, 1963, p. 107.

ominous threats of a previous villainous suitor, and the superstitious villagers' mistrust of the hero's new and strange ideas.*

Roumain sought to deepen his understanding of Haitian life by undertaking advanced study in cultural anthropology in Paris and New York. He brought the fruits of his study back to Haiti in 1941 by founding the nation's Department of Ethnology, devoted to what might today be described as "Haitian studies," and by publishing a number of scientific papers of his own.

Roumain despaired over the indifference of existing institutions—the Church, the Haitian government, the capitalist economic system—and over the deprivation of ninety per cent of the Haitian people. Marxist ideology seemed to him to offer the only hope. It is, therefore, not surprising that Roumain, like many people of conscience during the 1930s, became a communist, and in 1934 founded the Haitian Communist Party. In the years that followed, his countryman Jacques Antoine recalls, Roumain often went hungry, and suffered brutal beatings and imprisonment for speaking out against the Haitian government. It was doubtless these courageous stands that made him such a hero to the young, particularly to René Depestre, who is in so many ways Roumain's heir.

It is in the poems of *Bois d'ebène* (*Ebony Wood*), written in Brussels in 1939, though not gathered and published by his widow until 1945, that Roumain's relationship to the militant negritude poets (Damas, Césaire, and particularly the much younger Depestre and David Diop) can most clearly be seen. As Lilyan Kesteloot has noted, "All the great themes of black revolt are condensed in a few pages: slavery, exile, forced labor, lynching, segregation, colonial oppression, calling the Negro diaspora to the banner of revolution." In addition to the sense of identification with black peoples the world over, there is the broader expression of the brotherhood of all exploited peoples, typical of the rhetoric of socialist humanism during the late 1930s. Miners of Spain and South Africa, German steelworkers, Sicilian peasants, Indian untouchables, all are in the litany of capitalist victims enumerated in Roumain's last poems. From *Ebony Wood* we offer three of the best known and most representative excerpts.

The last eight lines of Roumain's "New Negro Sermon" beginning with the words "We'll no longer sing the sad, despairing spirituals . . ." have been quoted so often since their inclusion in Senghor's 1948 an-

---

* The book has been reissued in paperback with a new introduction by Mercer Cook. New York: Collier Books, Macmillan, 1971.

thology that they have literally become one of negritude's mottoes. The poem's title shows that Roumain, like Senghor, was an admirer of James Weldon Johnson, particularly of his poetic re-creation of old-time Negro sermons in *God's Trombones*, first published in 1927. Roumain's sermon is "new" by virtue of being written from outside the Christian faith rather than from within, and because it appears to be a direct response to Johnson's. If Johnson's sermons were encouragements to follow the way of the Lord, exhortations against sin but resignation as to its workings, Roumain's is a protest against the betrayal of Christian ideals by the institutionalized Church and an exhortation to revolt. Christ is seen as a Negro martyr, or, conversely, the black man as a kind of Christ. The theme is one on which later poets in this anthology— Senghor, Dadié, and Tchicaya U Tam'si—continue to make variations.

With no attempt at subtlety, Roumain communicates the irony of a society which proclaims the qualities of Jesus Christ (his poverty, his gentleness, his mercy, his hard work) as divine, only to utterly betray these attributes. In institutionalized Christianity, the remnants of His ragged clothes become "relics"; His "gentle song of poverty" becomes "the haughty thunder" of an organ; "arms that hauled cotton" become, in His name, those that "wield the sword"; forgiveness is greeted with scorn; and the ascetic ideal of self-imposed poverty is betrayed by clergy who "count the interest" on Judas's thirty pieces while the multitudes go hungry. At last the "bleeding man" who was made into a "bleeding god" is so transformed that a statue of his passion on the Cross—stretched arms limp, head hanging—casts the hideous shadow of a vulture. Christianity itself is betrayed, and the black man in his poem is seen as its chief victim. "We will pray no more," the poem declares, surging to a close with Roumain's well-known call to arms. Perhaps it is from these lines of Roumain's that Fanon took the title of his best-known work, *The Wretched of the Earth*.

From the very metaphor of its title, David Diop's "Vultures" is a direct descendant of "New Negro Sermon" and "Ebony Wood." The two poets' images are similarly powerful and unfinished. The architecture of nearly all David Diop's poems, in fact, follows closely that of these two by Roumain, though Diop's diction and rhythmic sense are often superior to his mentor's. The "New Negro Sermon" also illustrates the transformation of color symbols remarked on in Sartre's "Black Orpheus": black becomes the positive, and white the negative. Christ is "black," a "poor nigger," a "glowing coal" among "white roses," his "black face whitened" by cold white spittle. One finds the same reversal in the Toussaint Louverture section of Césaire's *Cahier d'un retour au pays natal* (*Notes on a Return to the Native Land*). Again, Roumain may have been influenced by James Weldon Johnson, whose poem "The White Witch" (included in Johnson's *The Book of Negro Poetry*) portrays a beautiful, fair-haired, blue-eyed young woman as the pernicious embodiment of all that is evil and will lead to disaster.

The known facts about Jacques Roumain's life are so sparse as to make a biographical résumé of his career extremely difficult. We do know that he wrote the poems of *Ebony Wood* in 1939, the same year that Césaire's *Notes* was published, and only two years after the appearance of Léon Damas's *Pigments*. Was *Ebony Wood* composed completely independently, or did the Damas poems have some influence upon it? Had Roumain ever met Senghor, Césaire, Damas, or Alioune Diop? Did he know their work? These are questions we cannot answer for sure. What is certain, however, is that Roumain was not only the leading Haitian writer of his generation, but also one whose influence reached far beyond the confines of his island to the whole black French-language world.

Guinea

It's the long road to Guinea
death takes you down.
Here are the boughs, the trees, the forest.
Listen to the sound of the wind in its long hair
    of eternal night.

It's the long road to Guinea
where your fathers await you without impatience.
Along the way, they talk,
They wait.
This is the hour when the streams rattle
    like beads of bone.

It's the long road to Guinea.
No bright welcome will be made for you
in the dark land of dark men:

Under a smoky sky pierced by the cry of birds
around the eye of the river
    the eyelashes of the trees open on decaying light.
There, there awaits you beside the water a quiet village,
and the hut of your fathers, and the hard ancestral stone
    where your head will rest at last.

—Translated by Langston Hughes

When the Tom-Tom Beats . . .

Your heart trembles in the shadows, like a face
    reflected in troubled water.
The old mirage rises from the pit of the night
You sense the sweet sorcery of the past:
A river carries you far away from the banks,
Carries you toward the ancestral landscape.
Listen to those voices singing the sadness of love
And in the mountain, hear that tom-tom
    panting like the breast of a young black girl.

Your soul is this image in the whispering water where
    your fathers bent their dark faces.
Its hidden movements blend you with the waves
And the white that made you a mulatto is this bit
    of foam cast up, like spit, upon the shore.

—Translated by Langston Hughes

THREE POEMS FROM *Ebony Wood*

Dirty Niggers

Well then
here we are
we negroes
we niggers

we dirty niggers
we won't accept it any more
we're simply
done
in Africa
in America
with being
your negroes
your niggers
your dirty niggers
we won't take it any more
that surprises you
after our: yes, sir
polishing your shoes
yes, father
to the missionary whites
yes, master
harvesting for you
the coffee
cotton
peanuts
in Africa
America
like the good negroes
poor negroes
dirty negroes
that we were
that we won't be any longer. . . .

Ebony Wood (excerpt)

Negro peddler of revolt,
you know all the roadways of the world
since you were sold in Guinea. . . .

Here is an echo of flesh and blood for your voice,
black messenger of hope,
beginning with the worksongs of the age-old Nile.

You remember with each word the weight of Egypt's stone;
the urging of your misery raised the temple columns
like the pulse of sap within the reeds.

Stumbling procession dizzy from mirages,
along the trail the caravans of slaves
raise thin branches of shadow chained to sunlight,
arms implore our gods,
Mandingo Arada Bambara Ibo,
moaning chants, choked by iron collars

(and when we reached the coast
Bambara Ibo
out of all of us
the Bambara Ibo grain
hardly a fistful was left
in the hand of the sower of death).

O my people, when
spreading storms of birds,
of ashes, when
in ardent winters
will I see your hands revolt?

How I listened in the Indies
to that black girl singing!
Who taught you such a song of boundless pain,
black woman of the isles, of the plantations,
that lament
as desolate
as the breathing of the sea
compressed into a conch?

But I also know a silence
of twenty-five thousand corpses
from twenty-five thousand crossings of ebony wood
on the Congo-Ocean railroad.
I know shrouds of silence in the cypress
petals of black blood clotted in the brambles
of those woods in Georgia where
they lynched my brother. . . .

The silence
more harrowing than a windstorm of spears,
louder than the thundering of wild beasts
howling,
rising,
calling for
vengeance,
castigation,
a tidal wave of pus and lava
on the world's crime
and the tympany of sky
bursting
beneath the fist
of justice.

Africa, I have kept your memory, Africa,
you are within me

like the thorn in the wound,
like the guardian fetish
at the center of the village,
make me the stone in your sling,
make my mouth the lips of your wound,
my knees the broken columns of your humiliation.

New Negro Sermon

In His face they spit their icy scorn,
As at a black flag flying windswept by snow
To make of Him, poor nigger, the god of those in power,
From His rags, relics to embellish altars;
From His gentle song of poverty,
From the trembling lamentation of His banjo,
The haughty thunder of the organ;
From His arms that hauled the heavy cotton
On the river Jordan,
The arms of those who wield the sword;
From His body, worn like ours from the plantations

Like a glowing coal,
Like a black coal burning in white roses,
The golden necklace of their fortune;
They whitened His black face beneath the spittle
    of their icy scorn,
They spit on Your black face,
Lord, our friend, our comrade;
You who parted on her face long hair that hid the harlot's tears,
Like a screen of reeds;
They the rich, the Pharisees, the owners of the land, the bankers,
From the bleeding man they made the bleeding god;
Oh, Judas snicker;
Oh, Judas laugh;
Christ, like a torch between two thieves,
At the summit of the world,
Lit the slaves' revolt.
But Christ today is in the house of thieves
And his spread arms in the cathedral spread a vulture shadow,
And in the monastery vaults priests
Count the interest on the thirty pieces
While church bells shower death on hungry multitudes.

We do not pardon them because they know what they do:
They lynched John who organized the union,
They chased him through the wood with dogs like a savage wolf,
Laughing there, they hanged him to the sycamore.
No, brothers, comrades,
We will pray no more.
Our revolt will rise like the stormbird's cry,
Above the putrid lapping of the swamps.
We'll no longer sing the sad, despairing spirituals!
Another song will spring forth from our throats
Our red flags we shall unfurl,
Stained by the blood of our upright brothers.
Beneath this sign we shall march,
Beneath this sign we are marching,
Standing tall, the wretched of the earth!
Standing tall, the legions of the hungry!

HAITI (1908–   )

Emile Roumer

EDUCATED IN FRANCE AND ENGLAND, EMILE ROUMER
is a lawyer by profession. His first book of poems, *Poèmes de Haiti et de
France* (*Poems from Haiti and France*), was published in 1930, when
he was twenty-two. While later poems appeared in *La Revue indigène*,
of which he was a founder and the first editor, he seems to have stopped
writing after 1935. *"Amour paysanne"* ("The Peasant Declares His
Love") has a delicious sensuality that characterizes most of his poetry.
Roumer, like all the Haitians except Roumain and the younger René
Depestre, is considerably influenced by classical French models.

The Peasant Declares His Love

High-yellow of my heart, with breasts like tangerines,
you taste better to me than eggplant stuffed with crab,
you are the tripe in my pepper-pot,
the dumpling in my peas, my tea of aromatic herbs.
You are the corned beef whose customhouse is my heart,
my mush with syrup that trickles down the throat.
You are a steaming dish, mushrooms cooked with rice,
crisp potato fries, and little fish fried brown. . . .
My hankering for love follows you wherever you go.
Your bottom is a basket full of fruits and meat.

—Translated by John Peale Bishop

Ten Lines

To me you are infinitely distant. . . .
Some strange tropical unknown perhaps
insinuates itself into your soul, rousing
cooling palms above bright whiteness of a mosque.
Of me you know nothing. Am I Arab? sheikh?
By your race you are infinitely distant. . . .
I dream that were the beauty with the golden
hair to wake to some slight tremor of my lute
she would refuse her lips to me and stain
the love of this black prince with her derision.

Charles Pressoir

CHARLES PRESSOIR, LIKE ROUMER A LAWYER BY PROFES-
sion, was educated in France and England and later did graduate work
in economics at Columbia University in New York.

The title of his book of poems, *Au rythme des Coumbites (To the
Rhythm of the Coumbites)*, published in 1933, alludes to the coopera-
tive work sessions of rural Haiti, where people gather to help plant or
harvest a neighbor's field. They work in rhythm to drums and all kinds
of songs, and their labors are rewarded at the end by a festive meal. Like
the youthful lyrics of Roumain and Roumer, and like so much of the
poetry of this group, many of Pressoir's poems appeared first in *La Revue
indigène*.

Pressoir's "Country Graveyard" focuses on African survivals in
Haitian peasant life, and the haunting question of what happens after
death: "Do the dead go then forever,/ To Heaven or to Guinea?"

Country Graveyard

> *"This is the long way to Guinea."*
> —*Jacques Roumain*

In the high, high grass of Guinea
    The little houses hide,
Gray stone, moss-grown and thickly,
    Like dun hair that floats beside.

Sometimes the ground curves slightly
    In a long, vague, pebbly wave,
Which the weeds veil but lightly—
    Some poor wretch's fresh-made grave.

At the foot of the Cross suspended,
    Lest the dead should know *grangou;*
A tiny grain, some fish, foods blended,
    At feet of Christ you find voodoo.

So they follow the two faiths ever—
    The white, the bone-bred deeply.
Do the dead go then forever,
    To Heaven or to Guinea?

—Translated by Edna Worthley Underwood

10. *Grangou:* The Creole word for hunger.

Black Island

Women of my country, black and barefoot girls
Whose catchy tunes are sung to lively drums,
If I flee the town to wander in your fields,
It's seeking you, and your unknown charms.

I'd like to delve into your very soul,
Seemingly so open, yet so strange.
You offer up to love those panting breasts
Coiling like Damballah as you swoon.

Though I cannot see your bare, brown legs,
In the flame that lights those almond wicks,
Brightening dark corners of the street,
Your shining eyes flicker to a voodoo beat.

You are a living Africa to me,
Surviving in this place since slaveship days,
When your forebears, carried to America
From Guinea, stood chained along the quays.

When evening comes you call upon their ancient laws,
When sickness comes you turn to juju.
What is this island but a part
Severed from the continental homeland?

8. Damballah: A voodoo snake god.

GUADELOUPE (1917–   )

Guy Tirolien

GUY TIROLIEN WAS TWENTY-THREE, A WEST INDIAN student serving in the French Army, when he met Léopold Senghor in 1940 in a German prison camp. Both had been captured during the fall of France. Released later on, Tirolien went to Paris for the remainder of the Occupation, joining, at Senghor's suggestion, the group of black intellectuals that was forming around Alioune Diop, the future editor of the not-yet-founded *Présence Africaine*. Tirolien was among the sixteen poets represented in Senghor's 1948 anthology. But it was not until thirteen years later that a little collection of his poems, *Balles d'or* (*Golden Bullets*), was brought out by his friends at *Présence*.

"The Soul of the Black Land" is a lyrical evocation of West Indian Africanisms, composed in the tradition that began with *La Revue indigène*. "Marie Galante," named for the island near Guadeloupe where Tirolien grew up, recalls both his childhood and the history of the island itself, discovered by Columbus in 1493. The "I" in the poem stands, of course, for the author's whole race, forcibly emigrated to grow "gold" (in the form of sugar cane) that "they," the first European explorers, more than a century later, had hoped to mine but had to plant and harvest instead. "A Little Black Boy's Prayer" is probably Tirolien's best-known poem, perhaps because it is so universal. "Ghetto," the last poem included here, sounds a new note. Despite his respect for the African past, and his awareness of historical scars, Tirolien good-humoredly refused to be confined to the limits of any "ghetto of the exotic." He will partake of life and other cultures as he wishes.

Tirolien made a long-dreamed-of "return to his sources"—by which he meant Africa, rather than his Caribbean islands—soon after World War II ended. He joined the administration of what were then the French Overseas Territories, serving in the Cameroons and later in Sudan. Following independence, Tirolien settled in West Africa, and later was named the United Nations Representative to Mali.

FOUR POEMS FROM *Golden Bullets*

The Soul of the Black Land

Your breasts of shining black satin,
your long, supple, undulating polished arms,
the white smile
of eyes
in your dark face
awake in me tonight
the muffled rhythms,
clapping hands,
languid chants,
that rouse our sisters back in Guinea
black and bare
to rapture;
they awake in me
tonight
negro twilights
heavy with a sensual excitement,
for
the soul of the black land
where the ancients sleep
lives and speaks
tonight
in the anxious power of your empty loins,
the indolence of your proud walk
which leaves behind
when you are past
the savage call of nights
that swell and fill
with a great pulse of feverish tom-toms,
and, most of all
your voice,
your voice with its nostalgic sound,
remembering,
trembling, weeping
here tonight

for the soul of the black land
where the ancients sleep.

Marie Galante

Is this rapture that your rums have filled me with,
or perhaps the magic of a homeland rediscovered?
The old volcanoes of my past
faintly, faintly rumble;
look at them expand,
pale flowers,
exploding in the evening peace
with all the ghosts that once were me.
It was by error that their caravels came here
and that many died beneath the manzanilla trees
from having wished to taste the sweetness of its fruit.
They didn't find the gold they came in search of;
but me, I came to make gold grow,
from where I don't remember any more;
one day I came to make gold grow,
I don't remember when,
but whips have whistled since that spotless morning
and the sun has drunk the perspiration of my blood.

A Little Black Boy's Prayer

Lord, I'm tired
I was born tired.
And I've walked a long way since daybreak
and the hill that leads to their school is a high one.
Lord, I don't want to go to their school any more.
Fix it, please, so I don't have to.
I want to follow my pa down into the cool ravines
when night still hovers in the mystery of the woods,

where spirits steal about that the dawn will chase away.
I want to go barefoot along red paths
the noon sun cooks to broiling.
I want to doze beneath the mango trees
and waken
when the white man's whistle sounds
and the factory over there
anchored like a ship
on a sugar-cane ocean
spills its black crew
across the fields.
Lord, I don't want to go to their school any more.
Fix it, please, so I don't have to.
They say a little black boy has to go
to get like
city guys,
fine gentlemen from town,
but I don't want
to get to be . . .
a gentleman from town.
I'd rather loaf on by the sugarworks
where the sacks are fat
with sugar, brown as my brown skin.
And at night when the moon whispers sweet-talk
to the coco palms
I'd rather listen to the reedy voice
of some old man
telling about Zamba and Br'er Rabbit
and lots of other things that aren't in books.
You know black folks work too hard already!
So why should I need to learn in books about things
that aren't from here?
And anyway, it's really sad,
their school.
Sad as
those city guys,
those gentlemen from town
who don't dance in the moonlight no more,
who never walk on their own bare feet no more,

who don't know how to tell the evening tales no more.
Lord, I don't want no more school.

Ghetto

Why should I confine myself
to the image
they would fix me in?
For pity's sake,
I'd suffocate
segregated as exotic.

I'm no idol made of ebony
breathing phony incense
in museums of the primitive.

I'm no sideshow cannibal
rolling ivory eyeballs
to make the kiddies shiver.

If I shout a shout
that burns my throat,
it's when my belly
feels my brothers' hunger;
and if sometimes
I howl with pain
it's when my toe
is stuck beneath somebody's boot.

The nightingale sings many notes,
my monotone laments are done.

I'm no perspiring actor,
arms lifted to the sky,
sobbing out his pain
before the camera's eye.

I'm frozen in no pose of militance
or of damnation either.
I'm a living creature,
beast of prey
ever poised to leap

to seize life
which mocks at death;
to pounce on joy
which needs no passport;
to spring at love
when it happens by my door.

I'll talk of Beethoven,
stone deaf amid the tumult,
because it was for me,
yes, me (who could understand him better),
that he unleashed his storms.

I'll sing of Rimbaud
who wanted to be black
to speak to man
of primogenial matters.

I'll praise Matisse
and Braque and then Picasso
for having found
the ancient secrets of
the rhythmic song of life
beneath the rigidness
of elemental forms.

Yes, I'll praise mankind,
all men!
I go forth to them
with a heart full of song,
hands heavy with friendship,
for they are made in my image.

GUADELOUPE (1917–1962)

Paul Niger

LIKE HIS CLOSE FRIEND GUY TIROLIEN, PAUL NIGER
was born in Guadeloupe in 1917, had his higher education in France,
and was active in the wartime group in Paris that eventually gave rise
to *Présence Africaine*. The lines translated here by Samuel Allen first
appeared in Senghor's 1948 anthology. Niger is a pen name the poet
took from that of the great West African river. He served in Dahomey
with the French administration, writing two novels based on that experi-
ence, *Les Puissants* (*The Powerful*) and *Les Grenouilles de Mont
Kimbo* (*The Frogs of Mount Kimbo*), as well as *Initiations,* a book of
verse, before his untimely death in 1962 in a plane crash.

Initiations (excerpt)

What?
a rhythm
a wave in the night through the forests,
    nothing—or a soul reborn
a drum
a chant
the power
the surging
an intense vibration which slowly in the shuddering
    marrow
brings down an old flagging heart
seizes it by the waist
and pierces it
and turns it

and lives again its mounting fury in the hands
in the loins
in the thighs
and in the quickening womb.

—Translated by Samuel Allen

FRENCH GUIANA (*1912–*)

Léon Damas

TWENTY YEARS BEFORE FRANTZ FANON HAD MATURED it into psychoanalytic theory, *Pigments,* a book of poems published in 1937 by Léon Damas, revealed the anguish of what has come to be known as "the colonized personality." The feelings so succinctly transformed into art in Damas's subtle, incisive, ironic poems—feelings of oppression, of the discomfort Sartre called *mauvaise foi,* and of an accompanying anger and revolt were elaborated by the Martiniquan psychiatrist Fanon into the broader portrait of a cultural type only a generation later. Fanon's thought was nourished on the insights of the negritude poetry, of which Damas's *Pigments* was the first major work.

Like two of his distinguished countrymen, René Maran and Félix Eboué, Léon Damas came from a comfortable middle-class mulatto family of French Guiana. He was born in the town of Cayenne in 1912. Once known chiefly as the site of Devil's Island, the tiny French outpost in South America is today an important space-research station of the French government, and, since 1946, a *département* (a status similar to American statehood) of metropolitan France.

Damas often contrasts himself with Maran and Eboué, both of whom were some twenty-five years his elder, and both of whom he much admires. The candor of Maran's *Batouala* cost him the security of a civil-service career, leaving the proud, sensitive author the difficult task of earning a living entirely from his writings. Félix Eboué, on the other hand, climaxed a long and successful career in colonial administration when, as governor of the Tchad in 1940, he offered it to General Charles de Gaulle as the first territory of "Free France" rather than surrender to the Germans. This gesture earned Eboué his appointment as governor-general of all French Equatorial Africa, and his eventual burial in the Panthéon.

Each in his own way, Maran (1887–1960) and Eboué (1884–1944)

39

epitomized the phenomenon of French cultural assimilation. Both were educated in France, prized the values of its civilization and culture, and modeled their lives upon them. Both were humane and compassionate persons; neither denied his African or Negro heritage, but each felt so removed from his ancestral past as to consider himself as French first and foremost and only incidentally as black.

Damas's background was very similar. After primary school in Cayenne, he too attended a French lycée on the island of Martinique, and was later sent to Paris for his higher education. Everything in his upbringing prepared him for a distinguished career. When Damas reached Paris, however, it was no longer simply the center of French intellectual and artistic life. Since the close of World War I it had witnessed the dadaist and surrealist upheavals, which challenged all traditional values. The high principles of the Russian Revolution, still in its infancy, seemed to offer hope of a new form of government that would guarantee a better life to "the wretched of the earth." Damas became acquainted with a Martiniquan student several years older than he, Etienne Léro, who was violently rejecting French cultural assimilation on the grounds that it meant turning one's back on the riches of the Negro heritage, and ignoring the misery of the illiterate Caribbean masses. Léro's group issued a manifesto, *Légitime Défense,* which rejected the writings of previous West Indians and endorsed communism, surrealism, and the American Negro Renaissance. It called for a literature which would expose the real condition of Caribbean blacks and militate for improvements. The Léro group did not itself produce such a new literature, and its review, appearing in one issue in 1932, was immediately banned. But its ideas greatly stimulated Damas and some of his friends.

As students in Paris in 1934, Aimé Césaire of Martinique and Léopold Senghor of Senegal joined Damas to found *L'Etudiant noir* (*The Black Student*). This little magazine was one of several short-lived reviews established by French-speaking blacks for exploring American-derived ideas of a Negro renaissance. It was the forerunner of a new cultural and literary movement within the French-speaking world, which would insist on Negro-ness and its values. Inevitably, it was also linked to African independence, which in those years still seemed very remote.

It was not until a decade later, in about 1945, that the ensemble of these ideas came to be known, after the term in Césaire's poem *Notes on a Return to the Native Land,* as negritude.

Damas was the first of the three founders to publish his own book of poems. Rejecting what he termed "tracing-paper poetry"—pale copies of outmoded white-French models—Damas was looking for a new language, a fresh style and form with which to express new preoccupations about life—themes that were not only profoundly and personally his, but also those of a much larger Negro group of which he was a part. He found the means in several sources: the ideas of the French surrealists; the poetry of contemporary black Americans such as Langston Hughes and Sterling Brown; the striking rhythms and tunes of American blues and jazz; and the closed, mysterious shapes of African sculpture. All were popular in Paris during the 1930s.

When *Pigments* appeared in 1937, it caused a sensation. Claude McKay's lines, "Am I not Africa's son / Black of that black land where black deeds are done," which Damas chose as an epigraph, and implications of the title itself were underlined in Robert Desnos's introduction.

> His name is Damas. He is a Negro. Let's clear the ground a bit. With Damas, there is no question of his subject matter or how he treats it, of the sharpness of his blade or the status of his soul.
>
> Damas is Negro and insists on his Negro-ness and on his condition as a Negro. This is what will raise the eyebrows of a certain number of civilizers who deem it right that in exchange for their freedom, their land, their customs, and their well-being, persons of color ought to be honored by the name of "black."
>
> Damas refuses the title and reclaims his own. What this own consists of will be revealed to you in the poems that follow. . . . They do honor, these poems, to the whole immense native proletariat of our colonies. They signify that the time has come for us to seek the conquest of these lands and of these peoples.
>
> Are they not exploited just as ours are, these lands? And are these people not exploited? Notice where the pen and common sense are leading us.
>
> These poems are therefore also a song of friendship offered in the name of his whole race by my friend Damas the Negro to all his white brothers.
>
> A gift from the field to the factory, from the plantation to the farm, from tropical workshop to European foundry.

The racial terms used by Desnos were the reverse of American usage today: "blacks" ("*noirs*") was the nonpejorative term used by white Frenchmen; "*nègre*"—before Damas—hovered somewhere between the American "nigger" and "Negro." Damas's insistence on the term was a direct response to the pride with which the "New Negro" movement in America had endowed the word since the late 1920s. *Pigments* marks the beginning in France of a trend giving a truly positive emphasis to the word *"nègre."* Within a year or two, Césaire would complete the process by coining the word *"négritude."* In 1937 in France, then, *"noir"* was something of an Uncle Tom expression, while *"nègre"* marked the awareness and acceptance of one's condition.

It is interesting, too, that Desnos introduces Damas's poems exclusively in a political or social-humanitarian, rather than an artistic or literary, context. Desnos views Damas as a spokesman for his race, a "proletariat" of the lands colonized by France, one more example of a working class, like the French working class itself, "exploited" for the profit of the few. The "conquest" of the colonies that Desnos calls for is, by inference, a revolutionary one. Like many surrealist poets during the 1930s, Desnos had departed from the primarily artistic and aesthetic concerns that had launched the movement to reflect an increasing sense of social engagement.

As for Desnos's characterizing *Pigments* as Damas's "song of friendship . . . to his white brothers," this is true only by the most generous extrapolation. The short poems of *Pigments* do reveal compassion for fellow sufferers other than the black man (the Jews under Hitler, for example). But they are a bitter testimony, variations on themes of *pain;* anger, tenacity, and a certain despair are the prime elements in this first book of poems, this first major work of the negritude group.

In a blunt, dry, vivid style, marked by fresh images, unashamedly plain language, staccato rhythms, and acridly witty puns, Damas's short poems lay bare their author's often violent rejection of white European "ci-vi-li-za-tion." His language is always informal, close to the spoken word. The poems are built on the repetition of key phrases, images, rhythms and word play.*

We present fifteen poems from *Pigments,* one less than half the volume, in the order in which they appear in the French edition. "The Black Man's Lament," "They Came That Night," "Sell Out," "Blues,"

---

* These were similar to the techniques of other French surrealists of the time— Damas's friend Desnos, for example, and the popular Jacques Prévert. Damas absorbed, hammered, and perfected them until they were his own style, perfectly fused with what he had to say. Readers may be interested to know that Folkways Records (701 Seventh Avenue, New York City) has made a long-playing record of Damas reading from his poems in the original French.

"Reality," "If Often," "Whitewash," and "Shine" could well have been written by a black American today. "Obsession," "There Are Nights," and "Position," on the other hand, express intimate moods of despair, disgust, and depression not limited to any racial group. The ironic references to "my ancestors the Gauls" and to that specifically European dance, the waltz, in "Sleepless Night" are, of course, associated with the poet's childhood. Throughout the French colonies, the history books in primary and secondary schools were exactly the same as those used in France. Cro-Magnon ancestors were spoken of as if they were everyone's. Waltzing, similarly, was simply a part of the etiquette any well-bred French child would acquire. The reference to Hitler clearly dates this poem to the eve of World War II. And the mock-affectionate allusion to "Uncle Gobineau" refers to the nineteenth-century Frenchman whose notorious *Essay on the Inequality of Human Races* first solemnized the long undisputed belief in white European cultural supremacy.

"Et Cetera," the last poem in *Pigments,* which closes our Damas selections, also reflects its historical moment. Senegalese soldiers were long known as among the best in the French Army. Here the poet exhorts them to fight for their own independence, "to invade Senegal," rather than defend their colonial masters against the Germans. Doubtless this was among the Damas poems recited in Baoulé translation by rioting African draft resisters in the Ivory Coast in 1939. As a result, *Pigments* was quickly banned throughout French West Africa.

As a noted critic has remarked, Damas still has a voice like no other negritude poet. His cryptic style is quite different from the "rich drapery" of Senghor's verse, or the extended explosions of Césaire's. Senghor once described Damas's poems as "charged with an emotion concealed by humor." "Hiccups," for example, portrays the childhood frustrations of a little boy whose mother is ever vigilant in her demand for the very best and most correct "French" behavior. But the poem can be understood in more universal terms as well: as the age-old revolt by children against the standards of parents; and as analogous to the situation of many a minority group socially pressed to banish undesirably "ethnic" habits. Perhaps the sacrifice "of all that once was ours" need not always be the price of upward mobility in a world dominated by others.

Reveling in the freedom of his student years, Damas at first studied law and Oriental languages. But, along with Senghor and Césaire, he too had an enthusiasm for the new anthropology of Africa, and for the better world envisioned in radical politics. He had a great curiosity about people. It was not long before his parents, scandalized by his associations, cut their son off from financial support. Until he eventually secured a scholarship, Damas took on all kinds of odd jobs to make a living. He worked in a factory, toted vegetables at a wholesale produce market, bused dishes, and peddled newspapers, all the while writing, thinking, pursuing his new interests—ethnic, aesthetic, literary, and political.

Pigments was followed in 1938 by a prose account called *Retour de Guyane* (*Return from Guiana*), and, in 1943, by a book of Negro tales, the result of ethnographic field studies by Damas in his native land. After the war, Damas was again the first of the *Etudiant noir* trio to publish an anthology of poets from black Africa, the West Indies, and French colonies in the Far East. Ample, well edited and thoughtful, the Damas anthology was unfortunately overshadowed within the next year by Senghor's briefer collection, concentrating on black poets alone, which had one special advantage: a stunning introductory essay, "Black Orpheus," by Jean-Paul Sartre.

Like many French colonials who were also writers (Senghor, Césaire, Sissoko, Rabémananjara, and the elder U Tam'si), Damas served in the French Assembly (1945–1951), as deputy from Guiana. But unlike his friends Senghor and Césaire, he seems to have found himself temperamentally unsuited to the political life and was not re-elected for a second term. He joined the French Overseas Radio Service, and later UNESCO, traveling and lecturing in Africa, the United States, Haiti, and Brazil.

Damas's *Poèmes nègres sur des airs Africains* (*African Songs of Love, War, Grief and Abuse*), 1948,* adaptations of traditional African oral poems, were a departure from his other work. But *Graffiti* (1952), *Black Label* (1956), and *Névralgies* (*Neuralgias*) (1966) return to the style characteristic of *Pigments*. While one cannot pretend to do them critical justice in so short a space, the later poems are extensions of the themes that have always haunted Damas.

As a contributing editor of *Présence Africaine* and senior adviser to the Society of African Culture, Damas has traveled on numerous projects to Africa, the Americas, and in Europe. Among his current works-in-progress are new poems, a French-language biography of the late Langston Hughes, and new French translations of Hughes's poems.

In 1970, Damas and his Brazilian wife moved to Washington, D.C.,

---

* Translated by M. Koshland and U. Beier (Ibadan: Mbari Publications, 1961).

where he is professor of modern literature at the new Federal City
College.

They Came That Night

For Léopold Sédar Senghor

They came that night as the
    tom
        tom
            rolled
                from
                    rhythm
                        to rhythm
                            the frenzy

of eyes
the frenzy of hands
the frenzy
of statue feet

How many of ME ME ME
have died
SINCE THEN
since they came that night when the
    tom
        tom
            rolled
                from
                    rhythm
                        to rhythm
                            the frenzy

of eyes
the frenzy
of hands
the frenzy
of statue feet

Obsession

A taste of blood comes
A taste of blood rises
Irritates my nose
eyes
throat

A taste of blood comes
A taste of blood fills me
nose
eyes
throat

A taste of blood comes
acridly vertical
like
the pagan obsession
for incense

There Are Nights

For Alejo Carpentier

There are nights with no name
there are nights with no moon
when a clammy
suffocation
nearly overwhelms me
the acrid smell of blood
spewing
from every muted trumpet

On those nights with no name
on those nights with no moon
the pain that inhabits me
presses
the pain that inhabits me
chokes

Nights with no name
nights with no moon
when I would have preferred
to be able no longer to doubt
the nausea obsesses me so
a need to escape
with no name
with no moon
with no moon
with no name
on nights with no moon
on nameless nameless nights
when the sickness sticks within me
like an Oriental dagger.

Position

For J. D.

The days themselves
have taken on the shape
of African masks
indifferent
to any profanation
of quicklime
the homage of
moonlit sighs
any size
played on a piano
the refrain
repeated in
shrubbery
gondolas
et cetera

Hiccups

For Vashti and Mercer Cook

I gulp down seven drinks of water
several times a day
and all in vain
instinctively
like the criminal to the crime
my childhood returns
in a rousing fit of hiccups

Talk about calamity
talk about disasters
I'll tell you

My mother wanted her son to have good manners at the table:
    keep your hands on the table
    we don't cut bread
    we break it
    we don't gobble it down
    the bread your father sweats for
    our daily bread

    eat the bones carefully and neatly
    a stomach has to have good manners too
    and a well-bred stomach never
    burps
    a fork is not a tooth-pick
    don't pick your nose
    in front of the whole world
    and sit up straight
    a well-bred nose
    doesn't sweep the plate

And then
and then
and then in the name of the Father
        and the Son
        and the Holy Ghost
at the end of every meal

And then and then
talk about calamity
talk about disasters
I'll tell you

My mother wanted her son to have the very best marks
        if you don't know your history
        you won't go to mass
        tomorrow
        in your Sunday suit

This child will disgrace our family name
This child will be our . . . in the name of God
        be quiet
        have I or have I not
        told you to speak French
        the French of France
        the French that Frenchmen speak
        French French

Talk about calamity
talk about disasters
I'll tell you

My mother wanted her son to be a mama's boy:
        you didn't say good evening to our neighbor
        what—dirty shoes again
        and don't let me catch you any more
        playing in the street or on the grass or in the park
        underneath the War Memorial
        playing
        or picking a fight with what's–his–name
        what's–his–name who isn't even baptized

Talk about calamity
talk about disasters
I'll tell you

My mother wanted her son to be
                very *do*
                very *re*

        very *mi*
        very *fa*
        very *sol*
       ·very *la*
        very *ti*
        very *do-re-mi*
        fa-sol-la-ti-
            do

I see you haven't been to your vi-o-lin lesson
      a banjo
      did you say a banjo
      what do you mean
      a banjo
      you really mean
      a banjo
      no indeed young man
          you know there won't be any
          ban-or
            jo
          or
            gui-or
              tar
                 in our house
They are not for *colored* people
Leave them to the *black* folks!

Sell Out

For Aimé Césaire

I feel ridiculous
in their shoes
their dinner jackets
their starched shirts
and detachable collars
their monocles and
their bowler hats

I feel ridiculous
my toes not made
to sweat from morning until night's relief
from this swaddling that impedes my limbs
and deprives my body of the beauty of its hidden sex

I feel ridiculous
my neck caught smokestack style
with this head that aches
but stops
each time I greet someone

I feel ridiculous
in their drawing rooms
among their manners
their bowings and scrapings
and their manifold need of monkeyshines

I feel ridiculous
with all their talk
until they serve each afternoon
a bit of tepid water and
some teacakes snuffling rum

I feel ridiculous
with theories they season
to the taste of their needs
their passions
their instincts
laid out neatly every night
like doormats

I feel ridiculous
among them
like an accomplice
like a pimp
like a murderer among them
my hands hideously red
with the blood of their
ci-vi-li-za-tion

Blues

For Robert Romain

Give them back
 to me
 my black
 dolls
 to dissipate the picture
 of pallid wenches
 merchandising love
 who stroll along
 the boulevard of my ennui

Give me back my black
 dolls
 to dissipate
 the never-ending image
 the hallucinating image
 of buxom puppets with big bottoms
 whose stinking misery
 is carried in the wind

 Give me the illusion I'll no longer
 have to satisfy
 the sprawling need
 for mercy
 snoring beneath the world's disdainful nose

Give my black dolls back to me
 So that I can play with them
 the simple games of my instincts
 instincts that endure
 in the darkness of their laws
 with my courage recovered
 and my audacity
 I become myself once more
 myself again
 out of what I used to be
 once upon a time
  once

without complexity
                    once upon a time
when the hour of uprooting came

Will they never know the rancor in my heart
opened to the eye of my distrust too late
they did away with what was mine
            ways
            days
            life
            song
            rhythm
            effort
            footpath
            water
            huts
            the smoke-gray earth
            the wisdom
            the words
            the palavers
            the elders
            the cadence
            the hands
            beating time
            the hands
            the feet
            marking time
            upon the ground

            Give them back
            to me
            my black
            dolls
            black
            dolls
            black
                    black
                        dolls.

The Black Man's Lament

For Robert Goffin

They gave it back to me
life
heavier and weary

Each of my todays has eyes that
look upon my yesterdays
with rancor
and with shame

The days
have never ceased to be
inexorably sad
at the memory of my mutilated life

Still there
my stupor
from the time gone by
of blows with the knotted cord
bodies burnt
charred from head to toe
dead flesh
branded
with red-hot irons
arms broken
beneath the lashing whip
beneath the whip that made plantations move
and quenched their thirst for blood my blood sweet blood
and the overseer's bravado as he swaggered it to heaven.

If Often

If often my feeling of race
strikes the same fear
as the nighttime howling of a dog

at some approaching death
I always feel
about to foam with rage
against what surrounds me
against what prevents me
ever
from being
a man

And nothing
nothing would so calm my hate
as a great
pool
of blood
made
by those long sharp knives
that strip the hills of cane
for rum.

Sleepless Night

For Sonia and Georges Gavarry

I've waltzed my friends
waltzed
more than any
of my ancestors
the Gauls
to such a point my blood
still beats
three-quarter time

I waltzed my friends
waltzed my childhood through
humming the Viennese tune
of some blue
        white
        red

green or
pink Danube
Red
green
pink
or blue
depending on your preference

I have waltzed friends
madly
waltzed
to such a point that often
I thought I had an arm
about the waist of
Uncle Gobineau
or Cousin Hitler
or that good Aryan gumming out his years
on some park bench.

Whitewash

For Christiane and Alioune Diop

It may be
they dare to
treat me white
though everything within me
wants only to be black
as Negro as my Africa
the Africa they ransacked

White

Abominable insult
that they'll pay me dearly for
when my Africa
the Africa they ransacked
is determined to have

peace
peace
nothing else but peace

White

My hatred grows
around the edges of their villainy
the edges of the gunshots
the edges of the pitching
of the slave ships
and the fetid cargoes of the cruel slavers

White

My hatred swells
around the edges of their culture
the edges of their theories
the edges of the tales
they thought they ought
to stuff me with
from the cradle onward
while all the while
everything within me
wants only to be black
as Negro as the Africa they robbed me of.

Shine

For Louis Armstrong

With others
from the neighborhood
a few rare friends
till now I've kept
the conical ancestral faith
high among the rafters of my hut

And the automatic arrogance
of masks

masks of living chalk
never has been able to remove
anything
ever
of a past
more hideous
here
at the four corners of my life

And my face gleams with the horrors of the past
and my dreadful laughter would repel
                              the specter of the hounds
                                    pursuing runaways
And my voice which sings for them
is sweet enough to soothe
the soul saddened by their
              por–
                 no–
                 gra–
                     phy

And my heart keeps watch
and my dream feeding on the noise of their
              de–
                 pra–
                     vi–
                     ty
is stronger than their clubs besmeared with foulness.

Reality

From having done nothing up to now
destroyed nothing
built nothing
dared nothing
like the Jew
or the yellow man

for the organized escape
from mass inferiority

I look in vain for
the hollow of a shoulder
in which to hide my face
my shame of the
> Re–
>> al–
>>> i–
>>>> ty.

Their Thing

They did their thing so well
they did their thing so well
that one day we let all
all that once was ours go
we threw it all away

They did their thing so very well
so very well indeed
indeed
that one day we had let it all
all that once was ours slip away
just disappear

And yet it wouldn't take much more
not very much
not much
for finally everything to go
for all of it
to go
everything that's ours I mean
belonging to our race

It wouldn't take much more
not much
not much.

Et Cetera

*In response to the German threat, the
Senegalese Veterans of War have
cabled an expression of their unre-
mitting loyalty to France. . . .*

                                   (*From news reports*)

To the Senegalese veterans of war
to future Senegalese soldiers
to all the Senegalese veterans or soldiers
that Senegal ever will produce
to all the future veterans
former and future regulars
what–do–I–care future former
      pensioners
      n.c.o.'s
      broken-down
      decorated
      mutilated
      poison–gassed
      disabled
      disfigured
      alcoholic
      amputee
      past and present soldiers
      et cetera et cetera

Me
I say SHIT
and that's not half of it

Me
I ask them to
shove
their bayonets
their sadistic fits
the feeling
the knowing
they have
filthy

dirty
jobs to do

Me
I ask them
to conceal the need they feel
to pillage
rape
and steal
to soil the old banks of the Rhine anew

Me
I ask them
to begin
by invading Senegal

Me
I call on them
to leave the Krauts in peace!

MARTINIQUE   ✳   *(1913–   )*

Aimé Césaire

THOUGH LITTLE OF HIS WORK HAS THUS FAR BEEN translated into English, Aimé Césaire is an important figure in contemporary French literature.

Césaire was born in Martinique. French planters who colonized the tiny, volcanic island have grown wealthy since the eighteenth century on sugar cane and rum. Except for the few upper-class Europeans, the population of this rich, fertile, but disaster-prone isle—repeatedly hit by hurricanes, tidal waves, earthquakes, volcanic eruptions, fire, famine, and drought—is largely black. In this lush climate, most live close to the subsistence level.

Césaire's family was of a slightly more prosperous class. His father was a minor government clerk, his mother a dressmaker. From an early age, their son attended, on scholarship, a school frequented by the children of far richer families. Césaire soon became aware of the "moral leprosy" of his native land, where, as in so much of the West Indies, the gradations of color were observed on each rung of the socioeconomic ladder.

Césaire had but one desire: to escape the confines of this narrow, monotonous life. At eighteen, already known as a brilliant student, he was sent on a scholarship to France. After studying at the Lycée Louis-le-Grand, he went to the prestigious *Ecole Normale Supérieure,* where he earned a *licence ès lettres.*

It was at Louis-le-Grand, in 1931, that Césaire met Léopold Senghor and "discovered Africa." In this reserved, reflective Senegalese, who was seven years his elder, he found "an immense certitude, that seemed to come from having had a whole continent beneath his feet, traditions, his own language . . . a past he had no need to be ashamed of."[*] Senghor introduced Césaire to the modern European writers—Proust,

[*] Armand Guibert, *Léopold Sédar Senghor* (Paris: Seghers, 1962), p. 22.

James Joyce, Virginia Woolf—the surrealist poets, the American Negro Renaissance. The two students explored and discussed the pioneering work of the French and German anthropologists Delafosse and Frobenius, who were propounding the astonishing idea that Africa had civilizations, a history, art, and cultures of its own.

Despite the differences in their personalities and background, the Senghor-Césaire friendship was immediate and close, and, despite their political differences, one that has withstood the test of time. When they joined with Damas to found *L'Etudiant noir* (*The Black Student*) in 1934, however, the two friends' goal was "to reunite black people who are considered French by law and nationality to their own history, traditions, and languages, to the culture which truly expresses their soul." Not until a decade later, with the *Présence Africaine* group centering around Alioune Diop, did the leaders begin to see the concerns of negritude as encompassing all persons of African descent. Not until the 1960s was the concept further enlarged to stress the role of black cultures on a universal basis.

While the triumvirate and their friends were launching the new movement, they were also involved in their own personal quests for artistic expression.

For Damas, this work had been *Pigments* (1937). For Senghor, it would be the early poems later collected as *Chants d'ombre* (*Songs of Darkness*). For Césaire, it was *Notes on a Return to the Native Land*, a book-length, free-form, free-verse poem written in 1938 when Césaire was twenty-five years old, on the eve of his return home from seven years of schooling abroad.

Notes is the only possible introduction to Césaire's work. It summarizes his emotional, moral, and intellectual journey from adolescence to manhood. In the painful year he spent writing it, one senses that some mysterious crystallization of the self occurred. Refusing the part of his education that had "stuffed him with lies," he assimilated its tools in order to transcend it, to reassert his whole self, to achieve equilibrium and direction both as a man and as an artist. Despite the lack of regular paragraphs, chapters, stanzas, *Notes* soon reveals itself as highly organized. Leaving the meters, rhythms, and metaphors of classical French verse behind, inspired by the aesthetic freedom proclaimed by surrealism, the voice which speaks has created its own language, its own vocabulary, imagery, beat, and alterations of rhythm.

It was this extraordinary power of language that so impressed André

Breton. In his preface to *Notes,* Breton called it "nothing less than the greatest lyric monument of our time." *Notes* marks the first full orchestration of group themes only sketched, only hinted at by the earlier West Indian poets.

Since its first appearance in a full-length edition in 1947—nine years after it was written—Césaire's *Notes* has won a unique place among French-speaking black students. Curiously, it is with Césaire, the West Indian, and above all the Césaire of *Notes,* rather than the African Senghor, that young Africans still identify today. "Whole passages of this masterpiece," says Alioune Diop, "are recited by heart in francophone Africa by young people, sometimes barely literate themselves, but burning with [its] intensity." The Nigerian critic Abiola Irele writes, "No other single work has had so profound an influence . . . shaping the very spirit . . . determining the very movement of contemporary attitudes within the French-speaking Negro world." The Belgian literary historian Lilyan Kesteloot describes *Notes* as absorbing "in the same surge of love and revolt, black people of the West Indies and the United States, those of Africa and Europe, those of the past and the present, slaves and heroes. Césaire's has truly been the voice of Negro awareness, of its sufferings and its needs." It is, she has said, "the national anthem of blacks the world over."

In excerpting from *Notes,* the problem was to preserve the flow and architecture of the entire poem. The present abridgment—approximately one-third the length of the original and incorporating a number of the major passages—was made with this goal in mind. Though obviously no abridgment can replace the whole, one can distinguish several major movements.

First, an evocation of the native land; second, the quest for "what is mine"—a catalogue of portions of the world that bear the black imprint, ending with a vision of the dying Toussaint Louverture imprisoned in white; third, the confrontation between the poet's childish imaginings of a glorious African history, his personal dream of heroism, and the ugly truths about him; fourth, the revelation ("What strange pride illuminates me suddenly?"); fifth: an ascent to the famous celebration of negritude ("My negritude is not a stone," etc.); sixth, the prophecy and dedication, in which the poet's anger against the lies and crimes of the West, which have dehumanized his race, are subsumed in his refusal to hate, his insistence on the "burning immensity of love" that fills him; and, seventh, an affirmation of the poet's own vision of the world.

Césaire's poetry since *Notes* is much admired by critics, but far less known than his early work. His language and imagery have become increasingly hermetic, the syntax and sense often difficult. The later, short poems we include here are taken from the sampling of poems from *Les Armes miraculeuses* (*Miraculous Weapons*), 1946; *Soleil Cou Coupé* (*Beheaded Sun*), 1948; *Ferrements* (*Shackles*), 1959; and *Cadastre* (*Land Survey*), 1961, translated by Clayton Eshleman and Denis Kelly and published in a private edition titled *State of the Union.**

Césaire retired from teaching in 1944, after he was elected to the twin post of deputy to the French National Assembly for Martinique and mayor of its capital, Fort-de-France. He has been re-elected each term since. Unlike the former French colonies of Africa, or the Caribbean islands once ruled by the British, Martinique has never become independent. At a referendum in 1946, citizens of the island voted to move from the marginal status of colony to that of statehood. Legally, the population of Martinique now enjoys full equality of citizenship with metropolitan France.

In 1956, after twelve years as a member of the French Communist Party, a disillusioned Césaire resigned. His *Lettre à Maurice Thorez* (*Letter to Maurice Thorez*) remains a classic statement of the discrepancies between theoretical Marxism and the actual workings of the Party apparatus. "What I wish is that Marxism and communism were made to serve black peoples, and not black people to serve Marxism and communism, that the doctrine and the movement were made for men and not men for the doctrine and the movement," he commented. Today Césaire leads his own independent, liberal party. He continues to work for economic and social reforms and to erase the apathy and resignation of his islanders. But he takes an interest in far less parochial issues as well.

Césaire has always been a lucid and provocative essayist. He has written on European colonialism; the Harlem Renaissance poets; and the political, economic, and cultural situation of the West Indies. His study of the eighteenth-century Haitian revolutionary *Toussaint Louverture* appeared in 1962. He has also written more and more for the theater. *La Tragédie du roi Christophe* (*The Tragedy of King Christophe*), 1963, and *Une Saison au Congo* (*A Season in the Congo*), 1966, are plays based on historical figures. The first focuses on Henri-Christophe, the Haitian ruler who succeeded Toussaint Louverture, crowned himself

* *State of the Union: Twenty-Eight Poems by Aimé Césaire,* translated by Clayton Eshleman and Denis Kelly (Cleveland, Ohio: Asphodel Book Shop), 1965.

king, imitated the excesses of European court life, drove his people as relentlessly as any European tyrant, and finally committed suicide when his physical powers began to fail. The second play is a dramatization of the life and death of Patrice Lumumba.

What most interests Césaire about these leaders—seen not at the point of their victory over imperialist powers but at the next stage, that of decolonization—is the problem of newly freed peoples trying to cope with the responsibilities of self-government. The leader's solitude, his dreams for his people, the difficulty of awakening and motivating them, his own uncertainties and internal demands, conflicting priorities, internecine struggles, the betrayals, the interference of outsiders: these are the forces that overwhelm Césaire's visionary but also very human heroes.

Dramatist, essayist, teacher, political and intellectual leader, Aimé Césaire is, first and foremost, a poet. As André Breton put it, Césaire has "that unmistakably major tone which distinguishes great from lesser poets."

Notes on a Return to the Native Land (abridgment)

This flat city shortly after dawn, exposed, stumbling commonsensically along, inert, breathless beneath its geometric burden of crosses eternally renewed; intractable before its fate, mute, thwarted in every way, incapable of growing according to the essence of this earth, cut down, encumbered, reduced, ruptured from flora and fauna.

Shortly after dawn, this city, flat, exposed. . . .

And in this inert town the noisy crowd so surprisingly missing the point of its noise, just as the town misses the point of its movement, its meaning, making insouciant detours from its true cry, the only cry one would want to hear because one feels it *is* this town's, belonging to it alone, because one senses it alive in some deep refuge of darkness and pride here, within this inert city, within this crowd that overlooks its cries of hunger, misery, revolt, and hate: this crowd so strangely talkative and mute.

Within the inert city this strange crowd which doesn't crowd, which doesn't mix, ingenious at discovering the disengagement point, elusive, evasive. This crowd that doesn't know how to be a crowd, this crowd, one realizes, so perfectly alone beneath this sun. . . .

And neither the teacher in his classroom nor the priest at catechism can get a word out of this sleepy little nigger, in spite of the energetic way they both have of drumming on his close-cropped head, for his voice is caught in a quicksand of hunger (a-word-just-one-word-and-we'll-forget-Queen-Blanche-of-Castille, just-one-word, look-at-this-little-savage-who-doesn't-know-a-single-one-of-God's-Ten-Commandments)

for his voice is forgotten in a quicksand of hunger

and there is nothing really nothing to be had from this worthless little nobody

but hunger, a hunger that no longer cares to clamber up the rigging to his voice,

dull, sluggish hunger,

a hunger buried in the deeper hunger of this famished hill.

. . . the time went quickly, very quickly

August gone, of mangoes decked in crescent blossoms; September, begetter of cyclones; October, igniter of cane; November, of purring distilleries; Christmas was beginning.

It disclosed itself first in a teasing of desires, a need for brand-new tenderness, a burgeoning of vague dreams—Christmas—then it took flight suddenly with the purple rustling of its great wings of joy, and then it was rampant in the city, its giddy climb bursting the life in the shacks like a too ripe pomegranate.

Christmas was not like other feasts. It didn't lend itself to running in the streets, dancing in the public squares, sitting astride wooden horses, profiting from the throng to pinch the women, or setting off fireworks by the tamarind trees. Christmas had agoraphobia. It needed a whole day of bustling preparations, cookings, cleanings, worryings

> that there may not be enough
> that this-or-that is missing
> that maybe we'll be bored

Then in the evening a little unintimidating church, amiably filling up with laughter, whisperings, secrets, scandals, declarations of love and the guttural cacophony of an energetic singer, and also happy men and open-hearted, buxom girls and shacks with innards rich with all things succulent, and no one stingy with them and twenty people stopping by, and

the street deserted and the town nothing any longer but a garden of sing-
ing, and one feels good inside and eats good things and drinks good
cheer, and there is pudding, the thin kind that rolls easily on two fingers,
the mild, dumpy kind that tastes of wild thyme, the violent kind, in-
candescent with spices, and piping hot coffee and sugared anise and
punch with milk in it and the liquid sunshine of the rums, and all sorts
of good things that forcefully impose themselves upon your mucous
membranes, or that you rapturously distill, or that weave their fragrances
around you, and you laugh and sing, and the choruses run on and on like
coco trees as far as the eye can see

ALLELUIA

KYRIE ELEISON . . . LEISON . . . LEISON

CHRISTE ELEISON . . . LEISON . . . LEISON

And it's not just mouths that sing, but hands, feet, hips, genitals, the
whole creature liquefies in sound and voice and rhythm.

Reaching the peak of its ascent, the joy bursts like a cloud. The sing-
ing doesn't stop, but rolls along now heavily, uneasily, past the valleys of
fear, through the tunnels of anguish, the fires of hell.

And each begins to pull the nearest devil by his tail, until the fear
dissolves insensibly into the fine sand of dreams, and truly one lives as in
a dream, and drinks and shouts and sings as in a dream, and dozes too as
if in a dream, with rose-petal eyelids, and daylight comes velvety as
sapodilla, with the smell of liquid dung from the cacao trees, and turkeys
picking their red pustules in the sun, and the obsession of the bells, and
the rain,

the bells . . . the rain
going plink, plink, plink,

Soon after dawn, the city—flat, exposed.

.   .   .   .

. . . And this long-ago joy, bringing me awareness of my present misery,
a bumpy road quilting its way through a hollow in which it scatters
several shacks; an indefatigable road that charges full speed up a hill to
sink abruptly in a sea of ramshackle cabins; a road climbing crazily,
descending recklessly, and the carcass of wood comically perched on
minuscule paws of cement that I call our "house," its tin mane rippling
in the sun like a skin laid out to dry, the dining room, rough floor with
nailheads glinting, rafters of pine and shadow that run across the ceiling,

chairs of phantom straw, the dull lamplight, the rapid gleam of roaches that hum until you ache.

. . . .

Shortly after dawn, another stinking little house on a very narrow street, a tiny house that harbors in its guts of rotting wood tens of rats and the turbulence of my six brothers and sisters, a cruel little house whose intransigence made us panic at the end of every month, and my temperamental father, gnawed at bit by bit by a single misery, I've never known what, an unpredictable sorcery quiets into melancholy tenderness or excites to flames of anger; and my mother, whose limbs for our tireless hunger pedal, pedal day and night, I am even awakened at night by those tireless limbs that pedal through the night and by the bitter bite into the soft flesh of the night of a Singer that my mother pedals, pedals for our hunger day and night.

Shortly after dawn, surrounding my father, my mother, the shack, blistered like a peach tree suffering from blight, and the worn roof, patched with bits of kerosene cans that make swamps of rust in the stinking gray straw; and when the wind whistles these disparities make a bizarre sound, like the crackling of frying at first, then like a burning log plunged in water that sends off streaks of steam and flying sparks . . . and the bed of planks from which my race has sprung, my whole race sprung from this bed of planks with its kerosene-can feet, as if it had elephantiasis, the bed, and its goatskin and dried banana leaves and rags, a nostalgia of a mattress, my grandmother's bed (above the bed in a pot filled with oil a faint light whose fat flame dances like a beetle . . . written on the pot in gold letters: Thank You).

A disgrace, this rue Paille,
an appendix as disgusting as the shameful parts of this city extending to the left and right all along the colonial highway, the gray mass of its shingled roofs. Here there are only roofs of straw, darkened by the spray, plucked at by the wind. . . .

. . . .

To leave.
As there are hyena-men and panther-men I would be a Jew-man
a Kafir
a Hindu from Calcutta
a voteless man from Harlem

The hungry man, insulted man, the tortured man that anyone at any time can seize and beat and kill—yes, absolutely kill—without being accountable to anyone or needing to apologize. . . .

I would retrieve the secret of great combustions and great communications. I would say storm. I would say river. Tornado I would say. I would say leaf. I would say tree. I would be watered by all rains, dampened by all dews. I would rumble onward like frenetic blood on the slow stream of the eye my words like wild horses like radiant children like clots like curfew-bells in temple ruins like precious stones so distant as to discourage miners. He who would not understand me would not understand the roaring of the tiger either. . . .

.   .   .   .

To leave. My heart murmured emphatic generosities. To leave . . . I would arrive young and polished in this country of mine, and I would say to this country whose slime is a part of the composition of my flesh: "I have wandered long and I return to your hideous, deserted wounds."

I would come to this country of mine and say to it: "Embrace me without fear. . . . And if all I know how to do is speak, it is for you that I shall speak."

And I would say more:
"My lips shall speak for miseries that have no mouth, my voice shall be the liberty of those who languish in the dungeon of despair. . . ."

And as I came I would tell myself:
"And above all, my body, as well as my soul, beware of crossing your arms in the sterile attitude of spectator, for life is not a spectacle, a sea of pain is not a proscenium, a man who cries out is not a dancing bear. . . ."

And here I am!
Once again this life limping before me; not this life, this death, this death without piety or purpose, this death whose magnitude runs pitifully aground, the dazzling insignificance of this death, this death that limps from insignificance to insignificance, these serving spoons of petty greediness from the conquistador, these scoops of tiny flunkeys on the great wild thing, these shovelfuls of shabby souls on the three-souled Caribbean, and all these futile deaths. . . .

This is mine, these few thousand humiliated souls circling round inside a calabash isle, and mine too the archipelago curved as if anxiously seeking to deny itself, in a maternal anxiety one might say to protect the more delicate slenderness separating one America from the other, and their flanks secreting the Gulf Stream's good liquor for Europe, one of the two incandescent versants through which the equator funambulates toward Africa. And my unenclosed island, its bright audacity upright at this polynesia's tail end; Guadeloupe in front of it, bisected at the dorsal line, suffering our sickness too; Haiti where negritude first stood up and said it believed in its humanity, and the comic little tail of Florida where a Negro is being strangled, and, gigantically caterpillaring toward the Hispanic foot of Europe, Africa, in whose nudity Death cuts a wide swath.

And I tell myself Bordeaux and Nantes and Liverpool and New York
and San Francisco,
there is no place on this earth without my fingerprint,
and my heel upon the skeleton of skyscrapers, and my
sweat in the brilliance of diamonds!
Who can boast of more than I?
Virginia   Tennessee   Georgia   Alabama
Monstrous putrefactions of inoperative
revolts,
swamps of putrid blood,
trumpets absurdly stopped,
red lands, sanguine,
consanguine.

This is mine too: a little
cell in the Jura Mountains,
a little cell,
the snow lines its bars with white,
the snow is a white
jailer standing guard before a prison.
This is mine,
a man alone
imprisoned in white,
a man alone who defies the white
cries of white
death
(TOUSSAINT, TOUSSAINT
LOUVERTURE),

a man who fascinates the white
hawk of white
death,
a man alone in a sterile sea of white
snow,
an old darky standing tall
against the waters of the sky.
Death traces a shining circle
above this man,
gently sprinkling stars about his head.
Death breathes like a mad thing
in the ripe roughness of his arms.
Death gallops in the prison like a white
horse.
Death gleams in the darkness
like a cat's eyes.
Death hiccups
like the water under coral reefs.
Death is a wounded bird.
Death wanes,
wavers.
Death is a great shady tree.
Death expires in a white
pool of silence.

Puffs of night
at the four corners
of this dawn.
Convulsions of stiffening
death.
Tenacious destiny.
Will the splendor
of this blood
not burst mute earth
with its upright cries?

.   .   .   .

I refuse to take my bombast for authentic glories
and I laugh at my childish old imaginings.

No, we were never Amazons to the king of Dahomey, or Ghanaian princes with eight hundred camels, or doctors in Timbuktu when Askia the Great was king, or the architects of Djenné, or Madhis, or warriors. We do not feel the armpit itch of those who once upon a time bore lances. And since I've sworn to leave out nothing of our history (I who admire nothing so much as the sheep browsing in his afternoon shadow), I want to admit that for all time we have been rather wretched dishwashers, shoeshine boys with little scope, let's make it even plainer, rather conscientious conjurors, and the only indisputable record we have held is that of endurance to the whip. . . .

And this country cried out for centuries that we were rude beasts; that the pulsing of humanity stopped at Negro doors; that we are a walking dunghill morbidly promising tender cane and silky cotton, and they marked us with red-hot irons, and we slept in our excrement and they sold us in the public squares, and a bolt of English cloth or a side of salted meat from Ireland cost less than we did, and this land was calm, tranquil, proclaiming the spirit of the Lord was in its actions.

We, vomited from slaveships.
We, hunted in the Calebars.
What? Stop up our ears?
We, sotted to death from being rolled, mocked, jeered at,
Stifled with fog!
Forgiveness partner whirlwind!

From the hold I hear the curses of the chained, the coughs of the dying, the sound of someone thrown into the sea . . . the howling of a woman in labor . . . the scrape of fingernails in search of throats . . . the snigger of the whip . . . the scampering of vermin in the weariness. . . .

Nothing could ever urge us toward noble, desperate adventure.
So be it. So be it.
I am of no nationality foreseen by chancelleries;
I defy the craniometer. *Homo sum et cetera*
That they serve and deceive and die.
So be it. So be it. It was written in the shape of their pelvis.

And I, and I,
I who sang the hard fist,
You must know how far I let it go, my cowardice.
One evening in the trolley across from me . . .

A Negro as big as an ape was trying to make himself very small on a trolley seat. He was trying to dispose of his gigantic limbs and his trembling, hungry boxer's hands on this greasy trolley seat. And everything about him was falling apart. His nose looked like a peninsula adrift, and even his negritude was fading under the hand of a tireless tawer. And the tawer was Poverty. A sudden bat whose claws left scabby islands on his face. Or rather, it was a tireless worker, Poverty, laboring on some hideous scroll. The industrious, malevolent thumb, one could see, had shaped the forehead with a lump, pierced the nose with parallel alarming tunnels, elongated the huge lip, and, in a master stroke of caricature, had planed, polished, and varnished the tiniest, cutest little ear in all creation.

He was an awkward, ungainly Negro, without rhythm or proportion,

A Negro whose eyes rolled in bloodshot weariness,

An obscene Negro whose toes sneered in a rather stinking way from deep in the half-open lair of his shoes.

Poverty, one had to admit, had done its best to do him in.

It had hollowed out the orbit, filled it with a camouflage of rheumy dust.

It had stretched the empty space between the solid hinge of jaws and the cheekbones of an old, worn face. It had planted tiny, shining stakes of a several-days-old beard. It had disconnected the heart, and stooped the back.

All in all, he was absolutely hideous, a mumbling, sprawling, melancholy nigger, a nigger shrouded in a worn, old jacket, his hands joined in prayer on a knobby wooden stick. A nigger comical and ugly, and the women behind me tittered at the sight of him.

He *was* comical and ugly,

Comical and ugly, to be sure.

I unfurled a great big guilty smile,

My cowardice discovered!

I salute the three centuries that uphold my civil rights and my minimized blood.

My heroism, what a farce!

This town is just my size.

And my soul is asleep, sleeping like this city in its filth and mud.

This city, my filthy face,
I demand for it the brilliant commendation of spit! . . .

.   .   .   .

I live for the flattest part of my soul,
For the dullest part of my flesh.
Tepid dawning of ancestral warmth and fear
I tremble now with the common trepidation of our docile
blood pulsing in the madrepore.

And these tadpoles within me hatched of my prodigious ancestry!
Those who invented neither gunpowder nor compass,
Those who never vanquished steam or electricity,
Those who explored neither seas nor sky,
But who know in its uttermost corners the landscape of pain,
Those who've known no voyages other than uprootings,
Those who have been stupefied from falling on their knees,
Those who were Christianized and tamed,
Those who were inoculated with decay,
Tom-toms of empty hands,
Futile tom-toms echoing with wounds,
Tom-toms made absurd by atrophied betrayals.

Tepid dawning of ancestral warmth and fear;
Overboard, my peregrine riches,
Overboard, my authentic falsehoods,

But what strange pride illuminates me suddenly? . . .

O friendly light!
O fresh source of light! '
Those who invented neither gunpowder nor compass
Those who never knew how to conquer steam or electricity
Those who explored neither seas nor sky
But those without whom the earth would not be earth,
Protuberance so much more beneficial than deserted earth,
Earthier,
Silo preserving and ripening the earth's most earthy,
My negritude is not a stone, its deafness hurled against
The clamor of the day;

My negritude is not a speck of dead water on the earth's dead eye,
My negritude is neither tower nor cathedral,

It plunges into the red flesh of the earth,
It plunges into the ardent flesh of the sky,
It perforates opaque dejection with its upright patience.

Eïa for the royal *Kaïlcédrat!*
Eïa for those who never invented anything,
Who never explored anything,
Who never conquered anything,
But who abandon themselves to the essence of all things,
Ignorant of surfaces, caught by the motion of all things,
Indifferent to conquering but playing the game of the world,

Truly the eldest sons of the world,
Porous to all the breathing of the world,
Fraternal space for all the breathing of the world,
Bed without drain for all the waters of the world,
Spark of the sacred fire of the world,
Flesh of the world's flesh palpitating with the very movement of the
world. Tepid dawning of ancestral virtues

Blood! Blood! all our blood roused by the virile heart of the sun!
Those who know the oily body of the womanly moon,
The healing exaltation of antelope and star,
Those whose survival advances in the germination of the grass,
Eïa for the perfect circle of the world, enclosed concordance!

Listen to the white world,
Horribly weary from its enormous effort,
Its rebellious joints crack beneath the hard stars.
Its rigid, blue steel penetrates the mystic flesh;
Hear its traitorous victories trumpet its defeats;
Hear the grandiose alibis for its sorry stumblings,
Pity for our conquerors, omniscient and naïve! . . .

And here at the end of dawn is my virile prayer,
Eyes fixed on the beautiful city I prophesy:
May I hear neither laughter nor cries,
Give me the sorcerer's wild faith,
Give to my hands the power to mold,

Give to my soul the temper of steel,
I do not shrink. Make of my head a spearhead, and of my self, my heart,
make not a father nor a brother but *the* father, brother, son; not a hus-
band, but the lover of this single people;
Make me rebel against all vanity but as docile to its genius,
As the fist is to the arm;
Make me the servant of its blood,
The trustee of its resentment,
Make of me a man who terminates,
Make of me a man who initiates,
Make of me a man who contemplates,
But make of me as well a man who sows;
Make me the executor of these lofty works,
For now is the time to gird one's loins like a valiant man.

But in doing so, my heart, preserve me from all hatred,
Make not of me that man of hate
For whom I've only hate,
For to allot myself
This single race
You know my love to be tyrannical,
You know that it is not from hate
For other races
That I seek to be the plowman
Of this single race,
You know that what I wish
For the universal hunger,
For the universal thirst,
Is to shake it free at last,
To summon from its inner depths
The succulence of fruit.

.   .   .   .

Look, I am nothing but a man,
No degradation, no spit disturbs me.
I am nothing but a man who no longer accepts
being angry
Who has nothing in his heart any more
But a burning immensity of love.

I accept . . . I accept . . . entirely without reserve
My race that no ablution of hyssop and lilies could purify,
My race corroded with stains,
Ripe grape for drunken feet,
Queen of sputum and leprosies,
Of whippings and scrofula,
Queen of squasma and chloasma
(Oh, those queens I once loved in faraway spring gardens, against a
background of candlelit chestnut trees!).
I accept, I accept
The flogged nigger who says: Forgive me, master,
And the twenty-nine legal blows of the whip,
And the dungeon four feet high,
And the spiked iron collar,
And the hamstrings cut for my runaway audacity,
And the fleur-de-lys streaming from the brand iron
On my shoulder.

Look, am I humble enough? Have I enough callouses on my knees?
Muscles in my back?

Groveling in mud. Stiffening against the slickness of the mud. To
bear it.

Mud sun. Muddy horizon. Sky of mud.

Deaths in mud. O names to hold in the hollow of a hand, to warm
with feverish breath.

Annular islands, lovely constellation,
I caress you with my ocean hands,
I twist and turn
My tradewind words about you,
And I lick you with my tongues of algae,
And I steer you clear of pirates,

O death, your viscous marshes!
Shipwreck, your hell of debris! I accept them!

And my original geography, as well; the map of the world made
For my use, not painted in the arbitrary colors of scholars,
But in the geometry of my shed blood, I accept,

And the determination of my biology, not prisoner to a
Single facial angle, to one kind of hair, to a nose sufficiently

Flat, a color sufficiently melanian, and the negritude, no
Longer a cephalic index, or a plasma, or a soma, but measured
On the compass of pain.
And the Negro each day more base, more cowardly, more sterile,
Less profound, more scattered, more separated
From himself, more wily, less immediate with himself,

I accept, I accept all that.

And far from the palate sea that foams beneath the suppurating syzygy
of blisters, the body of my country marvelously recumbent in the despair
of my arms, its bones shaking and in its veins the blood hesitating like
the drop of vegetal milk at the wounded point of the bulb;

And now, suddenly, strength and life charge through me like a bull, and
the wave of life surrounds the papilla of the hill, and now all the veins
and capillaries swell with new blood, and the enormous, cyclonic lung
breathes, and the hoarded fire of volcanoes, and the gigantic, seismic
pulse beat now the measure of a living body in my firm embrace.

And we are standing now, my country and I, hair in the wind, my little
hand now in its enormous fist, and the strength is not in us but above us,
in a voice that pierces the night, and the audience like the sting of an
apocalyptic hornet. And the voice proclaims that Europe for centuries has
stuffed us with lies and bloated us with pestilence,
For it is not true that the work of man is finished,
That there is nothing for us to do in this world,
That we are parasites on this earth,
That it is enough for us to keep in step with the world,
But the work of man has only just begun,
And it is up to man to vanquish all deprivations immobilized in the
corners of his fervor,
And no race has the monopoly on beauty, intelligence, or strength,
And there is a place for all at the rendezvous of conquest,
And we know now that the sun turns around our earth illuminating the
portion that our will alone has determined and that any star falls from
sky to earth at our limitless command. . . .

FROM *Miraculous Weapons*

First Problem

When they grab my leg
I hurl back a jungle of lianas
Let them lynch me
I vanish into a row of figs

The weakness of most men
they don't know how to become a stone or tree

Sometimes I stick tinder between my fingers
for the sole pleasure of breaking out
fresh poinsettia all night long
reds, greens flaming in the wind
like our dawn in my throat.

—Translated by Clayton Eshleman and Denis Kelly

TWO POEMS FROM *Land Survey*

The Wheel

The wheel is the most beautiful discovery of man and the only one
the sun turns
the earth turns
your face turns on the axle of your neck when
you cry
but you minutes won't you ever rewind on the living
bobbin
the lapped blood
the art of suffering sharpened like tree stumps by the
knives of winter
the doe drunk from not drinking
which puts me on the well's rim unforeseen your
face of a dismasted schooner
your face

like a village asleep at the bottom of a lake
which revives in the daylight from the grass and the germ
year

—Translated by Clayton Eshleman and Denis Kelly

Magic

with a thin slice of sky on a hunk of earth
you beasts who hiss into the face of this dead woman
you free ferns between the murderous rocks
at the extreme of the island between conches too vast for their
destiny
when noon sticks its canceled stamps on the tempestuous
folds of the she-wolf
beyond the frame of all known science
and the mouth in the linings of the nest satisfied with islands gulped
like a sou

with a thin slice of sky on a hunk of earth
prophet of the islands forgotten like a sou
without sleep without watch without finger without stockade
when the tornado passes gnaws at the bread of huts

you beasts who hiss into the face of this dead woman
the beautiful ounce of lust and the operculate shell
languid glide of the summer squalls we were
beautiful flesh to transfix with the ara's trident
when the five-branched chancellor stars
trefoil in the sky like drops of fallen milk
reinstate a black god low born of their thunder

—Translated by Clayton Eshleman and Denis Kelly

FROM *Beheaded Sun*

Mississippi

Man too bad you don't notice that my eyes
remember
   slings and black flags
   that murder every time I blink

Man too bad you don't see that you see nothing
not even that beautiful signal-system of the railroad that
under my eyelids makes the red and black discs of the coral-
snake which my munificence coils in my tears

Man too bad you don't see that in the depths of the reticle
where chance has deposited our eyes
there waits a buffalo drowned to the guard of the eyes
of the marsh

Man too bad you don't see that you can't
prevent me from building for his sufficiency
islands to the egg head of flagrant sky
under the calm ferocity of the immense geranium our sun.

—*Translated by Clayton Eshleman and Denis Kelly*

TWO POEMS FROM *Shackles*

Beat It Night Dog

the sea drew back uninjured with the blood of giant squids
stranded on the sand
in the country which opens up always to heal over again I seek
a memory of tide a flower of water a murmur of fury
but too many trails tangle their caravans
too many jaundiced suns impale the trees with their rancor
too many lying portolan-charts are sucked
into watersheds always diverging

from tall ants polishers of skeletons
    of this fiery silence of the mouth of this sand
will nothing rise but the rotted tips of the dry forest

rage of an unwonted solstice, glowing beast at the barbaric limit
so faint from the sea
beat it night dog beat it
sudden and major at my temples
        you hold between your bleeding fangs

a flesh I recognize too easily

              —Translated by Clayton Eshleman and Denis Kelly

State of the Union

Gentlemen,

the situation is tragic;
beneath our soil we have left
only 75 years of iron
only 50 years of cobalt;

but what of the
55 years of sulfur,
20 years of bauxite
in the heart?

nothing   zero,
mine without vein,
cave where no man moves,
not a drop left
of blood.

EMMET TILL,
your eyes were a conch where the bottle
of wine of your fifteen-year-old blood
bubbled,
never had any age, these young men,
or it weighed them down

more than skyscrapers,
five hundred years

> of torturers
> of burners of witches

five hundred years

> of bad gin
> of big cigars
> of fat bellies
> filled with slices
> of rancid bibles

five hundred years

> of mouths
> of old women
> bitter with sins

They've had five hundred years, EMMET TILL,
five hundred years is the ageless age of the gallows of Cain.
EMMET TILL I tell you

> in the heart zero
> not a drop left
> of blood;

and your heart,
let it conceal my sun,
let it mix with my bread.

Boy from Chicago,
are you still worth
as much as a white man?

Spring, he believed in you,
yes even on the levee of night,
on the dikes of the MISSISSIPPI,
sweeping between high banks
of racial hate its jails its barricades
its tides of tombstones
in spring, whose sounds flow
in eyes of riverboats, the portholes.
In spring whistling stampedes
on savannas of blood.
In spring slipping its gloves from delicate hands
in explosions of shells and silica

which loosen the blood-clots of fear,
dissolve the blood-clots of hate,
swelling with age in the thread of rivers of blood,
rafting the hazardous rubric of beasts in ambush
        But They
were invulnerable slow mounted massive
on sinister immemorial billygoats
              BOY FROM CHICAGO
gone in the stuttering of racial winds
hear him in the blue grove of the veins
sing like the blood-bird
foretell above the banks of sleep
his climbing in the blue field grappling
Sun your furtive step vehement fish

Then night remembered in its arms,
soft flight of the vampire gliding suddenly
and the pistol of BIG MILLAM
wrote these words on a black living wall
in rusty letters wrote
State of the Union Message
zinc 20 years
copper 15 years
oil 15 years
           and in the 180th year of these states
           but what in the heart unfeeling clock
           nothing zero what not a drop of blood
           left in the putrid white and
           antiseptic heart?

—Translated by Denis Kelly

MARTINIQUE (1928–   )

Edouard Glissant

AS A TEEN-AGER DURING WORLD WAR II, EDOUARD
Glissant was Aimé Césaire's student at the Lycée Schoelcher in Fort-de-
France. Glissant and his classmates played roles in the 1944 political
campaign which resulted in the election of their popular professor as
mayor of Martinique's capital and deputy to the Assembly. Some years
later, Glissant wrote *La Lezarde* (*The Ripening*), a novel named for
the island's principal river, which described the inner and outer realities
of these predecent-shattering political events.

Glissant, who completed his university studies in France, now lives
and teaches there. But the West Indian scene is still the focus of his
literary efforts. He has published four book-length poems: *Les Indes*
(*The Indies*), 1956; *Un Champ d'îles* (*A Field of Islands*), 1953; *La
Terre inquiète* (*The Uneasy Earth*), 1954; and *Le Sel noir* (*Black
Salt*), 1960; a play, *Monsieur Toussaint,* 1961; *Soleil de la conscience*
(*The Sunshine of Awareness*), 1956; and *Le Quatrième siècle* (*The
Fourth Century*), 1964, a historical novel about several generations of
two black West Indian families.

For this volume we have chosen several pages from Glissant's epic
prose poem, *The Indies,* a lyrical evocation of Caribbean history.

The Indies (excerpts)

XLIX

They fastened a people to merchant ships. They sold, leased, bartered
flesh, old folk at the lowest price, men for the sugar harvests, women
for the value of their children. There is no longer any mystery, any
shock: The Indies were a market place of death. The wind howls it

now, righteously against the prow. Those who liquidated love and desire were the navigators. They turned their faces to the forest and mutely asked—once more the language violated—for muscle. O words, O empty language, mortuary grammar! A full set of teeth brought still more . . . at the Omega of the New World. I see Cyrus, long, long ago, leading his people to slaughter at the hour when you, Sun, redden with another hope. Cyrus, betrayed leader, who whips you, then insults you? The sea. Have you forgotten that pain is a slaughterhouse and the light a whip? I see hollow sun and weary sea, supported on the bleeding of the great and unmysterious Indies.

L

One of them, taking advantage of the crew's momentary carelessness, turns his soul toward the sea and lets it swallow him. Dehumanized, his body had no meadow, no river, no fire. Another dies in his excrement, consumed by the general fetidity. There's one here who knows his wife is chained nearby: he cannot see her but hears her growing weaker. And one, too, who knows his wife is bound to a post aboard another slaveship; he cannot see her, but he hears her being taken away. And another whose side has been wounded by a cudgel, but the sailor who's been reckless with the merchandise is roundly punished. Some are led about the deck once a week so their legs don't waste away. Another, who will not walk, who already has the immobility of death, is made to dance on hot sheet iron. One waits for starvation, refusing to swallow the salted bread. Then he is offered the bread or a red-hot iron from the fire. One actually swallows his tongue, choking, choking, until motionless in red spittle. There's a medical name for it that I can't recall, but surely every sailor knows it since that time.

LI

The child climbs to the island's highest point. He sees the ship grow large on the horizon: "It's a new one, arriving for the Lenten market." He sounds the giant conch, and the buyers down below make ready to bid for young males and females. Where is the passion, where the splendor in this new distribution of the world? The auctioneer rises; in his belt, the list he'll sell from. I have called the roll, made the harsh toll of those who sailed the sea of death. A levy of deprivation beyond measure, I am told. Ancient, unleavened history! Utterance and song with no depth or shadow! Come one, come all! Hawkers parade along the sidewalks, retailing human lives. The buyers hasten, the gentle child slides down the hill, leaving his crow's nest behind. This adolescent lookout for the future does not know that there will be other auctions, to the misfortune of the prophecies, that there will be furious fingers on nocturnal drums whose frenzy will prove: "We are descended from those who survived."

LII

O Sun! O age-old labor mutely mixed with ocean and this terrible color of love! A man opens his eyes each morning on the solitude in which he keeps himself. He has left flamboyances behind, wept over his dreams, abandoned the uncommon ecstasy of those who love and are loved. He observes, he is moved, the day is thick with noises, he will have to busy himself, won't he, with this knot of undivided lives, out of which he must make sense. After the crossing, the loneliness, the anger of the sharks, soon a field of sumptuous earth, of misery and fire and the shedding of black blood unfolds. In the heavy summer, the tumultuous constriction, the race will ripen, and what belongs to it will ripen. We tread on harsh ground. Each strives now to distinguish in the Rising Sun his pure Setting Sun. It has only been a question of this flow since the beginning. O Sun, and you, sea, we shall know your rhythm and your meaning! . . . and may it close upon this dream in which you are enclosed, with the dead and the centuries. May the song of Death where Darkness reigned be forever ended.

HAITI   ✖   *(1926–   )*

René Depestre

LIKE U TAM'SI FROM THE CONGO, MAUNICK OF MAURI-tius, and the late David Diop of Senegal, René Depestre belongs to the second generation of negritude poets. He was born in 1926 in the port town of Jacmel, in southern Haiti, and spent his early childhood there. Depestre's father died when he was a small child, leaving the widow to bring up a large family on slender means. For his secondary studies, Depestre went to the Ecole Tippenhauer in Port-au-Prince. As a teen-ager he met and much admired Jacques Roumain—both for his writings and the political ideals he represented. Depestre, who had known de-privation firsthand, wanted to see the continuing misery of his country and his people relieved. By the time he was twenty he had published two books of stirring, patriotic verse, *Etincelles (Flashes)* in 1945, and *Gerbe de sang (Spurting Blood)* in 1946. He had also become editor-in-chief of a small, revolutionary newspaper, *La Ruche (The Beehive)*, and was a leader of the group responsible for the overthrow of the Elie Lescot government in 1946. As a gesture of gratitude, the then new President of Haiti, Dumas Estimé, in 1947 awarded the young Depestre a scholarship to continue his education in France.

In 1950 the Estimé government fell, and was followed by the Ma-gloire regime. Five years later, Duvalier took over the presidency and remained in power until his death in 1971, when he was succeeded by his son.

Depestre never returned to his homeland to live. In the 1950s he traveled a great deal in Europe, sojourning here and there on both sides of the Iron Curtain, frequently appearing at leftist-oriented interna-tional youth festivals, such as those in Berlin (1951), Moscow (1957), Algiers (1969), to speak and to read his poems. He also traveled widely in Central and South America, visiting Haiti briefly again in 1959. At least once, the intervention of a fellow poet of quite different political

89

persuasion, Léopold Senghor, is said to have saved the "boilingly militant" Haitian—who had become a communist during his early years abroad—from being imprisoned for his political activities.

For some twenty years Depestre's poetry has continued to appear in France: *Végétation de clarté* (*Vegetation of Light*), in 1951; *Traduit du grand large* (*Translated from the Great Expanse*), in 1952; and *Journal d'un animal marin* (*Diary of a Sea Creature*), in 1965—all published by Seghers. *Minerai noir* (*Black Ore*) and *Un Arc-en-ciel pour l'occident chrétien* (*A Rainbow for the Christian West*) were published by *Présence Africaine* in 1957 and 1967 respectively. The last two books appeared since Depestre's emigration to Cuba.

When he is not writing, Depestre directs a library in Havana and makes regular radio broadcasts to Haiti, which has no diplomatic relations with its Cuban neighbor. Depestre is a passionate defender of the Cuban revolution, and poems and articles of his reflecting his political views appear from time to time in *Présence Africaine*.

At the heart of *A Rainbow for the Christian West* is a section called "Epiphanies of the Voodoo Gods." This "voodoo mystery poem," as Depestre subtitles it, deserves to have been published separately. Inspired by Haitian folk religion, it is a surrealistic fantasy touching the deeper social and psychological issues of black-white race relations and human destructiveness.

The "Epiphanies" begin as an imaginary confrontation with a mythical white American family. An Alabama judge, his wife, five sons, and five daughters symbolize for the poem's narrator America's collective betrayal of its ideals, both religious (personified by Jesus) and democratic (personified by Abraham Lincoln). This fictitious Southern judge's family is seen as "launchers of H-Bombs, lynchers of Negroes," weighted by the author with symbolic responsibility for the evils of capital punishment ("the electric chair"), the KKK, and the economic and human disgrace that constitutes so much of the racial situation not only in the United States but also in South Africa and elsewhere throughout the world.

To fully appreciate and understand Depestre's poem it would be helpful to know more about Haitian folk religion and its practices. The pioneering American anthropologist Melville Herskovitz has written well on voodoo, in his classical field study *Life in a Haitian Valley*,* as

* New York: Alfred A. Knopf, 1938; second edition, 1964.

has the French scholar Alfred Métraux in the more recent and more detailed *Voodoo in Haiti.**

While little is known about Depestre's early life, there is reason to believe that he was familiar with voodoo divinities and practice. The opening lines of his "Notes for an Autobiography," which appeared in *Présence Africaine* in 1970, strongly suggest at least one and perhaps two experiences of "possession"—at ages five and fifteen—religious experiences whose memory still evokes for Depestre a resonance of the marvelous:

> I was born at Jacmel in 1926.
> At five I had my first sojourn beneath
> the Caribbean Sea.
> At fifteen, for a whole night I was a horse
> to the naked beauty of my native land . . .

Actual voodoo ceremonies are usually organized by a single family or clan, with friends and neighbors joining only in the festivities that follow. Under the guidance of a voodoo priest or priestess, the family joins in the recitation of prayers to set the mood. Often they are Roman Catholic prayers, which voodoo has simply incorporated, whole or in part, into what were originally purely African-derived rites. In Depestre's poem, one finds frequent references to voodoo gods in a twin role as "saints," to the recitation of The Lord's Prayer, et cetera. After the necessary preliminaries there is general solo dancing to various drum and rattle rhythms, participation in group songs and incantations, the witnessing of offerings of ritual food and drink to please the gods, the sacrifice of chickens, goats, or other farm animals, according to the various *loas'*† well-known preferences. Ingredients of such rituals mentioned in the course of Depestre's poem are footnoted at their first occurrence.

In the highly receptive emotional state induced among believers by these stimuli, some persons simply feel moved by supernatural mysteries, while others actually become possessed by the gods, completely losing consciousness of self for a period of time and taking on the attributes and personality of locally popular divinities. Special drum rhythms may signal the "descent" or appearance of the best-known gods, just as certain kinds of movement (dancing in various postures, whirling, jumping,

---

* New York: Oxford University Press, 1959.

† *Loa:* in voodoo belief, a supernatural being; rather than a god or a divinity, a *loa* is actually a bountiful or malicious spirit.

climbing, plunging into the sea) or of utterance (cries, yelps, moans, bird and animal sounds, or human speech) are typical of each. (Damballah, for example, a serpent god, is often greeted with a hissing sound.) In the true state of possession, Herskovitz and other scholars observe, voodoo adherents will speak and behave in ways completely alien to their normal personalities. In the person of their god, they may perform acts of rage or aggression, they may request some article of personal adornment (jewelry or clothing), they may blurt out bits of highly interesting scandal, perform athletic feats quite beyond their usual prowess, tease their audience with comic antics, permitting themselves to be "horse" to a male divinity though they are women, or a female divinity though they are men. Despite having sometimes to be physically restrained (for example from climbing too high in a tree), or guided by others during the time they are "ridden" by a *loa,* they will generally have no recollection of it. Persons possessed by one of the water divinities may leap into the sea or a nearby river and remain underwater for incredible periods, before emerging safe and sound. On recovering consciousness, they feel a great release from psychic tension, and are considered especially fortunate to have had such divine visitation.

The phenomenon of possession in Haitian culture is so common that Herskovitz concluded it must be understood as normal. He viewed possession as analogous in degree, if not in frequency, to the religious ecstasies of saints, or to seizures during Protestant revival meetings. Such emotionally compensatory forms of religious cult behavior are likely to persist, Herskovitz believed, in societies where economic, social, and cultural disadvantages of group life are widespread and acute.

As Herskovitz and Métraux observe, voodoo offers the simple people of Haiti one form of dignity, the only way to transcend the sordid, unremitting hardship of their lives. Voodoo is a living, changing institution, whose practice has multiple aspects and diverse functions. In Haitian peasant culture it is the central avenue for uniting the religious and artistic impulse. The dance, the making and decoration of drums, costumes, and accessories, of places of worship, the creation of new gods and embellishment of rituals, the stylized role-playing during possession— all these provide not only emotional outlets but gratifying opportunity for self-expression, in which humor and the entertainment of onlookers also sometimes play a role. Voodoo, in short, satisfies the cultural needs of Haitian rural people in a hundred manifold ways—ways that Roman Catholicism, the official Haitian religion, cannot.

From his personal burden of anger, frustration, and hope, and from the living folk religion of his native land, René Despestre has fashioned, in "Epiphanies of the Voodoo Gods," one of black French-language literature's most original works. We also include from *A Rainbow for the Christian West* its touching closing poem, "Ballad for a Little Lamp," as well as the well-known title poem of his 1957 volume, *Black Ore,* closely related in theme, mood, and style to the work of his contemporary David Diop, and by its metaphorical title, to Jacques Roumain's *Ebony Wood.*

TWO POEMS FROM *A Rainbow for the Christian West*

Epiphanies of the Voodoo Gods   A Voodoo Mystery Poem

Prelude

It was a summer evening in an Alabama city. Naked I advanced across the field of my misfortunes. Slave ships were making tracks across my sky in all directions. Somewhere within me a loudspeaker was recounting the story of the childhood of my race. The words fell in flames. They crackled, thumping against one another like blind birds. Yet they gave rise within me to an unbearable hope. They opened a vast landscape of adventure before me. I felt I was walking toward a revelation meant to change my life. It is tonight or never, I told myself. And with burning black steps I started up the walk leading to the Whites' house. They were having dinner, the whole tribe. Everything about the house exuded ease, charm, well-being, peace, light. It radiated respectability. I rubbed my eyes in order to believe it better. This was truly the family of all white fairy tales. The captain of this shining company, a judge by profession, was the first to notice my arrival. A giant wave of bile suddenly arose in the life of this just man of Alabama. And the whole table began to pitch toward me. But not a single red corpuscle in my body wavered. I was a rock dominating this white tumult from a very great height. They were all there:

The cadet son from West Point.

The son set out to graze in the delusions of Yale University.

The future-Republican-Senator son.

The future-Ambassador-to-Panama son.

The son who would stay home to administer the holdings of the family imbecility. And then there was the female side, the always overwhelming women of the white Southern family.

The young widow-daughter of a colonel-husband killed somewhere in Korea defending the Christian West against the Reds.

The daughter educated at all the nation's finest schools, et cetera, et cetera.

The daughter queen-of-all-stadiums, including the bed with the most wonderfully lyrical womb in all creation.

The daddy's girl with a sticky hint of incest in her look, but otherwise of a pristinity beyond reproach.

The daughter rather badly thought of in this sainted family for having one day said that black men in the streets attracted her, and if they didn't watch out she might bring one home to celebrate her brand-new puberty.

There was also the mother of this violently Southern company: the mother, great arborescent breeder of ten creatures dropped from the right hand of God!

And the judge, by now quite at the bilious apex of his indignation!

A fine family upright in its scum!

A noble family knowing how to be familial

in order to impose itself upon the Negro enemy.

A truly American family,

participating deeply in all that

leads America toward catastrophe.

A family upright in its quicklime!

A family summoning to its rescue

at one and the same time

Jesus and the Ku Klux Klan,

the H-Bomb, the Electric Chair,

and the Statue of Liberty.

And, on this night of mine, behold how all are deaf to their summons.

And where on this night of mine is the Whites' tender Jesus?

Where has the KKK planted the yellow cross of its lubricities?

And the Electric Chair, remembering on this very evening how it spent its childhood in a Mississippi forest dreaming of gentle birdsongs in the shadows!

And the Statue of Liberty, which no longer remembers anything, even its fine days in the arms of one called Abraham.

The Abraham tonight is me!

Abraham, the joy of unfolding before your eyes the false treasure of your madness.

Abraham, the miracle of splitting the atom of this family.

Abraham, tonight, the rapture of burning the cards of white respectability!

His woodcutter's ax is my black man's arm.
Tremble in your branches and your fruit,
White Alabama family!

.   .   .   .

Tonight all your idols are pledged to silence. There will be only this sound of an ax in the primitive forest of your hypocrisies. The wood I have chosen for my orgy of light is you, handsome Southern family! I am going to lay a pyre with the fuel of your baseness, never weary of bathing in the waters of my innocence! Tonight all the magic of my race tingles in my hands! All its *loas* have descended into my head and my gestures of a discontented Abraham! Everything that engenders voodoo in my people is contained in the length of my arm and my sex! I possess a pink stone that indicates the place where you have buried the false treasures of your race! I choose for a horse tonight that one of your daughters who shows herself the most rebellious to my diamond. My life will ride upon the back of the young Alabama widow! Her alcohol and dynamite are suited to my temperament. On horseback I traverse the savanna of your mysteries. I dress your other daughters in bright red! They are my novices! And you, Alabama judge, out of your pride I make my *bagui!**
I trace my *vévé†* sign smack in the middle of your living room. I cover the great family table with a red cloth on which I stretch the beautiful musculature of my ax. And your five sons are the five tapers of my libations! And your noble spouse is the *zin††* in which I burn oil in homage

* *Bagui:* A room in the voodoo sanctuary where the altar of the *loas* is located.
† *Vévé:* The symbolical design that represents the attributes of a *loa* that one traces on the ground with wheat flour or corn flour, ashes, coffee grounds, or crushed brick.
†† *Zin:* A small caldron in which food offerings to the voodoo gods are cooked.

to the gods of my native village! And your receptacles of gold I fill with rum and black coffee! And your sumptuous abode I fill with sound and fury!

O sweet family, listen first to the story of a few of my metamorphoses! When I was a dog in a town without mercy, I spent my nights running the streets. At that time I wore large eyeglasses made of scales. A dog with glasses on, I used to read the evening papers. I looked for my daily bone in the classified ads. There never was one. Even the bones had fled from that country. The bones were in exile while I, I wore out my dog's eyes looking for them in the evening papers. For the sake of peace and quiet I changed myself into a cat. I was quite the most Socratic sort of cat. With my Greek philosopher's walk I rambled through the town. Sometimes I would run across Human Solitude sauntering along the walls in evening clothes. She was a ravishingly beautiful black girl, Solitude. I'm still wondering why she called me General Balthazar!

—Come here, General Balthazar. Imagine that I am reporting on the Haitian man. It is certainly necessary for me to speak of how he uses his time. Who is going to believe me on the other side of the sea if I write that Time has not yet reached black skin here? In Haiti for fear someone will throw him in prison or quite simply stick a knife in his liver, Time keeps out to sea along the coasts. Tell me, General Balthazar, you who have traveled so much, have you ever seen a Negro from this country clasp Time fully in his arms? Have you seen one of our men cover her body with kisses and enter her like a god to transform her into a Venus of the sea?

From my cat memory, dog memory, tree memory, memory of a sea urchin, memory of a topaz, memory of a red ant, I had not seen a Haitian Negro one by one remove Time's garments. Solitude practiced her way of the Cross. I practiced mine. Each time that chance threw us together of an evening she asked me the same disturbing question. That is why I became a tortoise. I bought myself a large chestnut horse. A tortoise riding horseback? Makes you laugh, daughter of the Alabama judge? I change your laughter into a twig that I toss into the fire. While I was a tortoise I attended mass each morning without dismounting from my horse. The faithful found it very edifying. There is a Negro who has at least the sense of the divine! How naïve they were. If at the time I had a feeling for anything, it was only for the music. I was a musician-tortoise. Above all I liked to listen to Gregorian chants. Likewise my horse: it was his greenest grass! The day jazz was discovered one stopped wearing hoofs and shells to church. Their allurements were hurriedly assigned to butterflies, rare birds, toads, baby goats, coconut palms, rivers, and the great gods of voodoo. A famous orchestra was equipped with them, which you will have an opportunity to hear this evening. . .

1.
Attibon Legba

I am Attibon Legba
My hat comes from Guinea
Likewise my bamboo cane
Likewise my ancient pain
And old bones
I am the patron saint of janitors
And elevator boys
I am Legba-Wood, Legba-Cayés
I am Legba-Signangnon
And the seven Kataroulo brothers
I am Legba-Kataroulo
I plant my resting place tonight
The great medicine-tree of my soul
In the white man's land
At the crossing of his roads
Three times I kiss his door!
Three times I kiss his eyes!
I am Papa Alegba
God of your thresholds
Tonight it is I
The master of your pathways
And your white man's meeting places
I the protector of the plants
And insects of your house
I am chief of all the gateways
To the spirit and the human body!

Title: In Haiti, as in African cults, Legba is the god who "opens the way" for other *loas;* here he is an arthritic old man with hat and cane, dusty after his long journey from mythical Guinea. When the proper rituals are performed, in order "to release . . . his truth" he will "mount" or "possess" the Alabama judge.

2. *Guinea:* Here it means Africa generally.

I arrive all covered with dust
I am the great black Ancestor
I see I hear what happens
On the pathways and the roads
Your hearts and your white man's gardens
Have hardly any secrets from me
Quite exhausted from my journeying I arrive
And hurl my great age
Along the paths where your white man's
betrayals are creeping
O you Alabama judge
I do not see in your hands
Either pitcher of water or black candle
I do not see my sign traced
On the floor of the house
Where is the good white flour
Where are my cardinal points
My old bones arrive at your house
O Judge, and they do not see
Any *bagui* to put their troubles in
They see white roosters
They see white chickens
Where are our spices Judge
Where is the pepper and the salt
Where is the peanut oil
Where the burnt corn
Where are our stars of rum
Where are my *rada* and my *mahi*
Where is my *yanvalou?*
The Devil take your tasteless dishes
Your white wine
Your apple and pear
The Devil take all your lies

54. *Rada:* A name derived from the town of Allada in Dahomey. A *loa* nation, the ritual of this particular kind of *loa*. In Depestre's poem it seems to refer to the costumes donned by those possessed by the *rada loas,* or to the *rada* drums.

55. *Yanvalou:* A voodoo dance done with the body bent forward, hands on bended knees with the shoulders undulating.

For my hunger I want yams
taro plants and pumpkins
Bananas and sweet potatoes
The Devil take your waltzes and your tangos
The old hunger of my limbs
Clamors for a legba dance
The old thirst of my bones
Clamors for the virile steps of man!

I am Papa-Legba
I am Legba-Clairondé
I am Legba-Sé
I am Legba-Si
I emerge from their fur
My seven brothers Kataroulo

I change my terra-cotta pipe
Into a sword
My bamboo walking stick
I also change into a sword
My tall hat from Guinea
I also change into a sword
My trunk of a medicine-tree
I also change into a sword
The blood of mine that you have shed!

O Judge here is a sword
For each door of the house
A sword for each head
Here are the twelve apostles of my faith
My twelve Kataroulo swords
The twelve *legbas* of my bones
And not one will betray my blood
There is no Judas in my body
O! Judge there is a single old man
Who keeps watch upon the way of men
A single old fighting-cock
O! Judge, who releases in your pathways
The great red wings of his truth!

2.
Ogou-Ferraille

I am Ogou-Ferraille
Or General Mait'Ogou
My right arm is fire
The tower where my sword keeps vigil
I know his secrets
His appetites his torments
I know his hates
I know what repels him
He does not like to be given
Human flesh to eat
He does not like
Solitude and
The human heart's despair
Thrown to him
Like bones
Fire does not draw fuel
From the black man's pain
Fire likes to sing and laugh and drink
To make love with the air
To work at expanding
The frontiers of man
His root is the human race
His joy and his heaven
His faith and his hope
Green leaves die within him
Each time a white hand
Hurls a black body
To his depths
He burns it devours it
Absorbs it digests it
But in his fiery soul
Mute tears
Choke green leaves
But in his fiery soul
The fire-child that he has been laments

Title: Ogore-Ferraille, Haitian *loa* related to the West African war god Ogun.

I am Ogou-Ferraille
I am come to say that fire
Has not a single spark of patience left
At the bottom of his incandescent soul
The fire-child is weary
Of crying
Of playing
with dead leaves!

3.
Damballah-Wedo

Here am I Damballah-Wedo
Aquatic Negro river Negro
I am the water's beating heart
I am the water's turgid sex
Holding a thunderstone in one hand
I dip a twig of basilique
In a glass of white wine
And sprinkle your pale faces
Baste your pale hysterias
I dilute the terror that is coiled within your eyes
I irrigate the cardinal points of your vices
I slither on my back I drag my *rada*
I slip I dance my *yanvalou* about your house
If you see a green snake
Dancing with the eldest of your daughters, it is I
If you see a rainbow furiously kiss her pubis
It is I once more
I transform your eldest daughter to a rainbow
Behold her creeping with my seven serpents
Behold her undulating in the sunlight of my strength
See her make the tour of my sweet waters
See her kiss three times my Damballah
And my Wedo my Wilibo my Willimin
I am rainbow-voodoo
And the eldest daughter of an Alabama judge
Will lose her white propriety along my banks!

4.

Agoué-Taroyo

I am Agoué-Taroyo
I press my symbols
On the naked belly of your wife:
A ship a fish and the vast ocean
Here I am her master and her pilot
Here I am her sails and her woman isles
She raises her Alabama head to me
To tell me with tears shining in her eyes
"Forgive us Papa-Agoué we are all your children
We are the scabbard of your saber of sweet water
We are the radar of your sweet fruits of the sea
Have pity on us, have pity on us
Oh! Papa-Taroyo! Oh! Good Papa-Woyo!
Forgive us our errors, pardon our sins"
No I tell her I am a Negro without forgiveness
My last pardon no longer has Negro eyes
To see you nor ears for your prayers
You lynched him you martyred him
You have dried up the last drop of dew
That glistened at the end of my forgiveness
I am the proud Agoué a *marine creature*
Who lives upon the earth and also knows how to fly
At my neck I wear a collar of green pearls
I am come to squeeze your spongy souls
Thirsty sponges in which the blood of my trees is weeping
I am come to scatter reefs of coral in your path
I am come to break your masts and oars
I am Agoué-Taroyo the great sea monster
Who drags you down beneath his undertow!

5.

Ogou-Badagris

I am Ogou-Badagris
I am the red laurel

Title: Ogou-Badagris, another *loa* related to Ogun, is depicted as an old-time Haitian general.

Who hollows out his proud canoe
In the white trunk of your stupidities
I am a cruel general
I flash my lightning into your very hearts
Tonight my sword calls out
For Alabama cocks and hens
Cocks trained at West Point
Cocks who are candidates for the Senate
Hens who have stunningly lyrical bodies
My sword with the absorbent qualities of sponge
My sword with magnet strength
My sword with the sucking power
Of the quickest quicksand
My sword is an implacable tide
For its thirst it craves
Warm female odors
For its evening thirst it calls for
Proud forbidden roundnesses of flesh

My sword casts its mocking gaze of pagan god
On your five daughters
My phallic sword of Ogou-Badagris
Teases the lascivious curiosity
Of five hens well trained
In hysterical clucking
My sword tightens its black embrace
About your languors
My sword is as old as the mystery of me
And the fecundity of the sea
For its potency my sword demands
The roundnesses of laying hens
My sword broods as it moves
On the terrible impatience
Of your Southern flesh!

6.
Guédé-Nibo

I am Guédé-Nibo
Sobadi Sobo Kalisso
I dance atop your table
Sobadi Sobo Kalisso
The obscene dance of my lamps
Sobadi Sobo Kalisso
My phallus is half-a-yard long
Sobadi Sobo Kalisso
It knows how to climb trees
Sobado Sobo Kalisso
It descends to the heart of the earth
Sobadi Sobo Kalisso
It lived seven years underwater
Sobadi Sobo Kalisso
And on its back it carries
Sobadi Sobo Kalisso
A marvelous tattoo
Sobadi Sobo Kalisso
A remarkable white cross
Sobadi Sobo Kalisso
Half-a-yard long
Sobadi Sobo Kalisso
And upon its head
Sobadi Sobo Kalisso
It wears a crown of thorns
Sobadi Sobo Kalisso

2. *Sobadi Sobo Kalisso:* An invocation to Guédé-Nibo, god of tombs and death, for his aid in some questionable project.

7.
Azaka-Médé

I am Azaka-Médé
Minister Zaka-Médé
Azaka-Thunder
General Zaka-Si
Azaka-Yombo-Voodoo

Commander Zaka-Médé
I am a black man marching with
Damballah-Wedo on my right
Ogou-Ferraille on my left
I am Sir Azaka Storm
My *manger-yam* tonight
Will be offered at the white folks' house
My gumbo tonight served
By the white hands of a judge
It is a white Alabama evening
Where are you going comrade general Zaka?
I am going to fuck around Oh! fuck around
Let's fuck around with all our gods
To the good tom-tom of Lord Zaka-Médé

11. *Manger-yam:* An eating yam; an offering of yams used during voodoo consecration rites.

8.
Cousin Zaka

I am Cousin Zaka
My red neckerchief salutes you
My machete salutes you
My vine-cutter salutes your heads
My cane-cutter salutes your arms
O Americans destroyers of dreams
On the banks of the Mississippi
On the eve of the battle
The smoke of my pipe salutes you
I am an inhabitor of hilltops
The word West Point evokes in me
Visions of explosives and funeral pyres
Visions of dirtied waters and tears
And I fight my thirst with the coolness
Of the words Playa Girón upon my tongue
With the words Playa Girón in my eyes
And I say that thunder will burn me
If in these words I do not find

Title: Cousin Zaka, a farmer *loa* carrying a machete, the long, flat-bladed knife for cutting cane and bananas.

The earth liberating vegetable angels
Herbal secrets and the green word
That must spring from the lips of our wounds
O Americans I am cousin to the water
Just a drop of water am I
The patience of a drop of green water
I have descended from the mountain
I am come to say that the West Point general
Will one day die of thirst I am come to prepare
For his mouth for his stars for his bones
The most beautiful thirst in all creation!

9.

Agassou

I am Agassou
I am a great maker of rain
O young white girl
If you plunge your two hands
To the bottom of my anguish
You will pull out a great crab
Who will say good day to you siren
I am a black creeper
And I creep! O young girl
In the great trees of your modesty
I creep along the vines
That hang from your eyes
I creep with crazy ivy steps
Up the beautiful stairway
That rises to the tip
Of your virginity
O! judge's daughter! White girl
Saint Agassou is a mirror
Which sees very far into man
I am *ago ago* I see what happens
In the stars
I am *ago ago* I see
The tidal wave unfurling
In the nautical heart of my race!

20. *Ago ago:* A ritual exclamation meaning: Attention!

10.
Captain Zombi

I am Captain Zombi
I drink through my ears
I hear with my ten fingers
I have a tongue that sees all
A radar nose that detects
The sound waves of the human heart
And a sense of touch that perceives
Odors at a distance
As for my sixth sense
It is a detector of the dead
I know where they are buried
Our millions of corpses
I am accountable for their bones
I am inhabited by cadavers
Inhabited by the rattling of their dying
I am a floodtide of afflictions
Of cries of pus of coagulations
I graze in the pastures
Of the millions of my dead
I am the shepherd of terror
I keep watch over
A troop of black bones
These are my sheep my cattle
My swine my goats my tigers
My arrows and my lances
My lavas and my cyclones
A whole hidden black artillery
Howling in the graveyard of my soul!

1. *Zombi:* A person whose soul has been removed by a sorcerer and who is reduced to slavery, in a state resembling living death. Captain Zombi is an attendant *loa* to Baron Samedi. (See next footnote.)

11.
Baron Samedi

I am the great Baron Samedi
Oh! Don't count too much on my

Title: Baron Samedi, patron of the dead.

Beautiful white beard
It is a nest of savage wasps
My beard is capable of the worst excesses
Tonight, O Southern family, you are the
Great repository in which I loose
The bats of my past
I sew for your five daughters
Robes of Siamese cloth
Sprinkled with little black crosses
As for the males to work my spells on them
I hold them upside down:
Naughty beasts viper tongues
White whales lynchers of Negroes
Launchers of H-Bombs *mazimaza*-whites
You shall all march from place to place
From village to village in this atrocious South
From prison to prison in this bestial South
From crazy-house to crazy-house
I am the Expediter-Saint
And affectionately send your insolences
To the Devil
Your hatred of black men
Your gaping wounds
I do not heed the three Our Fathers
You recite in my honor
I set the stone of Baron Samedi aflame
With the dismal alcohol of your destinies
And seven times West Point cadet
I strike you on the head
And seven times Alabama judge
I strike you on the head
and seven times student of Yale
I strike you on the head
And seven times future Senator
I strike you on the head
And seven times with a branch of Congo-peas
I strike seven times
With the wings of a black cock I strike

16. *Mazimaza:* Voodoo term for a two-faced, hypocritical person.

With the wings of a *zinga-chicken* seven times
I strike your faces without light
With blows of the whip I take
Your little souls O Alabama zombis
I carry off your little souls
I am the Baron of the rain
And you are less alive
Than the trees or termites of my household!

43. *Zinga-chicken:* The varicolored chickens favored by Legba; they have markings like a guinea fowl.

12.
Shango

I am Shango exhaler of lightning
Eagle makes his nest in my voice
I seize your two hands without sun
Your judge's hands that waste the days
And red globules of my people
Slowly I pass them across
The flaming alcohol of my breath
Slowly I burn away their thorns
And now the moment for arranging
The bellies of each of the females of your house
I take two halves of a Jacmel orange
And fill them with palma-christi oil
Shouting three times: I am Shango
The pure sky keeps no secrets from my eyes
The touch of me brings good fortune and light
I warm the oil with the high truth
At the lighted wick of my man heart
White Alabama girls prostrate yourselves
At the feet of my innocence
And remove all your garments
I plunge a hand in the hot oil
And very slowly rub your cursed breasts
Rub the rebellious ivory of your limbs
Which little by little emerge from the shadows

Title: Shango, a West Indian deity; like Legba's, his name survives in Haitian cults; he continues the purification rites.

And one by one I rub your rapturous genitals
Now you are forever as pure as my eyes
Now you are ready to carry in your wombs
All the bursting life of humanity's morning!

13.
Ti-Jean Sandor

I am Ti-Jean Sandor
I am Sandor the Prince
I am a fine-footed cock
I am a dry-footed Ti-Jean
I perch my heart
At the top of a palm tree
I make use of both hands
I walk backward
My arms crossed behind me
In front of me I make
Bursts of dynamite explode
Behind me I leave
A long wake of shackles
I transform my West Point cadet
Into a handsome pedigreed dog
That I bite upon the ear
I am a great devourer
Of white dogs I am
A bull with a hundred seeds
I am *bakoulou-baka*
I am Captain *Zobop*
I am a negro-*mazimaza*
My life is the forge in which my hate is tempered
My hatred of the white man
My hatred of his hate
The hate I bear
As a lion wears his mane

Title: Ti-Jean (little John) Sandor, a kind *loa,* who hops on one foot and climbs trees.
20. *Bakoulou-baka:* An evil spirit or genie that can be called upon by voodoo sorcerers, who will bargain and give something special in return for the life of a family member.
21. *Zobop:* A member of an evil-doing voodoo sorcerers' society.

As a rattlesnake wears his rattles
The hate that never leaves my bones
Or blood or skin
Even when I sleep at night
Its black star opens inside me
Eyes that are claws
If I am left to continue to the end
Of my night of spleen I shall bind
My muscles to cyclones
And earthquakes
To swallow up this bitter South
And the other South that has been opened
On the flank of my Africa
O HATRED my great health
I plunge my burning temples
Into the icy blueness of your waters
I plunge my naked people
Into this proud shining current
I plunge our tigers our lances
Our wounds our cries our thirsts
Our pens our knives our tears
Into this fount of blessed water
And herein we are forever baptized
All the world's black prisoners
Here we are at last
Ready to give our conspiracies
Great white wings
Like the orgies of hatred
In the white heart of the South!

14.
Agaou

I am Agaou native of Guinea
My lizard when he bites white flesh
Does not let go until the
Thunder of the revolution growls
I know the art of binding up
Your rains, your prejudice, your fantasies

I am the cannoneer of lightning
O Agaou my brother rise
Rouse yourself and spit
In the face of the judge from Alabama!

15.
Baron-la-Croix

I am Baron-la-Croix
The dog that howls at death
In your garden is me
The black moth
That flies about the table is me
One word too many and I'll transform
Your little Southern lives
Into as many little crosses
Forged in the iron of my soul!

16.
Loko

I am Loko and I come from far away
Loko-mirror, Loko-key
Loko-crossroads, I keep watch
Over the cardinal points
Of my people, I keep watch
Over the tree of their misfortunes
I keep watch my soul turned
Toward the great north of their wounds!

The Bath at Dawn

Now, dear Alabama family, drop your last illusions at my feet! I am
going to dissolve all the white dirt that human folly has accumulated
even in your hearts. I am a god in sixteen persons and tens of other minor
loas pulse on the same wave length as my blood. I make the tour of your
house mounted on a magnetic goat. Look at the eyes of my phosphores-
cent mount. They ask you the following two questions: What have we
done, we, the wretched black men of the earth, for these Whites to hate
us so? What have we done, Brother Depestre, to weigh so little on their

scale? By way of an answer I suddenly transform your old Southern perversities into a large bathtub which I fill with water from the sea. Ladies and gentlemen, look at the sea! The same foaming sea we crossed in irons, three centuries ago! The same green surging waves in which we tossed the last rose of black hope! And now it has become the very water of your pre-dawn bath! This water will do battle with your hysterias, your manias, your treacheries, your moral frailty, your white superstitions, and all the supposedly incurable cannibalism which in each of you Southern men and women cries out its old dissatisfaction in the desert. I bestow on your vices an acid made to their measure: the water of the ocean we once crossed to discover in our turn the splendors of America! And into your new day's bath each of the *loa*s here present will pour a dewdrop of his Haitian wisdom!

.   .   .   .

I say that this water is what will defeat your deliriums. I say that this water will extinguish the nuclear fuse you train on the world. I say that this water is the voice of humanity's future, that it speaks in the name of all men! I say that this water advances with all the allurement of hope. I say that this water carries within itself the infancy of human joy! I say that this water will move you one day to the side of the human! I welcome this water which comes from the confines of pain! Let all of us welcome this water come from the depths of the sea! This water is glorious, I say, a zodiac to vanquish all the monsters of our night!

Ballad of a Little Lamp

> *Thy dusky face I set among the white*
> *For thee to prove thyself of highest worth;*
> *Before the world is swallowed up in night*
> *To show thy little lamp: Go forth, go forth!*
> —Claude McKay

There is no salvation for mankind
Except through a great dazzling
Of man by man I affirm it
Me an unknown Negro in the crowd
Me a wild and solitary blade of grass

I shout it to my century
There will be no joy for man
Except by a pure radiance
Of man by man a proud
Leap of mankind toward his destiny
Which is to shine very high
With the star of all men
I shout it I do that defamation
Of the harelip has
Relegated beasts of prey to the last row
I toward whom the lie always
Points its poisoned claws
I whom mediocrity night and day
Pursues with wild boar hoofs
I at whom hatred in the streets
Often aims the finger
I proceed the shepherd of my revolts
I advance with great diamond steps
I clasp to my wounded heart
A faith so human that often at night
Its crying wakes me
Like some newborn babe's that
One must soothe with lullabies and milk
And tenderly at night I rock
My Helen my sweet faith my life falls
In springtime waters on her body
I cherish human dignity
And give to it the rhythm of the rains
That fell my child nights through
I move forward the bearer of an
Insular and bearded faith, the sower
Of a faith untamed untamable
No great poem on bended knees
Before the altarstone of pain
But a little Haitian lamp
That wipes its tears away with laughter
And with a single flex of wings
Rises to the edges of the sky
To be a man forever

Standing tall and free
As the verdant innocence
                of all mankind!
Christian West my terrible brother
Here is my sign of the cross:
In the name of insurgency
and tenderness
and justice
                May it be so!

Havana, December 1964–June 1965

FROM *Black Ore*

Black Ore

When Indian sweat was suddenly soaked dry by the sun
When gold fever had drained the last drop of Indian blood from the
                                                            markets
So there was no longer a single Indian left to mine the gold
They turned to the muscular river of Africa
To renew the despair
Then the rush began toward the inexhaustible
Treasury of black flesh
Then the surge commenced toward the shining noon of black bodies
And the whole earth echoed with the sound of picks striking layers of
                                                            black ore.
And chemists almost thought of ways to make some precious alloy
Of black metal
And ladies almost dreamed
Of saucepans and tea sets of West Indian nigger
And a priest or two
Very nearly promised his parishioners
A bell resounding with the sound of black blood
And some good Father Christmas
May even have thought of little black lead soldiers
For his yearly visit

Or some brave captain may
Have made himself a sword
Of the ebony metal
The whole earth shook with the shock of the drills
In the guts of my race
Piercing the muscular deposits of black man
And thus for many centuries
The wonders of my race have been extracted
O metallic layers of my people
Inexhaustible ore of human dew
How many pirates have explored the depth of your dark flesh
With their weapons
How many robbers have hacked their way
Through the vegetation of your gleaming body
Littering your years with pools of tears
And withered branches
Plundered people, people tilled
From top to bottom like earth beneath the plow
People stripped for the enrichment
Of the world's great markets
Let the fire damp fester in your body's secret night
No one any more will dare
Smelt coin or cannon
From the black ore
Of your swelling rage.

African Poets in French

 Senghor

 Birago Diop

 Sissoko

 Bolamba

 Dadié

 David Diop

 Yondo

 Sinda

 Ouloguem

 U Tam'si

SENEGAL ⚘ (*1906–*)

Léopold Sedar Senghor

LÉOPOLD SÉDAR SENGHOR, WHO HAS BEEN PRESIDENT
of the Republic of Senegal since its establishment in 1960, is also con-
sidered the leading poet of French-speaking Africa. While the emphasis
of his poetry is usually personal and contemplative rather than ideological,
in his public life and prose writings Senghor has, for almost forty years,
championed the contribution of black civilizations to the twentieth-cen-
tury world. His essays on political and cultural topics mark him as one of
Africa's, and the black world's, foremost intellectuals. "Culture," or the
sum total of the way in which a people live, Senghor declared in an
address at the 1966 World Festival of Negro Arts, "is the first requisite
and the final objective of all development. . . . The humanism of the
twentieth century," he continued, "which can only be the Civilization of
the Universal, would be impoverished if it excluded a single value of a
single person, a single race, a single continent." Senghor is persuaded
that the meaningful political, social, and economic development of people
of African descent the world over will occur only when the special values
of Negro cultures are accorded their full place.

Born in Joal, a tiny village on the coast of Senegal, Senghor came
from a large and prosperous family. His people were Serers, members of
a minority tribe among the more numerous Wolofs. And, in a land where
Islam and indigenous animist religions had been dominant since the
Middle Ages, the Senghors were Catholic. Though young Léopold at-
tended a rural mission school from the age of seven, the world he grew
up in until he was in his teens was, outside the classroom, entirely
African, a life still steeped in traditional ways, largely untouched by the
European presence.

This childhood paradise—a peaceful, mysterious world punctuated
by seasonal rites and dances, and ceremonial visits—is the background,
source, and central reconciliation point which much of Senghor's poetry

121

evokes and to which it often returns. "Since I must explain my poems," he wrote in an epilogue to *Ethiopiques* (*Ethiopics*), "I'll confess that nearly all the beings and things they evoke are from my canton: a few Serer villages lost among the sandflats, the woods, the channels, and the fields. I need only mention their names to revive the kingdom of my childhood. I lived then in this kingdom, saw with my eyes, with my ears heard the fabulous beings beyond things; the ancestral spirits in the tamarind trees, the crocodiles, guardians of the springs; the sea cows, who spoke to me, initiating me in turn to the truths of night and noon."

At fifteen, Senghor left this "kingdom" for Senegal's capital city, Dakar. There he went to secondary schools, where his teachers were Alsatian priests and most of his classmates European. Senghor was an avid reader, with a natural aptitude for study. Yet, even as a teen-ager, he reacted strongly to one professor-priest "who told me we were savages, that we had no traditions, no civilization, that we were merely responsive to the hollow sound of words, without putting ideas behind them." In an interview during his state visit to the United States in the fall of 1966, Senghor recalled, "That Father was really my teacher, because I reacted against the things he told me. I was a child. I had no reasoning. But I had an intuition about black African civilization, the intuition that we had roots in a profound spiritual tradition. At the same time, I took in the Father's lesson. I believe this is the reason I have always taken care to put an idea or an emotion behind my words. I have made it a habit to be suspicious of the mere music of words, precisely because I am extremely sensitive to it. All this," Senghor continued, "made me want to defend the civilization [my teacher] was denying us, made me want to demon-strate and illustrate it. I was only perhaps fifteen at the time, and my ideas were rather confused. But I believe my whole direction in life was set about then. At that point I had two goals: first, I wanted to be a priest in order to save my people; second, I wanted to be a professor in order to teach them."

It was the latter course the twenty-two-year-old Senghor thought he had chosen when, in 1928, armed with a half-scholarship from the French government, he sailed for Europe. In Paris, at the Lycée Louis-le-Grand, Senghor met Aimé Césaire and Georges Pompidou, both of whom were to become Senghor's lifelong friends. The atmosphere of the city, the subjects Senghor and other black colonial students found of such passionate interest, have been described earlier in this volume. The short–lived radical journal *Légitime Défense* (1931) and *La Revue du monde noir,* a Haitian-edited "review of the black world" which ran to six issues in the early 1930s, were among the catalysts that put the students in touch with the situation of the black man throughout the world and introduced them to the ideas of West Indian and black American writers. A second great influence on Senghor was the work of Frobenius, Delavignette, and Delafosse, European anthropologists who were the first to lend serious weight to the teen-age "intuitions" he had had about the value of African civilizations. These same ideas had had a similar, stunning effect on a Haitian student named Jean Price Mars, who, in 1928, produced *Ainsi parla l'Oncle* (*Thus Spake Our Uncle*), another landmark work whose ideas Senghor absorbed at about this time.

Soon the young African focused on three pursuits: 1) the career of professor of languages and grammar, which he was to abandon for politics only after World War II; 2) the vocation of poet; and 3) the intellectual investigation of Negro–African cultures, or, as they collectively came to be called in the word coined by Aimé Césaire, of "negritude."

By 1934, having earned his *licence,* Senghor became the first black African to succeed at the extremely competitive examinations for the degree of *agrégé d'université,* roughly equivalent to an American Ph.D. After a triumphal visit to Senegal, he accepted a post as professor of Latin, Greek, and French in a high school in northwest France. He was also writing poetry and articles, and working with Césaire and Damas on their magazine, *L'Etudiant noir.* When Hitler's forces attacked in 1940, Senghor was in the French Army. He fought during the six-week defense of France, and then spent two years as a German prisoner of war. Some of the poems in *Songs of Darkness* and many from *Hosties noires* (*Black Host,* or *Black Victims*) were inspired by these wartime experiences. Eventually released by the Germans, the bespectacled young professor returned to Paris to teach, work for the French underground, and join Alioune Diop and other African and West Indian friends who were already planning *Présence Africaine,* the ambitious magazine they were to found when the war was over.

After the liberation of France, Senghor became the first African to be named professor at the National Training College for administrators of the French overseas territories. Since his subject was to be African languages and cultures, it was an ideal opportunity for him to proselytize his ideas about black civilizations. With the publication of his first two books of poems in 1945 and 1948, and in the latter year as well of his *Anthologie de la nouvelle poésie nègre et malgache* (*Anthology of New*

Negro and Malagasy Poets), Senghor established a name for himself in French literary circles.

But the postwar 1940s were a time of political upheaval and change, not only in metropolitan France but throughout its empire. The first pre-independence currents began to be felt. Suddenly, there were unprecedented opportunities—and in fact a compelling need—for new political leaders to represent the colonies in Europe. So the relative quiet of academic and literary life was no longer to be Senghor's. In 1945 Senghor was elected deputy from Senegal to the French National Assembly, soon serving on the General Council of Senegal and on the Grand Council of French West Africa as well. At home, his popularity steadily increased in a series of vigorous electoral campaigns. There, and in Paris, he was developing into a skillful and intelligent political leader. For a time Senghor was part of the French delegation to the U.N. His poem "To New York" was doubtless inspired by actual experiences of the city dating from this time.

Despite the pressures of his increasing public responsibilities, Senghor continued his intellectual pursuits. His speeches, statements, and articles on literary, cultural, and political topics, and particularly on the idea of negritude—the sum total of African cultural values—were collected in 1964 in a volume called *Liberté I—négritude et humanisme*. (*Liberty One—Negritude and Humanism*).

But what of the other Senghor, Senghor the poet? His use of language—typically a formal, almost Biblical tone—is quite unlike the trenchant, ironic Damas's, or the incendiary Césaire's. Unlike Damas or Césaire, Senghor has produced no single work of poetry with the far-reaching impact of *Pigments* or *Notes on a Return to the Native Land*, which so miraculously encompass the passion and revolt of the black man in the Western world.

Senghor is essentially a poet of meditation, of nostalgia, a weaver of songs about what is closest to his heart. Stylistically, he blends a highly cultivated sensitivity to the French language and its literature with an esteem for the age-old oral traditions of his Serer kinfolk and their Wolof neighbors. Western critics with a background in the written literatures of Europe and America quickly see Senghor's resemblance to such French poets as Paul Claudel and St. John Perse—with their preference for long, flowing elegiac lines of verse—or to Walt Whitman. But anyone who has seen African poets and praise-singers perform—with all their variations of gesture, rhythm, and tone—to the accompaniment of drums and varied musical instruments—stringed ones like the kôras and khalams, or the wooden, xylophone-like balafongs—can imagine a whole other side to Senghor's poetry, derived from local traditions. This African aspect is oral. It can only be experienced in actual performance and is only suggested to the uninitiated who merely read from the printed page.

Senghor's best lyric poems are pure enchantment. Like his "Night of Sine," they operate insidiously on the reader, slowly enfolding him into a world rich with unfamiliar sights, scents, tastes, feelings. To fully appreciate much of Senghor's poetry, one has to acquire a whole new vocabulary of Senegalese allusions, to become acquainted with places, persons, customs, the natural and supernatural, the past and present, of another world, another culture.

"French Garden," a very early poem that remained unpublished for a long time, poses the European–African duality that will later become one of his major themes. "Night of Sine," the first of seven poems from *Songs of Darkness,* and one of Senghor's most memorable, is the lyrical re-creation of an African village at night. "Joal" paints further memories of his village; sunsets by the sea, religious feasts that blend pagan and Christian elements, the presence of mysterious green-eyed *signares,** cere-monial dances and athletic feats, and the final interruption of an "orphan" jazz which the poet hears in Europe, whose "sobbing" has perhaps set him to reminiscing.

A meditation on the timeless beauty of a "Negro Mask" follows, although the poet also seems to evoke the perfect balance of the bronze heads of Benin. He calls this sculpted face, however, Koumba Tam, the Serer goddess of beauty, and dedicates his poem to Picasso. "Prayer to the Masks" continues the meditation on these African religious objects, opening with the poet's salute to his forebears. With the phrase "you who have arranged . . . this face of mine . . . in your image," he counts himself an heir to the spiritual tradition these carved ancestral faces embody. In the second half of the poem, published just after the end of World War II, the narrator predicts the passing of colonial em-pires in Africa, and confides to the ancestral faces a hope that their children, though now subjugated, will prove "the yeast white flour needs."

"The Totem" is another striking poem of personal affirmation. Its final allusion to "the arrogance of lucky races" once again underlines the

* *Signares:* Women of mixed blood—half-African, half-European—generally of upper social strata.

contrast between the poet's cultivated outer self and the inner, African self symbolized by the totem.

Another evocation of the childhood kingdom comes from a long poem Senghor dedicated to René Maran, "Ode for Three Kôras and Bala-phong," one of the major pieces in *Songs of Darkness*. The concluding portion of the poem is set on the eve of World War II. The narrator appears to be in the French Army. The evidence of war is all about. In this violent confusion, the poet is consoled at night by his "migratory humor," reminiscences of the Senegal he remembers, the lore of fauna and flora that Tokô-Waly, the favorite uncle who was so often his child-hood companion, once taught him. In the final lines, as in so many of Senghor's poems, night is portrayed as a time of deliverance—here from war, from "slaughter humanized." But night is nearly always for Senghor a time when all that is unbearable—tensions, conflicts, "contradictions"— is mercifully, if temporarily, resolved.

Last from *Songs of Darkness*, we choose the ending of "Return of the Prodigal Son," which also concludes the book itself. Doubtless this half-mocking depiction of himself as an ungrateful son, who has for-gotten or neglected his family and cultural roots, was inspired by Senghor's vacation in Senegal after winning his *agrégation*. Visiting the people he grew up with, paying his respects at the pagan shrine of Mbissel near Joal, however, Senghor is reminded more than ever of the great historical places and persons of his ancestral past, and the values they represent. One by one he calls them forth, as if to draw upon their virtues, to arm himself with their strength: the elephant at Mbissel, an ancient sacred totem; Timbuktu, the inland city in what is present-day Mali, once a medieval center of Moslem culture and learning; Soni Ali, a fifteenth-century monarch, under whose leadership the West African Songhai Empire was vastly expanded; the Keitas, a ruling family of the Mandingo Empire, renowned for its learning, who built the cities of Timbuktu, Djenné, and Gao during the fourteenth century; the Guel-wars, a noble and courageous warrior people of the Serer region, the land of Senghor's birth; the Tyédos, soldiers of the royal bodyguard of the King of Sine, the last of whom was a friend of Senghor's father.

The first stanza thus ends with Senghor's rededication to his people. His work will be not just to teach them but to teach about them to others, as their ambassador. The final stanza once again evokes the earliest, tender memories of his childhood. It recalls his life in the women's quarters with the other little children, their father who was nicknamed "the Lion," the memory of being tucked into bed when very small "by the black hands so dear and . . . the white smile of my mother." It concludes with the abrupt realization that tomorrow the narrator must set out once more for Europe.

Senghor's second book of poems, *Black Host,* strikes an entirely different note from the lyrical nostalgia of his past. *Black Host* is the single best rebuttal to those who sometimes accuse him of not being militant enough, of being too much a poet of reconciliation, too easy on his "blue-eyed brothers." The very title of the book, with its double meaning—"black host" or "black victims"—suggests a Christlike sacrifice of black peoples, as in the Roman Catholic mass, and is an indictment of Europe, particularly of France, for its ruthless exploitation of the black man. One poem alone, the "Prayer for Peace," brilliantly summarizes the volume's themes, positions, emotions.

Dated "Paris, January 1945," it was written a scant four months after the city's liberation from four years of Nazi occupation. The poem is dedicated to Georges and Claude Pompidou, close friends of Senghor's since their student days. Senghor casts his indictment of France, but also paradoxically his pardon—and ultimately his faith in the French—in the form of a prayer, offered "as a ciborium of suffering."

From Senghor's third book of poems, *Ethiopics,* published in 1956, we have chosen two poems,* "New York," and one of his own favorites, "I Know Not When It Was . . .". "New York" opens by gathering what surely were the poet's actual impressions of the formidable metropolis. The poem concludes with a plea that the cold, steely city listen to its black voices, this great percussive jazz symphony of the senses. The trumpet, trombone, saxophone, and drums are all clearly reminiscent of James Weldon Johnson's *Trumpets of the Lord,* an American poem Senghor knew well. Make your rigid, rusty city supple once again, he begs. Loosen it up with a life-giving infusion of black blood, and the heritage of primal unity it brings from Africa. Here again, as in the last lines of the earlier "Prayer to the Masks," Senghor alludes to the special values he feels negritude can contribute to the automated, industrialized but dehumanizing West.

Senghor described the inspiration for his next poem, "I Know Not When It Was . . .," in a film about his work made on location in

---

* Other portions in *Ethiopics* that could not be represented, for reasons of space, are "Chaka," his dramatic poem for many voices; "Congo," and the love poems called "Letters to the Princess of Belborg."

Senegal several years ago.* As his voice begins to recollect the circumstances, the camera fades to a reenactment of the original incident. Senghor used to come home from boarding school in the city to visit his family in the country when he was a teen-aged student. On one such vacation, after paying his respects at the tomb of his ancestors at a nearby holy place, he set out for home on foot at high noon. According to local belief, this hottest time of day is a kind of witching hour when few people venture outdoors. The heat of the brutal African sun is at its apex, bouncing from the earth in waves one can often actually see in the transparent air. Unlike in the benevolent "Night of Sine," when friendly spirits come to visit, this is the hour when evil spirits stalk. One can avoid their pernicious influence only by skirting the pathways, keeping in the shade. As in the nighttime poem, with which the present song for African guitar (the khalam) makes a beautiful contrast, a woman is present who brings comfort and refreshment. This time it is a young girl, who emerges from a nearby house when the student finally stops to wait for a bus. Thoughtfully, she brings out a stool for the young man to sit on, and something cool for him to drink. She stands smiling and courteously chatting, to keep him company until his bus arrives.

From the memory of this simple incident, Senghor fashioned his poem many years later. He evokes the courtly ways of an ancient Senegalese past, as if he had been a traveling prince instead of a weary student, and the young girl a princess offering the handsome passer-by her royal hospitality, discreetly accepting his chivalrous gifts, and returning his admiration with compliments of her own about his noble lineage. And then the memory fades once more, with the poet's words: "I know not when it was. I still confuse the present and the past the way I mix up Death and Life—a bridge of sweetness links them."

Nocturnes was published in 1961, after Senghor had become president of Senegal. It won the International Grand Prize for Poetry from the Poets and Artists of France. Particularly outstanding in this volume are a group of about twenty love lyrics, some of them composed much earlier, known collectively as "Songs for Signare." Here we are far from the poet as spokesman for the politician, deep instead in the pure, intensely romantic lyricism that is surely his highest literary achievement.

---

* The half-hour Senghor film, one in a series devoted to contemporary artists from all over the world, is available for rental through National Educational Television Films, Bloomington, Indiana.

The poems of *Nocturnes* tend to be briefer, more tightly controlled than the earlier works. In each poem a single dramatic and melodic line of emotion is spun from beginning to end.

"Midnight Elegy," the last Senghor poem included, offers us a remarkably candid portrait of this complex man of two cultures. He is in a state of acute mental tension. He hasn't slept in several days. He feels surrounded by the blinding, unbearable brightness of lights, all kinds of lights he is powerless to extinguish. "The splendor of honors," for indeed he has reached a point in his life where honors are many, "is like a Sahara, an immense void." He feels like Father Cloarec, a Christian missionary who suffered years of scorn from the Serers among whom he lived. The images of emptiness and pain are interrupted by the sudden hallucination that a leopard is leaping at the poet's throat, that the roomful of books surrounding him are so many thousands of staring, unblinking eyes. The nightmare feelings of despair are momentarily alleviated by a sudden elation, a surging sense of strength and virility, climaxing in the brief fantasy of making love to a beautiful woman peacefully sleeping nearby. But the poet's anxiety is such that neither love nor poetry can lessen it. He thinks of suicide, but that would surely bring a hell as painful as the waking hell he is already enduring. His only hope for deliverance, once again, seems to be the "childhood kingdom that hummed with dreams." These images alone bring solace, the assurance that sleep will come with dawn, when at last he will find rest, with his beloved in his arms.

"The equilibrium you admire in me is an unstable one, difficult to maintain," Senghor once told the French critic Armand Guibert. "My inner life was split very early between the call of the Ancestors and the call of Europe, between the exigencies of black-African culture and those of modern life. These conflicts are often expressed in my poems. In fact, they are the very crux of them."

French Garden

Calm garden
Grave garden
Garden with evening eyes
Lowered for the night

Troubles and noises
All the city's rustling anguish
Reaches me, slipping down the slippery roofs
Arriving at my window
Bent, strewn with tiny, tender, pensive leaves.

White hands
Delicate motions
Soothing gestures

But the tom-tom's call
                    bounding
                            over continents
                                    and mountains

Who will quiet my heart
Leaping at the tom-tom's call
                            violently
                                    throbbing?

1934

SEVEN POEMS FROM *Songs of Darkness*

Night of Sine

Woman, rest your balsam hands upon my brow, softer your hands are
                                                            than fur.
Above, the swaying palms rustle faintly in the evening breeze.
Not quite a lullaby.
May the rhythmic silence cradle us.
Let us listen to its song, listen to our dark blood beat,
Let us listen to it beat, the deep pulse beat of Africa in the mist of lost
                                                            villages.

Lazily the moon inclines into her slack sea bed.
Laughter dies away, and even storytellers
Begin to nod their heads like sleepy children dozing on their mothers'
                                                            backs.

Title. Sine: A river; also name of the Senegalese province where Senghor was born.

The dancers' feet grow heavy now, as the alternating choirs cease.

It's star time, and dreamily the Night leans her elbows on this cloudy
hill, draped in her long, milky robe.
Tenderly the rooftops gleam. What are they confiding to the stars?
Within, the fire burns low in the privacy of odors sharp and sweet.

Woman, light the limpid butter lamp, so around it ancestors can come
to chat like parents when their children are in bed.
Let us listen to the ancients of Elissa. Exiled, like us.
They did not wish to die, or lose their fertile torrent in the sands.
Let me listen in the smoky hut where friendly souls have come to visit,
My head upon your breast, warm as couscous newly steaming from the
fire.
Let me breathe the odor of our Dead, let me gather and repeat their living
voices, let me learn
To live before I sink, deeper than a diver, into the lofty depths of sleep.

15. Elissa: The region in former Portuguese Guinea where Senghor's family orig-
inated.

Joal

I remember
Joal!

I remember *signares* in the green darkness of verandas,
Signares with eyes surreal as shafts of moonlight on the sand.

I recall the pageantry of sunsets,
Where Koumba N'Dofène would have cut his royal cloak.
I remember funeral feasts steaming with the blood of slaughtered herds,
The noise of quarrels, the *griots'* rhapsodies.

I remember pagan voices beating out the *Tantum Ergo,*
And the processions and the palms and the triumphal arches.
I recall the dancing of the nubile girls,
The battle songs—and oh! the final dance of the young men, chests
slender,

6. Koumba N'Dofène: The King of Sine, a friend of Senghor's father.
8. *Griots:* West African ministrels.
9. *Tantum Ergo:* A benedictory hymn of the Roman Catholic Church.

Bent, and the women's pure love cry
—*Kor Siga!*

I remember, I remember . . .
My head in motion with
What weary pace the length of European days where now and then
An orphan jazz appears sobbing, sobbing, sobbing.

14. *Kor Siga:* Champion or protector of Siga, the term for a sister or fiancée.

Negro Mask

to Pablo Picasso

She sleeps and rests on the candor of the sand,
Koumba Tam sleeps. A green palm veils the fever of her hair, bronzes
her brow, curves
The closed eyelids, a double cup with wellsprings sealed.
In this fine crescent, the darker, scarcely heavy lip, where is the smile of
woman accomplice?
The patina of the cheeks, the line of the chin sing of silent agreement.
Mask face, closed to the ephemeral, eyeless, without substance,
Perfect bronze head with its timeworn patina
That neither paint nor redness nor wrinkles nor the trace of tears or
kisses stain.
O face as God made you even before the memory of the ages,
Face of the world's dawn, show no tender throat to rouse my flesh.
I adore you, O Beauty, with my monochordal eye!

Prayer to the Masks

Masks! O Masks!
Black mask red mask you white-and-black masks,
Masks at the four points the Spirit breathes from,
I salute you in silence!
And not you last, lion-headed Ancestor,
You guard this place from any woman's laughter, any fading smile,

Distilling this eternal air in which I breathe my Forebears.
Masks of maskless faces, stripped of every dimple as of every wrinkle,
You who have arranged this portrait, this face of mine bent above this
altar of white paper
In your image, hear me!
Now dies the Africa of empires—the dying of a pitiable princess
And Europe's too, to whom we're linked by the umbilicus.
Fix your immutable eyes on your subjugated children,
Who relinquish their lives as the poor their last garments.
May we answer present at the world's rebirth,
Like the yeast white flour needs.
For who would teach rhythm to a dead world of cannons and machines?
Who would give the shout of joy at dawn to wake the dead and
orphaned?
Tell me, who would restore the memory of life to men whose hopes are
disemboweled?
They call us men of cotton, coffee, oil.
They call us men of death.
We are men of dance, whose feet take on new strength from stamping
the hard ground.

The Totem

In my innermost vein I must hide him,
My ancestor with the lightning-scarred, the stormy skin.
I must hide my guardian animal
Or a scandal will break out.
His is my faithful blood, requiring my fidelity
To protect me from my naked pride,
And the arrogance of lucky races. . . .

Ode for Three Kôras and Balaphong (excerpt)

for René Maran

After this day's hope—see how the Somme, the Seine, and the wild Slav
                rivers run red beneath the Archangel's sword.
My heart weakens at the winy smell of blood but I have orders and my
                duty to uphold.
May I be consoled each night at least by the migratory humor of my
                other self.
Tokô-Waly, my uncle, do you remember those long-ago nights when my
                head grew heavy on your patient back?
Or how you took my hand in yours and guided me through signs and
                shadows?
The fields blossom with glowworms; stars alight on grass and trees.
There is silence all around.
The only stirrings are the perfumes of the bush, hives of russet bees that
    dominate the crickets' thin vibrato and muffled tom-tom, the distant
                respiration of the night.
You, Tokô-Waly, you hear what is inaudible
And explain to me the signs our Forebears make in the marine serenity
                of the constellations,
The Bull, the Scorpion, the Leopard, the Elephant, and the familiar Fish
And the Spirits' milky splendor in the infinite celestial tann.
But here as veils of darkness fall is the Goddess Moon's intelligence.
African night, my black night, mystical and bright black and brilliant,
You rest in concord with the Earth, you are the Earth and the harmonious
                hills.
O classic beauty, line not angular but elastic, elegant and slender,
O classic face! From brow arching under perfumed forest and wide
                oblique eyes to a graceful bay, the chin, and
The ardent outburst of twin hills! O sweet curves, melodic visage!
O my lioness, my black Beauty, my black Night, my Black one, my Bare
                one!
Ah! How often you have made my heart beat like an untamed leopard's
                in its narrow cage!

    Title. *Kôra:* A Senegalese harp, made with from sixteen to thirty-two strings.
Balaphong: An African xylophone made of thin wooden slats.
    12. Tann: Great sand flats along the Senegalase coast.

Night delivering me from reasons, salons, sophisms, from pirouettes and
          pretexts, from the calculated hatred of slaughter humanized.
Night dissolving all my contradictions, melting contradictions in the
          primal unity of your negritude.
Receive this child, a child twelve years of wandering have not aged.
I bring from Europe but this child who is my friend, the brightness of
          her eyes amid the Breton mists.

Château-Gontier, October–December 1939

Return of the Prodigal Son (conclusion)

Elephant of Mbissel, hear my pious prayer.
Give me the fervent science of Timbuktu's great doctors.
Give me the will of Soni Ali, son of the Lion's foam, a tidal wave to
          conquer a continent.
Breathe on me the wisdom of the Keitas.
Give me the Guelwar's courage and gird my loins with a Tyédo's strength.
Let me die for the cause of my people, in the stink of gun and cannon
          if need be.
May the love of this people stay fast and take root in my liberated heart.
Make me your Master of Language; no, make me his ambassador.

Blessed be my fathers, who bless the Prodigal!
I want to see the women's house again, I played there with the doves and
          my brothers, the sons of the Lion.
Ah! To sleep once again in my childhood's cool bed,
Tucked in once again by the black hands so dear,
And once more the white smile of my mother.

Tomorrow I set out again for Europe, on the diplomatic path,
Homesick for the Black Land.

FROM *Black Host*

Prayer for Peace (for great organs)

to Georges and Claude Pompidou

> . . . *forgive us our trespasses as we*
> *forgive those who trespass against us* . . .

I

Lord Jesus, at the end of this book which I offer you as a ciborium of
suffering,
As this great year begins with the sunshine of your peace on the snowy
roofs of Paris
—I know my brothers' blood will run red once more on the Pacific shore
of a yellow East beset by storms and hatred.
I know this blood is the spring libation with which Great Publicans have
fattened the lands of Empire these seventy years.
Lord, at the foot of this cross—this tree of pain no longer You but beyond
the Old and New Worlds, Africa crucified,
Whose right arm stretches over my land, and whose left casts shadows on
America,
Haiti at its heart, which dared proclaim its Manhood to the Tyrant's
face—
At the foot of my Africa, crucified these four hundred years, yet
breathing,
Lord, let me repeat its prayer of pardon and of peace.

II

Lord God, forgive white Europe!
It is true, Lord, that for four centuries of enlightenment she threw her
foaming, yelping dogs upon my lands.
And that Christians, in denial of Your word and the mildness of Your
heart,
Lit their campfires with my parchments, put my seminarians to torture,
sent my doctors and my learned men to exile.
Their gunpowder crumbled proud fortresses and hillsides like lightning,
And their cannon crossed the backs of nations broad as daylight from
Western shore to the horizon of the East,

And set fire to our sacred woods as if to hunting grounds, pulling out
        our spirits and our forebears by their peaceful beards.
And they transformed these mysteries into the Sunday recreation of a
        sleepy bourgeoisie.

Lord, forgive those who made guerrillas of the Askias, who turned my
        princes into sergeants,
Made houseboys of my servants, and laborers of my country folk, who
        turned my people into a proletariat.
For You must forgive those who hunted my children like wild elephants,
Who trained them to the whip and made them the black hands of those
        whose hands were white.

You must forget those who stole ten million of my sons in their leperous
        ships
And who suppressed two hundred million more.
A lonely old age they've made me in the forest of my nights and the
        savanna of my days.
The glass before my eyes grows misty, Lord.
And the serpent Hatred stirs his head within my heart, the serpent I'd
        thought dead . . .

III

Kill it, Lord, for I must proceed upon my way, and strangely, it is for
        France I want to pray.
Lord, among the white lands, set France upon the Father's right.

Oh, I know she too is Europe, she too like some Northern cattle rustler
        raped my children to fatten cane and cotton fields, for
        Negro sweat is like manure.

She too brought death and cannons to my villages, she too set some of
        mine against the others, like dogs fighting for a bone.

She too treated the unyielding ones like criminals and spat upon the-
        heads-that-had-great-aims.

Yes Lord, forgive France, who expresses the right way so well and makes
        her own so deviously,
Who invites me to her table, and tells me to bring my own bread, who
        gives to me with her right hand while the left takes half back again.

Yes Lord, forgive France, who hates all occupations, and imposes hers so
heavily on me,
Who throws open her triumphal routes to heroes and treats her Sene-
galese like hired hands, making them the black dogs of her empire,
Who is the Republic and delivers whole countries to the concessionary
companies
That have made my Mesopotamia, the Congo, a vast cemetery beneath
the white sun.

IV

Oh Lord, dismiss from my memory the France that is not France, this
mask of pettiness and hate upon the face of France,
This mask of pettiness and hate for which I've only hate—but surely I
can hate the evil
For I am greatly fond of France.

Bless these captive people who twice have known how to liberate their
hands and dared proclaim the advent of the poor to those of
royal lineage,
Who made these daytime slaves into men of liberty, equality, fraternity,
Bless these people who brought me Your good tidings, Lord, and opened
my heavy eyelids to the illumination of Your faith,
And opened too my heart to knowledge of the world, bringing me a
rainbow of new brothers.
I salute you, brothers: Mohamed Ben Abdallah, Rasafymahatratra, and
also Phan-Manh Toung,
All of you from peaceful seas and enchanted forests
I greet you with a universal heart.

Oh! More than one of your messengers, I know, tracked my holy men
like animals and destroyed our sacred images.

And yet they well could have put up with them, for these images were a
Jacob's ladder from our earth toward Your heaven,
The limpid butter lamp that guides the way to dawn, the starlight that
anticipates the sun's.

Many of your missionaries blessed the instruments of violence, I know,
and compromised with banker's gold,
But there always will be imbeciles and traitors.

V

O bless these people, Lord, who seek for their own face beneath the
mask, and labor hard to know it,
Who seek for You amid the cold, amid a hunger that gnaws at bones and
innards.
The young betrothed who mourns her widowhood,
The boy robbed of his youth,
The wife who laments her husband's absent eye, and the mother who
seeks her child's dreams in the rubble.
O bless these people who break their bonds, bless these people reduced
to their last extremity who confront the wild greed of the powerful,
the torturers,
And with them bless all of Europe's peoples, Asia's, Africa's, and
America's,
Who sweat blood and pain. Among these waving millions, see the motion
of my people's wooly heads
And may their warm hands entwine the earth like a belt of brotherhood
Beneath THE RAINBOW OF YOUR PEACE.

Paris, January 1945

TWO POEMS FROM *Ethiopics*

New York (trumpet solo for jazz orchestra)

1

New York! At first I was confounded by your beauty, those tall long-
legged golden girls.
Timid at first before your metallic blue eyes, your frosty smile,
So timid, and my anguish at the bottom of your skyscraping streets,
raising owl-eyes toward the blacked-out sun.
Sulfurous your light and the livid shafts whose heads smash up against
the sky.
Skyscrapers whose steely muscle and bronzed stony skin challenge
cyclones.

Fifteen days on Manhattan's naked sidewalks
—at the third week's end the fever grabs one with a jaguar's leap,
Fifteen days without wellspring or pasture, birds falling suddenly dead
从 from sooty rooftops.
No blossoming child's laughter, his hand in my cool one.
No maternal breast, nyloned legs. Legs and breasts without odor or sweat.
No tender word in the absence of lips, nothing but artificial hearts paid
for at high prices.
And no book in which to read wisdom. The painter's palette is bedecked
with coral crystals.
O insomniac Manhattan nights! So stirred up with lively lights, while
auto horns blare forth the empty hours
And murky waters carry past hygienic loves, like flood rivers, the bodies
of dead children.

2

Now is the season for renderings and accounts,
New York! Yes, now is the time for manna and hyssop.
Only listen to God's trombones, let your heart beat to the rhythm of
blood, your blood.
I have seen in Harlem, humming with sounds, ceremonious colors and
flamboyant scents
—at teatime in the drugstores.
I have seen the festival of night in preparation at the flight of day. I
proclaim the night more truthful than the day.
This is the pure hour when God makes immemorial life spring forth in
the streets,
Its amphibious elements radiating like suns.
Harlem! Harlem! This is what I've seen—Harlem, Harlem!
A green breeze of wheat springing from pavements plowed by barefoot
dancers waving silken rumps and spearhead breasts, ballets of
waterlilies and fabulous masks.
At the feet of police horses, the mangoes of love rolling from low houses.
And I have seen along the sidewalks rivulets of white rum, rivulets of
black milk in the blue fog of cigars.
I have seen snowfalls at night of cotton flowers, seraphic wings and
sorcerers' plumes.

Listen, New York! Oh listen to your virile, copper voice, your vibrating
    oboe's voice, hear the stopped-up anguish of your tears fall in great
        clots of blood.
Hear the distant beat of your nocturnal heart, rhythm and blood of the
    tom-tom, tom-tom blood and tom-tom.

3

New York! I say New York, let black blood flow in your blood,
Let it rub the rust from your steely joints, like a life-giving oil
Till it gives your bridges the curves of buttocks and the suppleness of
    vines.
For then will be refound the unity of ancient times, the reconciliation of
    Lion, Bull, and Tree,
Idea linked to act, ear to heart, and sign to sense.
There are your rivers rippling with musky crocodiles and mirage-eyed
    manatees. And no need to invent any Sirens.
But it is enough to behold an April rainbow
And to hear, especially to hear the Lord, who with a saxophonic laugh,
    created heaven and earth in six days.
And on the seventh, slept a great Negro sleep.

I Know Not When It Was

(for *khalam*)

I know not when it was, I still confuse childhood and Eden
The way I mix up Death and Life—a bridge of sweetness links them.

I was coming home from Fa'oye, having drunk there deeply at the solemn
    tomb
Like sea cows soaking up the waters at Simal.
I was coming back from Fa'oye, and the witching hour had reached its
    peak.
It is then that one sees spirits, when the light becomes transparent
And one skirts the pathways to avoid their deadly and fraternal hand.

3. Fa'oye: Village near Senghor's birthplace.
4. Simal: A regional holy place.

The soul of a village throbbed on the horizon. Were its people dead or
living?
"May my poem of peace be calm water on your feet and your face
And may the shade of our courtyard bring refreshment to your heart,"
she said.
Her polished hands clothed me in a silken robe of honor.
Her words charmed like delicious food, with midnight milk's sweetness,
And her smile was more melodious than her praise-singer's lute.
The morning star came to sit among us, and deliciously we wept.

—Exquisite sister mine, take these golden beads to celebrate your throat's
dark splendor. . . .
—Chosen brother mine, tell me then your name. It must resound like a
sorong
Gleaming redly like a saber in the sun. Oh! Only sing your name!
My heart is a coffer of precious wood, my head an agèd parchment from
Djenné.
Sing but of your lineage that my memory may give answer.

I know not when it was. I still confuse the present and the past
The way I mix up Death and Life—a bridge of sweetness links them.

16. *Sorong:* A Fulani harp.

TWO POEMS FROM *Nocturnes*

Five Songs for Signare

(for *khalam*)

Long, long between your hands you held the warrior's black face
As if some fatal twilight lightened it already.
From the hill I saw the sun set in the bay of your eyes.
Homeland, when shall I see again the pure horizon of your face?
When shall I seat myself anew at the table of your dark breast?

Sweet resolutions nest in the penumbra.

I shall see other skies and other eyes,
I shall drink from the spring of other lips fresher than lemon,

I shall sleep beneath the roof of other hair, seeking shelter from the
storms.
But each year, when the rum of Spring sets memory aflame,
I shall mourn my native land and the rain from your eyes on thirsty
savannas.

(for *khalam*)

I walked you to the village where the granaries are at the threshold of
Night,
And I was speechless at the gold enigma of your smile.
A brief twilight fell upon your face, by some divine caprice.
From high on the last hilly refuge of light, I saw the brightness of your
robe go out
And your hair plunge like the sun into the ricefield's shadow,
When the anguish seized me, ancestral fears more treacherous than
panthers

—The mind cannot dismiss them any longer after dark.
Then must it be forever night? Oh! the leave without leavetaking?
In the darkness I shall weep, in the Earth's maternal hollow
I shall sleep in the silence of my tears
Until my brow is gently grazed by the milky dawn that is your mouth.

(for *khalam*)

We shall bathe, my love, in an African presence.
Furniture from Guinea and the Congo, heavy and polished, somber and
serene.
Masks primordial and pure upon the walls, distant yet so present!
Stools of honor for hereditary guests, for the Highland Princes.
Musky scents, and mattings thick with silence,
Cushions dark and leisurely, the sound of peaceful water.
Classic utterance; and from afar songs that alternate like the robes of
Sudanese.
Then you, friendly lamp, to soften the obsession of this presence
Black white and red, oh! red as the earth of Africa.

(for *khalam*)

Your face, the beauty of a time long past evokes the perfumed robes in
faded hues,

Souvenir of times without a history. They came before our birth.
We were coming back from Dyonewar, our thoughts lingered on the
channels
Where wings of rhythmic eulogies, a silken echo shone,
As mangrove beasts lay waiting them ecstatic as they passed,
And stars upon the concave sea were another divine echo,
And oars melodious and slow trickled shooting stars.
Statuesque, a figurehead bent above the sounding deep,
You sang in a dark voice praises to the upright Champion's glory
As the mangrove animals imbibed, voluptuous delight, your liquid
breath!
Through the bolongs we were coming back from Dyonewar and vaguely
Under its patina, your face of present times had the Eternal, black beauty.

(for two horns and balaphong)

She flees, she flees through flat white lands, as patiently I take my aim
Dizzy with desire. If she takes the bush to play the game,
The thorn and thicket passion, then hour after hour I'll run her down,
Inhaling the soft pant of her dark and speckled flanks,
And beneath the great dumb noonday sun I'll twist her glasslike arms.
Her jubilant antelope dying will intoxicate me like a new palm wine.
And long, long will I drink the rusty blood that flows into her heart,
The milky blood that brings damp earth scents to her mouth.

For am I not the son of Dyogoye? Yes he, the hungry Lion.

Midnight Elegy

Summer, splendid summer, nourishing the poet on the milk of your light,
I who sprouted like spring wheat, drunk from the water's greenness, from
its streaming greenness in the gold of time,
Ah! no longer can I stand the lamplight, your light, your atomic light
disintegrating all my being,
I can no longer bear the midnight light. The splendor of honors is like a
Sahara,

An immense void, without *erg* or *hamada,* without grass or a heartbeat or
a blinking of lashes.
Day after day this way, eyes wide like Father Cloarec's,
Who was crucified on stone by the serpent-loving pagans of Joal,
A Portuguese beacon revolves in my eyes, yes, for twenty-four hours and
twenty-four more,
Precisely, mechanically, unceasingly, until the end of time.

I leap from my bed, a leopard at my throat, choking from a sudden sandy
gust of wind.
—Ah! if only I could crumble into dung and blood, into nothingness.
I circle round among my books, who look at me from deep within their
eyes,
Six thousand lamps burning twenty-four hours on twenty-four more.
I am standing, lucid, strangely lucid,
And I'm as handsome as a hundred-yard sprinter, as a black Mauretanian
in rut.
My blood bears a seminal river to fertilize all Byzantium's plains,
And her hills, her stark hills.
I am lover and well-oiled locomotive.

Soft her strawberry lips, dense her stone body, sweet her secret fishing
grounds,
Her body, deep earth open to dark sower.
The feeling germinates beneath the groin, the birthplace of desire.
My sex is an antenna to the manifold center where lightning-like
messages flash.
The music of love no longer can appease me, nor can the sacred rhythm
of a poem.

Lord, I need all my strength against despair
—How sweet the dagger thrust to its hilt into the heart
As if in remorse. I'm not sure I'd die.
What if this were Hell, this absence of sleep, this poet's desert,
This pain of living, this dying of not dying,
This anguish of shadows, this passion over death and light,

5. *Erg:* A region of moving sand dunes in the Sahara.
5. *Hamada:* Strong plateaus in the Sahara.
6. Father Cloarec: A French missionary priest who greatly influenced Senghor as a child; he was not literally crucified by the people of Joal, but for years they treated him cruelly and hypocritically.

Like moths at night on storm lamps in the horrible decay of virgin forests.
Lord of light and darkness.
You, lord of the Cosmos, let me rest beneath Joal-the-Shady.
Let me be reborn into the childhood kingdom that hummed with dreams.
Let me be shepherd to my shepherdess on the tanns of Dyilor, where the
          dead lie blooming.
Let me burst into applause as Tening N'Dyare and Tyagoum N'Dyare
          join the circle;
Let me dance like the athlete at the drums for this year's dead.
This is but a prayer. You know my peasant patience.
Peace will come, dawn's angel, the song of wondrous birds will come,
The light of dawn will come.
I shall sleep the deathlike sleep that nourishes the poet.
—O you who give the sleeping sickness to the newly born, to Marône-the-
          Poetess, to Kotye-Barma-the-Just!—
I shall sleep at dawn, my rosy darling in my arms,
My darling with the green-gold eyes, with her speech so marvelous,
The very language of the poem.

  32. Joal-the-Shady: The repose of his childhood is encompassed in ideas of a huge tree in Joal.
  34. Dyilor: A village near Joal where Senghor's family lived.
  35. Tening N'Dyare and Tyagoum N'Dyare: Two Serer girls, with the family name of N'Dyare; they were especially fine dancers.
  40. Marône-the-Poetess: A Serer oral poet Senghor knew and admired since childhood. She lived near Joal from 1890 to 1950.
  40. Kotye-Barma-the-Just: A seventeenth-century Wolof philosopher and moralist, hero of many oral traditional tales.

Birago Diop

BIRAGO DIOP AND LÉOPOLD SENGHOR WERE BORN IN the same year. Diop grew up in the old city of Saint Louis, on the northwest coast of Senegal, and attended the Lycée Faidherbe there before going to France to take his degree in veterinary medicine at the University of Toulouse. He was one of the peripheral group around *L'Etudiant noir* during the late 1930s. His friend Senghor is credited with weaning the doctor away from imitating classical French poets and drawing him instead to Senegalese sources, traditional oral forms, rhythms, and styles, as well as subject matter. Birago Diop is perhaps best known for his three volumes of Senegalese folk tales. Many of them were learned from his family *griot* and retold by Diop in a French that retains much of the savor, imagery, humor, and wisdom of the original Wolof, the language of the major Senegalese ethnic group. A good selection of Diop's fables and legends was translated by Dorothy Blair for Oxford University Press in 1966 as *Tales of Amadou Koumba*.

Diop wrote poems early in his career. Our selections are taken from the slim volume, *Leurres et Lueurs* (*Gleams and Glimmers*), in which these early works were collected by *Présence Africaine* in 1960. Unlike many West Indians, whose poems often express the nostalgia for an Africa unknown to them, and unlike such Africans as Senghor or U Tam'si who fuse sophisticated Western literary forms and styles with African materials, Birago Diop's poems present purely and simply that Africa.

The materials for much of his writing, both prose and poetry, come not only from his Senegalese childhood but directly from his extensive travels in remote and untouched corners of the French Sudan. Again, unlike Senghor or U Tam'si, Birago Diop has spent most of his adult life not in Europe but in Africa. The annual rounds he made as practicing

147

veterinarian and chief of zootechnical services in the Upper Volta region gave him intimate contact for weeks—and even months at a time—year after year, with a traditional rural life which he observed and understood extremely well. Three of Birago Diop's poems, "Viaticum," "Spirits," and "Diptych," evoke the African reverence for the dead and the belief in their power to influence the world of the living. They are haunting re-creations of ancient African religious beliefs, of ways of looking at the world, explaining it, and attempting to control it. Langston Hughes made an abridged translation for his *African Treasury* of the poem we have translated as "Spirits." He called it "Forefathers." In French, the title is *"Souffles,"* which literally means "breaths." This idea of the pulsing, living, breathing presence of once human beings in trees, in the air, and in other elements of the natural world and its cycles is not only pervasive in African cultures but is also evident in many of the poems in this volume. We have preferred to present a longer version of "Spirits" as it originally appeared in Diop's short story "Sarzan."

As one can see from the opening lines, which recur with slight variations after each developing stanza in the poem, "Spirits" is a kind of call-and-response chant. It reads like a group poem, rather than one originating in the mind of a single narrator.

New editions of Birago Diop's folk tales—first published in 1947, 1958, and 1963—as well as the frequent reprinting of his poems and tales in anthologies and textbooks have given him a solid place in the new West African literature. At the time of Senegalese independence in 1960, President Senghor named his old friend ambassador to Tunisia, where he served for several years with distinction before retiring to private life in Dakar.

SEVEN POEMS FROM *Gleams and Glimmers*

Animism

When the land of El Kanesie awakens
Miracles will come to pass,
The light springing from your brows
Will restore to Africa its fervor.

When the whiteness of millennial bones
Has shaken free the soul
Held etherized and heavy,
When other rays bombard you,

You'll know then what your clay gods think,
What black-masked fetishes have said,
At flaming twilights, on beautiful nights,

You'll learn then what your scriptures are,
What the voice of things repeats to the great winds
From the dark forests to the distant east.

Kassak

To Léopold Sédar Senghor

The earth bleeds
as a breast bleeds
streaming with milk
the color of the setting sun.
The milk is red,
the sand is dark with blood,
the sky weeps
as a child weeps.

Who then made use of the sinister hoe?

The water pines
when the oar is dipped.
The canoe whines
at the water's kiss.
Hyena is pricked
passing through the hedge
and crow has broken
his feather in the wound.

Who then made use of the sinister hoe?

Title: *Kassaks* are age-old West African memory-training songs.

With the point of his assegai
the shepherd has wounded
the supple spine of the
brother-of-the-savanna,
and nothing remains
of all his handsome herd,
neither bulls, nor heifers
nor young calfs.

Who then made use of the sinister hoe?

Viaticum

Into one of three pots,
three pots to which on certain evenings
souls serene and satisfied return—
the breathing of ancestors,
ancestors who were men,
forefathers who were sages—
Mother dipped three fingers,
three fingers of her left hand:
the thumb, the first and middle fingers.

With her three fingers red with blood
with dog's blood,
with bull's blood,
with goat's blood,
three times Mother touched me.
With her thumb she touched my brow,
with her index my left breast,
and my navel with her third.

I, I held my fingers red with blood
with dog's blood,
with bull's blood,
with goat's blood,
I held these three fingers to the winds,
to the North winds, to the winds of the rising sun,
to the South winds, to the winds of the setting sun;

and I raised my three fingers toward the moon,
the full moon, the full and naked moon,
reflected in the bottom of the biggest pot.

Then I put these three fingers in the sand,
into the sand that had grown cold,
and Mother said: "Go, go into the World!
They will follow in your steps for life."

Since then I go my way
along the pathways,
the pathways and the roads,
across the sea and farther, farther still
beyond the sea and farther than beyond.
And when evil ones draw near,
men with black hearts,
when I approach the envious,
men with black hearts
before me move the Spirits of the Elders.

Desert

God alone is God! *Mohammed rassoul Allah!*
The muezzin's voice bounds from dome to dome,
Swells, spreads, dies out in the distance. . . .
The bodies of our men bend slowly, bowing low.

Wearily the muffled chorus keeps the rhythm,
Black tips of thatched roofs
Fringe a horizon we shall never reach.

In the infinity of the ages,
Stumbling thus through endless desert sands,
Will we reach far distant lands?

Does each day lead us toward tomorrow?
Toward the distant resting places, havens
Where our dreams will be no more than ashes?

Diptych

The Sun, hung by a string
deep in the indigo calabash,
boils up the kettleful of day.
The Darkness, frightened at the coming
of the Daughters-of-Fire, burrows
at the foot of fenceposts.
The savanna is bright and crisp,
shapes and colors, sharp.
But in distressing silences filled with hummings
and noises neither muffled nor shrill
a heavy mystery hovers,
a secret, shapeless mystery
frightens and surrounds us.

Nailed on with fiery nails, the dark cloth
spread above the earth covers up the bed of night.
Frightened at the coming of the Daughters-of-Darkness,
dogs bark, horses whinny,
man burrows deep within his hut.
The savanna is dark
shapes and colors, all are black.
But in distressing silences filled with hummings
pathways thick with mystery
slowly become visible
to those who have departed
and to those who will return.

Spirits

Listen to Things
More often than Beings,
Hear the voice of fire,
Hear the voice of water.
Listen in the wind,
To the sighs of the bush;
This is the ancestors breathing.

Those who are dead are not ever gone;
They are in the darkness that grows lighter
And in the darkness that grows darker.
The dead are not down in the earth;
They are in the trembling of the trees
In the groaning of the woods,
In the water that runs,
In the water that sleeps,
They are in the hut, they are in the crowd:
The dead are not dead.

> Listen to things
> More often than beings,
> Hear the voice of fire,
> Hear the voice of water.
> Listen in the wind,
> To the bush that is sighing:
> This is the breathing of ancestors,
> Who have not gone away
> Who are not under earth
> Who are not really dead.

Those who are dead are not ever gone;
They are in a woman's breast,
In the wailing of a child,
And the burning of a log,
In the moaning rock,
In the weeping grasses,
In the forest and the home.
The dead are not dead.

> Listen more often
> To Things than to Beings,
> Hear the voice of fire,
> Hear the voice of water.
> Listen in the wind to
> The bush that is sobbing:
> This is the ancestors breathing.

Each day they renew ancient bonds,
Ancient bonds that hold fast

Binding our lot to their law,
To the will of the spirits stronger than we
To the spell of our dead who are not really dead,
Whose covenant binds us to life,
Whose authority binds to their will,
The will of the spirits that stir
In the bed of the river, on the banks of the river,
The breathing of spirits
Who moan in the rocks and weep in the grasses.

Spirits inhabit
The darkness that lightens, the darkness that darkens,
The quivering tree, the murmuring wood,
The water that runs and the water that sleeps:
Spirits much stronger than we,
The breathing of the dead who are not really dead,
Of the dead who are not really gone,
Of the dead now no more in the earth.

> Listen to Things
> More often than Beings,
> Hear the voice of fire,
> Hear the voice of water.
> Listen in the wind,
> To the bush that is sobbing:
> This is the ancestors, breathing.

Omen

A naked sun—a yellow sun—
The pure yellow sun of hasty dawns
Pours waves of gold upon the bank
Of a pure yellow river.

A naked sun—a white sun—
A sun naked and white
Pours waves of silver
Upon a white, white river.

A naked sun—a red sun—
A sun naked and red
Pours waves of red blood
On a red, red river.

MALI ✖ (1900–1964)

Fily-Dabo Sissoko

UNTIL HIS MYSTERIOUS DEATH IN 1964 WHILE A political prisoner of Mali's independent government, Fily-Dabo Sissoko was one of the grand old men of French-speaking West Africa. The son of a Malinké chief, he was educated in local mission schools and graduated from the Lycée William Ponty in Dakar in 1918. A schoolteacher and local chieftain, Sissoko was an early participant in wider African political and cultural life during the colonial era. Like several of the other poets in this volume (Rabémananjara of Madagascar, Césaire of Martinique, Damas of French Guiana, and Senghor of Senegal) he was the first elected representative from his country to the French Assembly, serving from 1945 until 1958. He was three times a French delegate to the U.N. and for five years president of the Sudanese Territorial Assembly.

In 1962 Sissoko published a book of informal memoirs and meditations entitled *La Savane rouge* (*The Red Savanna*), a kind of personal diary or notebook recalling the principal events of his life in colonial Africa. The following year, Sissoko's *Poèmes de l'Afrique noire* (*Poems from Black Africa*), were collected in a new volume. Some date from the 1920s, others from much later. Although they defy easy classification, Sissoko's African vignettes depict scenes and situations clearly familiar to him, in a refreshing, deceptively simple style.

SEVEN POEMS FROM *Poems from Black Africa*

Grandmother

My grandma thinks only of me. The food that people bring her comes to
me. The chicken newly caponed is for me.

156

Already she is thinking of my future. All her worldly goods will come to
me.

All day long she frets to see me romping with my friends. Round the
huts we chase, armed with tiny bamboo bows and arrows, losing ourselves
in the bush with our dogs, hunting for does and palm-squirrels.

We come home filthy every time, dripping sweat from scalp and brow,
but ready to be off again at the least excuse.

This makes Grandma angry. But she dares not hold me back, knowing
what I want, I do.

When I'm naughty, no one in the family dares to scold me, still less to
hit me. The blows that come my way now and then, from a servant or
some older person, provoke real scenes.

The culprit, to my great delight, is roundly punished. As for me, I mock
him, cuddled—just in case—against my grandma.

If things had kept on like this with Grandma, I would have come to no
good end!

Dawn in the Valley

In the sun's path
three tongues of fire
stripe the azure sky.

Crowned in purple
full of fickle shadows
the valley prepares
its morning toilet.

Nothing moves
but the palm-squirrel
skipping from bush to bush
or the toucan
who clacks his beak
spinning from branch to branch.

The sun appears.
Its crimson robe falls
softening all the colors.
The valley decks itself in green
spangled with rust.
The wind blows
cool and aimless.

In a golden wake
a swarm of bees
hums past.

The Bombax Tree

Stripped of his crown
he stands
at the center of the town,
the crooks of his branches
heavy with enormous
warts.

Witness to the ages,
he has seen
generations,
ten, fifteen,
of warriors
filing by.

Often
homeward bound from battle,
vultures who had trailed the troops
perched upon his mutilated branches
drawing from their swollen crops
the hearts and livers of the fallen
still warm and quick
to offer them as nourishment
to those who stayed behind
recounting the vicissitudes of battle.

Today
on these same warts
each year
storks come
to clack their beaks.

Whirlwinds

Whirlwinds
nearly always
are born beneath a tree
at the hour when the sun
has reached its zenith.

In a column of burning dust
they climb straight into the sky
scouring everything
in their way.

Old seccos and mats,
calabashes with holes,
empty gourds torn away
fly in spurts
bumping into
hedges uprooted,
flapping roofs.

Sometimes
a fire starts
and panic grips
the village.

Women, children
beat on boxes and
anything that falls beneath their hands,
thinking to banish the evil spirit
with their racket.

And in fact
he does withdraw

moving toward the well
where everything
suddenly
dies
out.

Like a Flower

Like hibiscus
still unopened
preening in the sun;

Like water-lily petals
shimmering gold and flame,
springboard of the
water nymphs,

Love
blossoms
from a glance!

Meeting Bida

Taken by surprise
Bida throws his long black ribbon
on the ground.
His eyes shoot flame,
his forked tongue
flickers
like lightning.
Frozen where he stands
the traveler
is dead
even before he falls.

Title: Bida, a poisonous snake.

Brush Fire

At the onset of its sprint, the blazing circle climbs straight ahead, flooding the sky with globules of fire, dancing a saraband to dazzled eyes.

Beaten down in the last strong gusts, grasses carpet the underbrush in yellow. Shivering beneath, one feels the teeming life of animals and serpents, wild and small.

Come hunter or honey-seeker, the brush fire lights.

From crackling to crackling, closer and closer it tongues its way. Green grasshoppers, dizzy butterflies take flight. The wind rises, the trees howl death. Sheets of flame, suddenly tall, spring in gusts to storm the summits.

Nothing will stop the brush fire's furious race. Jumping over the thin curtain of greenery that runs along the riverbanks, it crosses streams, frightening does and palm-squirrels, pythons and panthers, cobras and elk.

Up to the naked foot of cliffs it creeps, to do final battle there with some fallen veteran whose ashes, dragged afar, will whiten the burnt earth.

Then, at night, here and there along the length of the horizon, one sees upon the slopes great spots of flame flickering in the debris.

For long days, brush fire has overcome the steppe.

Antoine-Roger Bolamba

BORN BEFORE WORLD WAR I IN BOMA, IN WHAT WAS until 1960 the Belgian Congo, Antoine-Roger Bolamba was educated in African primary and secondary schools. A journalist by profession, he was editor of *La Voix du Congolais* (*The Congolese Voice*), where his own articles and poems were frequently published. He now lives in the capital city of Kinshasa, formerly Léopoldville, and is Minister of Information and Tourism of the Congolese Republic, now known as Zaire. *Esanzo: chants pour mon pays* (*Esanzo: Songs for My Country*) is a book of Bolamba's poems published in 1956 by *Présence Africaine*. A preface by Léopold Senghor characterizes Bolamba's verse as "swollen with a truly African sap . . . a geyser of images that blow syntax to dust."

THREE POEMS FROM *Esanzo: Songs for My Country*

Bonguemba

Little drum
filled with the spirit
of ancestors,
singers
with bells on their ankles and wrists,
dance on your belly!
Toop-toop, toop-toop!

Women in labor
and nursing their young

Title. *Bonguemba:* The Lingala name for a little drum felt to contain ancestor spirits, which can be summoned by drumming. The drumming is a signal for dancing, which seems to bring emotional release.

become dizzy!
Toop-toop, toop-toop!

Treetops
and kettles
and small grass-roofed houses
are dancing
while misery, ragged and pitted
with purulent wounds,
dances too!
Toop-toop, toop-toop!

Worries and griefs
disappear,
toop-toop, toop-toop!
Bonguemba,
little drum,
you bring peace
with a secret concealed
in the sound of your voice!
Toop-toop, toop-toop!

The bones of the dead
in their tombs
are a-shaking!
Toop-toop, toop-toop!

In the river
the sea cows are
weeping for joy!
Toop-toop, toop-toop!

Bonguemba,
little drum,
ancestors breathing,
this is your message
Toop-toop,
Toop!

In a Storm

The river is rising, *Ngoho,* the river.
My canoe slips along on the crest of the waves.
Come, *Ngoho,* my love, come to my arms,
safe will it carry us.

The river is rising, *Ngoho,* the river.
A shiver is loose on the spine of the waves.
Hard must we paddle
to stay above water
to sail on the water
till dawn.

Morning will come with its delicate trotting
its dancing of flowers
its waltzing of cyclones
its *ngomo*
nkole
bisanzo
benguele
its *ngombi*
totola
bendundu
benguemba
basanga
that bring on man's madness.

The river is rising, *Ngoho,* the river.

1. *Ngoho:* Darling, or sweetheart.
14–22. *Ngomo . . . basanga:* These nine words are names for local dances and musical instruments.

Esanzo

Ding ding ding!
How pleasing are

Title. *Esanzo:* A musical instrument, played by pinching together steel blades, which doubtless produces the sound that punctuates each stanza.

the fireflies in blossom
on translucent leaves of night . . . ding!

How pleasing is the living gaze
behind the melancholy screen . . . ding!

How pleasing too
the headless neck,
the footless limbs,
the handless arms
of night's approach. . . ding!

Leaving her basket
of duties behind in the hut
daylight flees
winging dead memories away.
Ding ding ding!

What we need is the mating
of wood and of fire . . . ding!

What we need is a happiness bridge
where two hearts that are strangers
can make an exchange of their gifts . . . ding!

What we need is the milk
that thirsty desire
pours into us . . . ding ding!

Bernard Dadié

BERNARD DADIÉ IS THE LEADING WRITER OF THE IVORY Coast, though very little of his work has yet been translated into English. Primarily a prose writer, he has been prolific as a playwright and as a collector and reteller of African legends and folktales; he is the author of several travel books, an autobiographical novel, and two volumes of poems.

Dadié's entire education was received in Africa. He was born into a well-to-do family from Assinie and, though raised as a Catholic, grew up close to the roots of Agni-Ashanti tribal life. At sixteen, while he still was at school in Bingerville, he wrote, produced, and directed a short play called *Cities*. In 1936, as a third-year student at the Lycée William Ponty in Senegal, he wrote a three-act play on an eighteenth-century Ivory Coast warrior king, Assemien, which was performed the following year in Paris by African students.

After graduating from the Lycée Ponty, Dadié stayed on in Dakar for eleven years on the staff of the *Institut Français d'Afrique noire* (French Institute of Black Africa).* It was during his IFAN years that Dadié first met Senghor and Alioune Diop, who were both a few years older than he.

In 1947, at about the time *Présence Africaine* was being founded by his friends in Paris, Dadié returned from Senegal to settle in the Ivory Coast. He taught school and edited a periodical entitled *Réveil* (*Awake*). There were waves of political unrest in the French colonies during this period, and *Réveil's* outspoken criticism of the colonial regime earned Dadié a brief spell in jail. In 1950 his first book of poems, *Afrique debout!* (*Africa Arise!*), appeared in France, followed by two books of African tales, *Légendes Africaines* (*African Legends*) and *Le Pagne*

---

* Since independence, IFAN has been renamed; the "F" no longer stands for *Français* (French) but for *fondamentale* (fundamental or basic).

noir (*Black Robes*) in 1953 and 1955 respectively; by his novel *Climbié* in 1956 (translated into English in 1971), and the same year by a second book of poems, *La Ronde des jours* (*Dance of the Days*). From his sojourns in France came *Un Nègre à Paris* (*A Black Man in Paris*) in 1959; and his experiences in the United States produced *Patron de New York* (*A Fan of New York*) in 1964. In the book on New York, Dadié views Americans as if he were an African anthropologist studying the strange customs and characteristics of these curious "natives."

Shortly after the Ivory Coast won its independence, Dadié was made a cabinet minister. As director of arts and research, he leads the new nation's efforts to preserve and enrich its unique heritage in the performing, graphic, and literary arts.

In contrast to a poet like Birago Diop, Dadié does not draw on traditional folk sources for his poems. Nor does he, like Senghor or Tchicaya U Tam'si, attempt to blend the sophistication of European forms or poetic allusions with African subject matter. To Dadié, poetry is a popular art form imbued with social and moral purpose. His literary approach is simple, straightforward, direct. His early poems such as "In Memoriam" echo the well-known group themes: fervent protests against injustice and expressions of faith in the generosity of his people and in his country's struggle for a free and peaceful future.

Dadié's "I Thank You, Lord, for Having Made Me Black" is one of the negritude movement's best short poems. As Professor Mercer Cook recently pointed out, nearly fifty years of black history can be summarized in the contrast between the emotion Dadié expresses, intimately linked to the new black awareness of the 1950s, and Massillon Coicou's lament: "Why then am I a Negro? Oh, why am I black?" written in turn-of-the-century Haiti.*

Two Dadié poems, "Ode to Africa" and "A Wreath for Africa," are lush compared to his others. "Hands," "A World to Come," and several others illustrate his usual poetic style and his belief that "contemporary African poems ought to be a cry, an incentive . . . to surmount our problems." "In Memoriam," written much earlier, is notable for the force of its protest against an indifferent colonial regime. In the Ivory Coast, where the masses are just beginning to learn to read and write, and where French is a language that brings unity despite tribal and linguistic differences, Dadié's poems perform just this function. They inspire the

* *The Militant Black Writer* (Madison, Wis.: University of Wisconsin Press, 1969), p. 13.

"courage, strength, and ideals necessary to vanquish the difficulty of our times," reaching a vast audience through newspapers, radio broadcasts, and popular reprintings. He is also the author of two new plays: *Béatrice au Congo* (*Beatrice in the Congo*), and *Monsieur Thogo-gnini*.

FROM *Africa Arise!*

In Memoriam

"Starved to death,"
He died of hunger,
but it won't be written on his tomb
for they put him in an unmarked grave,
it won't be written there in stone
for the government rejects the truth.

He had gone to all the offices,
the factories, the farms:
no jobs . . .

And thread by thread, his clothing turned to rags.
This, with a thousand bales of surplus cloth nearby . . .
He slept beneath the stars.

And he was a man like you
a man like me,
a man like them,
and he lay beneath the stars,
this man, on the bare ground
before the palaces,
while on the docks mountains of cement were growing hard.
It won't be written there on stone
that he died
beside a palace
with hunger in his belly,
cold gnawing at his bones,
his flesh grown colorless and limp, his ribs collapsing,
the sockets of his bones rebelling.

It won't be written on his tomb
that he died of hunger, slowly,
slowly, while flour mildewed in the stores,
while behind the counters with the iron grills,
behind warehouses filled with goods
they were pulling in the profits . . .
A man is dying.
A man like you,
a man like me,
a man like them.
A man is dying of hunger,
starving, in the midst of plenty.

"Starved to Death"
won't be written on his tomb.
Dishonor on the government
that degrades mankind and brings him low.
It won't be written on his grave
"Dead, of Hunger."

But you, remember
that he starved to death,
slowly
died of hunger,

a man like them
a man like you
slowly
died of hunger
bit by bit
in the midst of plenty
staring at deaf heaven.

This was a man
like you,
like them,
a man . . .
Remember!

FOUR POEMS FROM *Dance of the Days*

I Thank You, Lord

I thank you, Lord, for having made me Black,
for having made me
the sum of all griefs,
for having put upon my head
the World.
I wear the livery of the Centaur
and I have carried the World since the first morning.

White is the color of the great occasions.
Black the color of everyday.
And I have carried the World since the first evening.

I am content
with the shape of my head
made to carry the World.
Satisfied
with the shape of my nose
made to inhale the four winds of the World.
Pleased
with the shape of my legs
ready to run to the end of the Earth.

I thank you, Lord, for having made me Black,
for having made me
the sum of all pain.
A thousand swords have pierced my heart.
A thousand brands have burned me.
And my blood has reddened the snow of all the calvaries,
and my blood, at each dawn, has reddened all horizons.

Yet I am content
to carry the World.
Happy with my short arms
  with my long arms
    with my thick lips.

I thank you, Lord, for having made me Black.
I have carried the World since the dawn of time

and in the night my laughter at the World
   creates the day.

A World to Come

Stars in profusion
     Pure
As the eyes of
     Wise men
Will be as brilliant
As the destiny of men.

We shall be one:
No more looks of anguish.
We shall be brothers:
No more looks of hate.

And if in the sky
There is a glow
It will be to light our love.
And if in the bush
There is a song
It will be to soothe our sleep.

We shall be brothers.
We shall be joined.
And the stars in profusion
     Pure
As the eyes of
     Wise men
Will be as brilliant
As our destiny.

Ode to Africa

I shall tune my lute to sing your litanies as the quiet hours pass,
limbering my hands to play the *griot's kôra*

along the straight and winding paths
to sing of dead and valiant bowmen.
I shall dress myself in velvet and in lilies
to glide in rhythm to the frantic drums
upon the gleaming ground that trails behind the stars.

I shall be shod in sandals of blue shadow
all decked with violets that loll upon the grass
to sketch in virtuoso steps
the ancient sabbath dances.

I shall glove myself in daybreak and in sighs
to praise on David's harp
the magic spell of life's first hours.

And on the marble of your courtyards
I shall dance bedraped in plumes
on a carpet made of fur from the kings of sea and bush.

On the threshold of your Eastern palace
I shall congregate the bards
to celebrate on instruments diverse
in chords harmonious and new
   your forests
      your savannas
         your grandeur
and your metamorphoses.

Beyond the world and windmoans in the doom palms,
beyond the incandescent desert sands
by pools of running water
where daytime seems forever chasing sirens,
I shall gather men and women
whose hands and laughter scan the strains
slipping from my lute onto the wing of time
in search of a last jewel for your azure throne.
And in ecstasy, before your fiery chariot,
from an amphora of virgin porphyra
I shall let flow
drop by drop

upon your feet
  the ambrosia
    of the gods.

A Wreath for Africa

I shall weave you a wreath
of laurel and hibiscus
set in a butterfly's wingspan
and the calm of underbrush in blossom.

I shall fashion you an emerald crown
with pearls from the treasures of Atlantis
sparkling with the moisture of my guileless tears
and a garland
from the song of rosy shoots and cool water.

I shall weave you a wreath
from the azure of the zephyr's web
and the babbling of the breeze
on dewy mornings when the breath
of living things is silhouetted in the air.

I shall weave you a wreath
from the harmony of my springtime songs
envied by the nightingale in bridal finery
and I shall give you sandals made of fur
from an angry lioness.

I shall fashion you a wreath
of pure flame mingled with the rainbow
of former times of fortune
enveloping
the heat of the millennial fire.

I shall fashion you a wreath
of blue dawns
and a necklace of pink gems
that Time
will never dare to tarnish!

I shall weave you a wreath
from the essence of flowers
with pendants of human life and wisdom.

I shall make you a crown
softly gleaming
with the brilliance of Tropical Venus
and in the orb of the feverishly shimmering
Milky Way.

I shall write
    your name
        in letters of
            fire,
                O Africa!

Hands

Free hands
Living hands
    made
for waking
and not for smothering
    for giving
    enriching
and not for taking away
    for keeping time
    for conquering hate
    Mason's hands
        rough and ready
        ditchdigger's
        woodcutter's
        cane
            cotton
                coffee-planter's hands
    Hands of a timber-hauler
        of a sawyer of wood

Outdoor hands
    black hands
    bare hands
      of a people stripped bare,

Hands that speak
      punctuate
      offer
      rise
      meet
      hold
        the bud of joy
      bound by Unity
        the knot of life.

Child's hands, blossoming with innocence
      old man's, wrinkled with wisdom,
      woman's, swollen with caressing,
Hands that wash and indicate
    reveal and flourish
            Hands!
      Black
      hands
made to mold Love
      calloused
to wear bitterness away,
I seek my share of the riches of the world.
Folded in the Cape of Tempests,
I tear the false gods' masks away
and crown you all in dreams and laughter.

    Black hands
    builder's hands
    men's hands
I plunge them
    into the Earth
    into the Sky
    into the light of Day
    into the diamonds of Night

I plunge them
       into the Morning dew
       into the gentle Twilight
       into Past   Present   Future
       into all that is Gleam and Sparkle
          that lives and sings
       into all that dances
          Black hands
          Brother's hands.

I take them out
strong and happy
full and radiant
to mix the colors
and beyond oceans and mountains
      to salute YOU
        Friend!

December 1963

SENEGAL *(1927–1960)*

David Diop

DURING HIS BRIEF LIFE DAVID DIOP PUBLISHED LESS than twenty poems. They have nonetheless earned him a secure place in modern African literature, and more widely as a poet of the black world. Diop brings to his poetry an intensity and a personal articulation of the ethnic themes that are peculiarly his own. He once wrote that his poems were meant "to burst the eardrums of those who do not wish to hear."

The third of five children, David Diop was born in Bordeaux, while his father was on a tour of duty in the French colonial service. The elder Diop is no relation to Birago Diop, though like him a Senegalese. As a child, David spent only brief periods in West Africa, living mostly in Europe. After his father's premature death, he and his brother and sisters were raised by his mother, a Cameroonian matriarch of indomitable character, in German-occupied wartime France. Despite the family's meager financial resources, David's eldest sister managed to earn her law degree at the University of Montpellier, and his youngest brother, today a surgeon in Dakar, completed his medical studies there. Another sister, Christiane, married Alioune Diop, and David, then in his teens, knew the negritude leaders and was close to the founding of the magazine, publishing house, and bookstores that bear the name *Présence Africaine.* Later on, David Diop contributed many short articles and reviews to *Présence* and participated in the historic black writers' conferences in Paris and Rome.

Léopold Senghor was David Diop's professor at the Lycée Saint-Maur-des-Fossées, near Paris. Several of Diop's earliest poems, written while he was still in high school ("Challenge" is one of them), first appeared in Senghor's landmark 1948 anthology. Years later, in a funeral oration for the young poet, Senghor recalled how as a youngster David's health had always been threatened by a recurrent tuberculosis. The sufferings, both physical and psychic, of his months on end in sanitariums

177

are recorded in several of the most personal and moving poems ("For My Mother," "The Hours," and "With You") that make up *Coups de Pilon* (*Pounding*), his single book. All but a few of these poems were written before David Diop was twenty-one, but were not published as a volume until 1956. In 1961 they were reissued in a revised and slightly enlarged edition.

When he was twenty, Diop tried a year of medical school at Montpellier, but he soon realized that his real talent and interest lay in literature. At length, despite a constant struggle against illness, he completed the demanding studies for the *licence ès lettres* that would qualify him to teach in secondary schools. In the late 1950s, with Senegal's independence already in sight, Diop returned with his wife and children to settle in Africa. Through his writing and teaching, he wanted to be part of building that new Africa, that new world for the black man of which his poems often sang. He began teaching at the Lycée Delafosse in Dakar, and a year later was named principal of a secondary school at Kindia in Guinea. He served there only two years before his tragic death in 1960 in an airplane crash, which foreshortened the contribution of one of Africa's most vital and promising young talents. Despite his slender output, David Diop remains at this writing one of Africa's most popular poets. His poems appear and reappear in anthologies of black-world and African writings, both in French and in various English translations.

The eleven poems that follow compose about half of David Diop's total poetic legacy. In the first six, the mood is revolutionary anger. "Challenge" makes a universal cry against injustice; "A Time of Martyrdom" expresses the same feelings in purely racial terms. "For a Black Child" (compare with Césaire's "State of the Union," p. 83) bemoans the ultimate injustice—a murder case so familiar to his audience that Diop had no need to name it. It is a withering indictment of moral gangrene, of that part of America where an Emmet Till could be lynched for a peccadillo, an imagined insult, victim of the violent racial and sexual phobias of a particular class of Southern whites. "Vultures," a metaphor Diop may owe to Roumain's *Ebony Wood*, exposes the irony and betrayal of civilizers who were all too often exploiters and destroyers.

"Listen, Comrades" calls on black men past and present "from Africa to the Americas" to mourn the death of Mamba, who seems incredibly real, although his name is purely a symbolic one to evoke all the African leaders who had met death in colonial repressions.

The poem pictures Mamba as someone well along in years, a man of vision who has inspired great affection and devotion among his followers, and whose martyrdom is seen as having almost Christ-like aspects. The poet hear "burning Negro voices" cry out in pain and anger at Mamba's passing, voices which at the same time are "The sign of dawn/ The brotherly sign, come to nourish men's dreams."

The "seven men from Martinsville," like the Emmet Till story, alludes to an actual American criminal case of the early 1950s that attracted international attention. In Martinsville, Virginia, seven blacks were convicted and executed for raping a white woman. At the time of their execution, an editorial appeared in the Lagos, Nigeria, *Pilot*. This African newspaper commented on the severity of the penalty, noting that rape was a crime for which no white American had ever paid with his life. Diop's third allusion, to "the Madagascan in the ghastly prison pale," was certainly inspired by his family friend Jacques Rabémananjara and others who were arrested after the uprising in 1947 (see p. 241).

"Negro Tramp," dedicated to Césaire and inspired by the old man on the trolley in Césaire's *Notes* ("He *was* comical and ugly/comical and ugly, to be sure"), addresses a pitiful old black man who seems to stand for his entire race. Whatever dreams for self-realization this shabby figure may have had are long since dead. Stooped by the knifelike northerly winds of the mistral, he has been the victim of ancient sufferings, this descendant of those who came in "caravels . . . torn away from Guinea," the same Edenic half-remembered Guinea of the Haitian poets Roumain and Pressoir. In the old man's weary eyes the narrator sees the endless, monotonous toil of those whose lives are spent in mines and cottonfields. The old man's past encompasses the larger past of a whole people, the forgotten heroes Soundiata and Chaka, the "tales of silk and fire," Africa's glory, that would seem to have been drowned in the Atlantic crossing. The allusion to bloodshed in snowy landscapes doubtless refers to the African troops who served in European wars, particularly World War II, about which Senghor also writes in *Black Host* as does Léon Damas in *Pigments*. But here again the image may well have a more pervasive meaning; the idea that all transplanted black men are victimized in white lands.

David Diop's poems often begin with an articulation of pain, either personal or general, contained in a succession of linked images. This development of themes continues, then is suddenly relieved or resolved by a group of concluding lines that alter the mood to one of intentful vision, of celebration, of hope, or of peace. This architecture is apparent not only in "Negro Tramp" and several other poems discussed above, but also in the poem "Africa."

Counterbalancing the bitterness and anger vented in many of David Diop's poems is the overriding faith and optimism embodied in such powerful images as that of the tree "patiently stubbornly rising again," the hurricane with which the future will be plowed, burning voices that are a sign of dawn, springtime that will grow beneath light feet, guitars and pestles that will sound forth into a portentous sky. Perhaps because of the suffering, anger, and humiliations implied in the opposing set of images in his poems, David Diop's optimism is not an easy or a facile one. It always seems blended with a certain wisdom, a wisdom that knows the taste of freedom will be bitter as often as it is sweet, that from delirium and impatience comes the working out of dreams, that days sparkling with joy are bought with "ragged" days, and with nights "with a narcotic taste." It is from these labors, both of the body and the spirit, that comes "the ever fertile seed of times when equilibrium is born."

Often, too, David Diop's poems are I-and-you poems, in which a single narrator sings of, or explores and defines, his relation to another. The "you," the other, is always a different one. It may be the comrades to whom he laments of the lost Mamba; it may be Africa itself; it may be the fictional black tramp, or the incarnation of black womanhood he calls "Rama Kam"; it may be the strange men who were not men but birds of prey; it may be his mother, heroine of one especially moving poem. In "With You" it is a beloved woman who is probably his wife, but who also may be Africa envisioned as a woman.

In these translations, we have tried to conserve the striking imagery of the originals and the compelling beat that is such a marked feature of David Diop's French.

ELEVEN POEMS FROM *Pounding*

Vultures

At that time
With great slashes of civilization
Spitting holy water on domesticated brows,
Vultures in the shadow of their claws

Built the bloody monument of a tutelary era.
At that time
Laughter died in the metallic hell of roads
And the monotonous rhythm of "Our Fathers"
Muffled the screams from profitable plantations.
Oh the acid memory of kisses sundered,
Promises maimed.
Strange men who were not men
You knew all the books but knew not love,
Or hands that fertilize the belly of the earth,
The roots of our hands deep as revolt.
Despite the proud songs amid your charnels,
The desolated villages of Africa dismembered,
Hope lived within us like a citadel.
And from the mines of Swaziland to European sweatshops
Springtime will bear flesh beneath our limpid feet.

Listen, Comrades . . .

Listen, comrades of the flaming centuries
To the passionate black shouts from Africa to the Americas.
They've killed Mamba.
Like the seven men from Martinsville,
Like the Madagascan in the ghastly prison pale
In his look, comrades,
Was the warm fidelity of a heart without anguish,
And his smile despite his pain,
Despite the wounds that striped his body,
Kept the colors of a bright bouquet of hope.
It's true, they've killed him,
White-haired Mamba
Who ten times poured us milk and light.
I feel his mouth upon my dreams
And the peaceful trembling of his breast,
And the memory hurts
Like a living thing torn from the maternal breast
But no . . .

What breaks out louder than my pain,
Purer than the morning when the wild beasts woke,
Is the shouting of a hundred peoples who crush them in their lairs.
And my long-exiled blood,
The blood they thought exhausted in a coffin made of words,
Finds once again the fervor to pierce fogs.
Listen, comrades of the flaming centuries
To the burning Negro voices from Africa to the Americas.
This is the sign of dawn,
The brotherly sign, come to nourish men's dreams.

Challenge

You who stoop, you who weep,
You who'll one day die, and not know why,
You who fight to guard Another's sleep,
You whose eyes no longer laugh,
You, my brother with the face of fear and pain,
Rise up and cry out: NO!

The Time of Martyrdom

The white man killed my father
For my father was proud.
The white man raped my mother
For my mother was beautiful.
The white man bent my brother beneath the roadway sun
For my brother was strong.
Then the white man turned to me,
His hands red with black blood,
Spit his scorn in my face
And with his voice of master called:
"Hey, boy! Bring me a napkin and a drink!"

For a Black Child

Life
At fifteen
Is a promise, a kingdom half glimpsed.

In the land where houses touch the sky
Although the heart remains untouched,
Where hands are placed upon the Bible
Though the Bible is unopened,
A fifteen-year-old life can allay the river's hunger,
A no-count god-damned nigger life . . .
A black boy on an August eve did perpetuate the crime,
Did dare the infamy to use his eyes and glance
To speculate about a white
Mouth and breasts and body,
A body, black boy, that only whites at orgies can ravish to the rhythm of
                                                                your blues
(the black man only sometimes in anonymous rooms).
Crime doesn't pay you'd often been told
And so justice could be done: there were two
Exactly two on the platform of the scale,
Two men against your fifteen years and the kingdom half glimpsed.
They thought of the crazy old blind man who saw,
Of their women besmirched,
Of the order that was tottering,
And your head flew off to the sound of hysterical laughter.

In air-conditioned mansions
Over cool drinks
Good conscience gloats
In its tranquillity.

For My Mother

When all about me memories arise,
Memories of anxious hangings on the edge of cliffs
Of icy seas where harvests drown;

When drifting days come back to me,
Ragged days with a narcotic taste;
When the word becomes aristocrat
To overcome the emptiness
Behind closed blinds;
Then Mother I think of you,
Of your beautiful eyelids burned by the years,
Of your smile on my hospital nights,
Your smile that told of old and vanquished miseries,
O Mother mine Mother of us all,
Of the Negro they blinded who once again sees flowers . . .
Listen listen to your voice,
This cry shot through with violence,
This song that springs only from love.

The Hours

There are times for dreaming
In the peacefulness of nights with hollow silences
And times for doubt
When the heavy web of words is torn with sighs.
There are times for suffering
Along the roads of war at the look in mothers' eyes,
There are times for love
In lighted huts where one flesh sings.
There is what colors times to come
As sunshine greens the plants.
In the delirium of these hours,
In the impatience of these hours,
Is the ever fertile seed
Of times when equilibrium is born.

Negro Tramp

For Aimé Césaire

You who walked like a broken old dream
Laid low by the mistral's blades,

Along what salty paths,
Along what detours muddy with suffering accepted,
Aboard what caravels from isle to isle planting flags of Negro blood torn
away from Guinea
Have you worn your cast-off cloak of thorns
To the foreign graveyard where you used to read the sky?
In your eyes I see you halt, stooped and in despair,
And dawns when cotton and the mines began again,
I see Soundiata the forgotten
And the indomitable Chaka
Hidden 'neath the seas with the tales of silk and fire.
All this I see . . .
Martial music and the clarion call to murder
And bellies gaping open in snowy countrysides
To pacify the fear cowering in the cities
O my old Negro harvester of unknown lands,
Sweet-scented lands where everyone could live.
What have they made of the dawn that used to open on your brow
Of your luminous stones and golden sabers?
Look at you naked in your filthy prison,
A dead volcano for others to laugh at,
For others to get rich on
To feed their awful hunger.
Whitey they called you, how picturesque,
Shaking their fat, high-principled heads
Pleased with their joke, not nasty at all,
But I, what did I do on your windy weeping morning,
That morning drowned in seafoam
When the sacred cows decayed?
What did I do seated on my clouds but tolerate
The nocturnal dyings,
The immutable wounds,
The petrified rags in the terror-stricken camps?
The sand seemed made of blood
And I saw a day like any other day
And I sang Yéba,
Yéba, like a raving animal.
O buried plants,
O lost seeds,

Forgive me Negro guide!
Forgive my narrow heart
The victories postponed, the armor abandoned.
Patience, the Carnival is done.
I am sharpening a hurricane to plow the future with;
For you we shall remake Ghana and Timbuktu
And guitars will gallop wildly
In great shuddering chords
Like the hammerblows of pestles
Pounding mortars
Bursting forth
From hut to hut
Into the portentous blue.

Africa

To my mother

Africa, my Africa!
Africa of proud warriors in ancestral savannas,
Africa my grandmother sings of on a distant riverbank,
I have never known you
But my face is filled with your blood,
Your beautiful black blood spread across the fields,
The blood of your sweat,
The sweat of your toils,
The toils of your slavery,
The slavery of your children.
Africa, tell me, Africa,
Is it yours this back that is bending
Bowed low by humility's weight,
This trembling red zebra-striped back
Saying yes to the whip on the sweltering roads?
Then gravely a voice answered me:
Impetuous son, this young and robust tree,
This very tree
Splendidly alone
Amid the white and wilted flowers,

Is Africa, your Africa, growing again
Patiently stubbornly rising again
And little by little whose fruit
Bears freedom's bitter flavor.

Rama Kam   song for a black woman

The wildness of your glances pleases me,
Your mouth has the taste of mango,
        Rama Kam.
Your body is the black pimento
That makes desire sing
        Rama Kam.
As you pass
The handsomest woman is made jealous
By the warm rhythm of your hips,
        Rama Kam.
As you dance
To the tom-tom, Rama Kam,
The tom-tom taut as my victorious sex
Throbs beneath the *griot*'s leaping fingers.
When you love me, Rama Kam,
A tornado shakes
In the fiery blackness of your flesh
And fills me with your breath,
        O Rama Kam!

With You

With you I have refound my name,
My name long hidden 'neath the salt of distances,
I have rediscovered eyes no longer fever-dimmed
And your laughter like a flame piercing the darkness
Once more has brought me Africa despite the snows of yesterday.
Ten years, my love . . .

Mornings of illusion and the remnants of ideas
And sleep inhabited by alcohol;
Ten years and the breathing of the world has poured its pain on me,
This suffering that weights the present with tomorrow's taste
And makes of love a boundless river.
With you I have refound the memory of my blood
And necklaces of laughter 'round my days,
Days that sparkle with joys renewed.

CAMEROON (*1930–*)

Elolongue Epanya Yondo

BORN IN DOUALA, THE PORT CITY OF THE CAMEROONS, Elolongue Epanya Yondo is a cousin of David Diop, who was three years his elder. While a student in Paris, Yondo lived for a while with the family of Alioune Diop and was much influenced by the negritude milieu. In 1960, *Présence Africaine* published a volume of his poems under the title *Kamerun! Kamerun! (Cameroon! Cameroon!)* The *Présence* edition of Yondo's poems included not only the French but also versions in the Douala tongue, which may make Yondo the first African to have published both in French and in his native language.

Yondo returned to the Cameroons, after finishing his law and sociology studies, where he is reportedly preparing for French translation a vast historical novel about his tribe.

FIVE POEMS FROM *Cameroon! Cameroon!*

My Country

Homeland! O beloved village,
I have heard the echo of your name
Endlessly repeated to the East
Like carillons pealing
To the East, there to the East.

Homeland, O village so beloved,
Once our elders' paradise
Bowing now
The proud and kingly brow

189

of yesteryear,
You will become O country,
Cameroon of whom we're proud . . .

Cameroon! Cameroon! Cameroon!
You are like the clump of palms
That neither smoking fields afire
Nor the shadow of fantastic monster fangs
Will ever smother;
In the noisy silence of the conquest
Prickly and elusive prey
Soon you shall see the day,
Beloved country,
Cameroon.

Lullaby

Sleep, my child, sleep.
When you sleep
You are handsome
As an orange tree in blossom.

Sleep, my child, sleep.
Sleep like
The high seas
Caressed
By the lapping breeze
That comes to die in *woua-woua*
At the foot of sandy beaches.

Sleep, my child, sleep.
Sleep, my beautiful black baby,
Like the promise of
A moonlit night
At the sight of dawn
Being born in your sleep.

Sleep, my child, sleep.
You are so handsome

10. An onomatopoetic soothing sound.

When you sleep.
My beautiful black baby, sleep.

To You

Like the buffalo
Who howls from thirst
My heart
Is thirsty for you, love,
You whose name
My song pours forth
All the length
Of my lament.
Love,
Hear my call.

Love

O night cold without your nearness,
O night so lonely far from you,
Where are you, love?
In vain
My heart seeks after you
In this great desert of solitude.
My body trembles
And I'm afraid tonight,
Afraid to never see you more.
In this night cold
Without you near
Forever you're within me.

Woman

Woman!
You're the sacred palm

I've chosen
out of all the plants
in the flora of the village
of my birth,
  eya-bolo.

Woman!
You are mistress
of all the full moon's paths
and when you dance the *bolo*
the slightest motion of your hips
is a delirium of
  bolobo-eya-bolo
that rocks
the cradle of your
life-colored flesh,
  eya-bolo.

Woman!
Here's a retinue in skirts
pointing fingers at you.
There are all the rivals
who scarcely reach your toe,
who spit as they go by
and whisper:
"What has she got
that we've not,
and to think that there are men
who'd sell a thousand cattle
just to have her,"
  eya-bolo.

Woman!
I like your brush-fire look
that reduces whims and waiting
into cinders.
But will you come tonight
behind the age-old Baobab,
black girl with the pulpy, palm-nut mouth?

7, 14. Eya-bolo; Bolobo-eya-bolo: Onomatopoetic words.

You are the sacred palm
I've chosen out of all the plants,
woman with the rhythm of
  bolobo-eya-bolo.

CONGO/BRAZZAVILLE ✳ (CIRCA 1930–)

Martial Sinda

MARTIAL SINDA'S EXACT BIRTHDATE IS NOT KNOWN. He was born near Brazzaville, in the former French Congo, sometime in the early 1930s. Along with David Diop, Epanya Yondo, Tchicaya U Tam'si, François Sengat-Kuoh, and others, he is one of the postwar generation of Africans who studied in France in the late '40s and early '50s. Caught up in the spirit and the group rhetoric of the times, nearly all of them wrote poetry, publishing in student reviews and sometimes in *Présence Africaine*. The two selections included here are from Sinda's book, *Premier chant du départ* (*First Song of Departure*), published in 1953.

TWO POEMS FROM *First Song of Departure*

To the Banquet of the Earth

To the banquet of the earth
You bring your kitchen knife
And your little spoons.

To the banquet of the earth
I bring my own white teeth
And my big black hands.

To the orchestra of the earth
You bring your accordion
And your harmonica.

To the orchestra of the earth
I bring my *n'tsambi*
And my quick black hands.

11. *n'tsambi:* Congolese drum.

194

To military processions
You bring your pom-poms
And your puny cheers.

To military processions
I bring my own white teeth
And my solid chest.

To the dances of the earth
You come in Sunday suit
To take some little steps.

To the dances of the earth
I come with *n'tsambi*
And my quick black hands

And my blood pulsing
And the voices of life
And my lively black feet

For this is my true language.

You Shall Walk in Peace! . . .

You shall walk in peace!
When you venture forth
At night
N'dila ho, do not listen
To the voice of the owl
                        the screech owl
For they presage Death.

You shall walk in peace!
For if upon your way
At night, *N'dila ho,*
You meet a mole,
If you breathe the odor
                        of a certain root

4. *N'dila ho:* A term of endearment.

The root with which cadavers are embalmed,
These things presage Death.

You shall sleep in peace!
If someone calls to you
At night,
If there is a muffled knocking
                    at your door,
Do not answer—
Never, ever, ever!
For it is your death that will be waiting!

You shall always be at peace,
O *N'dila ho,* if you sneeze
By daylight,
For at night
Sneezing
Is an evil omen.

MALI ❈ *(1940–)*

Yamba Ouloguem

YAMBO OULOGUEM IS THE YOUNGEST POET IN THIS anthology, and among French-speaking Africa's most promising new writers. His highly original novel, *Le Devoir de la violence* (translated as *Bound to Violence*), published when he was just twenty-eight, won the French Renaudot Prize in 1968. His second book, essays called *Lettre à la France nègre* (*A Letter to Black France*), appeared the same year. The poem "Dear Husband" was included in *New Sum of Poetry from the Negro World*, the anthology prepared by the editors of *Présence Africaine* for the First World Festival of Negro Arts, held in Dakar in 1966.

Dear Husband

Once your name was Bimbircokak
And everything was fine.
Then you became Victor-Emile-Louis-Henri-Joseph
And bought a dinner set.

I used to be your wife.
Now you call me spouse.
We used to eat together.
Now we're separated by a table.

Calabash and ladle,
drinking gourd and couscous
are banished from our daily fare
by your paternal order.

We're modern now, you say.

197

The tropic sun is hot, hot, hot!
But your cravat
never leaves the neck
it nearly strangles.

You frown
when I mention it,
never mind, I'll say no more.

But husband, look at me!

We eat grapes and
milk that's pasteurized
and imported gingerbread from France
and don't get much of any.
Isn't it your fault?

You used to be Bimbircokak
and everything was fine.
Becoming Victor-Emile-Louis-Henri-Joseph
as far as I can see
doesn't make you kin
to Rockefeller!
(Excuse my ignorance, I don't know much
about finance.)
But can't you see
Bimbircokak
—because of you—
once I was underdeveloped
now I'm undernourished, too!

Tchicaya U Tam'si

WITH EDOUARD MAUNICK, TCHICAYA U TAM'SI IS CON-sidered the most talented and original black French-language poet to have emerged since Damas, Senghor, and Césaire. Certainly he is the most prolific, having produced six major books before the age of forty. Born in 1929 at Mpili in the Central Congo, brought up in Pointe-Noire on the Atlantic Coast, U Tam'si came to France at the age of seventeen with his father, who was the first deputy from what later would become the Republic of Congo/Brazzaville. Since 1946, U Tam'si has lived entirely in Europe except for a brief and bitterly disillusioning return to Léopoldville in 1960 at the time of independence.

U Tam'si claims he became a poet by accident, simply because writing turned out to be the best way he could express himself without his father's knowledge. The elder U Tam'si had sent his son to a French lycée with the intention of preparing him to study law. But Tchicaya did not take to the prescribed program of history and mathematics. By his own admission, he became a discipline problem and eventually dropped out of school. Stubbornly independent, he left home to wander about Europe, picking up odd jobs on farms or doing carpentry to make a living. Though his formal education never went further, Tchicaya U Tam'si gradually came to know a great deal about European art, music, and literature. In an interview published in the magazine *Afrique* (December 1963), he described himself as a cultural "pillager." "Europe went to the four corners of the world for what it needed. Should Africa remain closed in upon itself? It is true Africa has a great deal, and must make an inventory of what it possesses. But to leave things as they are, that would be wrong. I would like to bring the Rhine to the Congo, the Louvre to the Congo. I would like us to be rich with everything mankind has ever produced."

U Tam'si's serious efforts to write began after he read and reread

199

Arthur Rimbaud, "an extraordinary being who remains for me the essential poet. . . . He was my first teacher and is still my teacher."

The title of Tchicaya's first volume of poems, *Le Mauvais Sang* (*Bad Blood*), published in 1955, is taken from a major section of Rimbaud's *Une Saison en enfer* (*A Season in Hell*). Critics also connect U Tam'si's work to Césaire and the French surrealists. He acknowledges them all as among the stylistic influences through which he developed his own poetic voice.

Since adolescence, of course, Tchicaya U Tam'si has been cut off from daily contact with his country, and it is impossible for a foreign critic to know exactly what influence Congolese oral tradition may have on his work. It appears to be slight. But just as Césaire finds all his central imagery in the landscape of Martinique, so does U Tam'si draw seminal images from the landscape—so different from any European landscape—in which he spent his childhood. "I write in order to discover something within myself," he has said. "It is always the same Congolese world that closes in upon me . . . with its familiar symbols that I attempt to seize. It is also the same questions recurring from poem to poem that give my work its continuity."

Senghor, in his preface to the first edition of U Tam'si's major work, *Epitomé* (*Epitome*), finds in U Tam'si ". . . the most authentic qualities of African poetry. The syntax of juxtaposition that unhinges all logic . . . an irrational syntax but one which translates the fluctuations of the heart; the outburst of inopportune passion with its syncopations, its repetitions that do not quite repeat themselves, its symmetrical parallels, its lines that run on, break off, turn themselves inside out. . . . For the image is the only thread that leads from one heart to another, the only flame that consumes and consummates the soul."

The English critic Gerald Moore has commented on the interlocking quality of U Tam'si's books, and on the fact that "the significance of his favorite images [tree and river, beast and bird, canoe and lurking fish] is extended and enriched by every poem, indeed, by every volume." Moore observes that U Tam'si ". . . borrows from the surrealists a technique largely innocent of punctuation and initial capitals, so that each poem presents a smooth unbroken stream of imagery in which the mind moves freely back and forth."

A second, seminal thread of images in U Tam'si's poetry, particularly evident in *Epitome,* centers around Christ, Christians, and Christianity. Ironic allusions to religious phenomena abound: the wound in Christ's left side upon the Cross, the crown of thorns, the hay in which Jesus was born of Mary, His betrayal by Judas, the road to Damascus, the mocking vision of animals giving absolution for sin, the temple defiled by those who sell the Cross, et cetera.

Mary Magdalene, Saint Anne of the Congo, and the Pope make their brief appearances in Tchicaya's* dream-poem, but so do Hamlet and Ophelia, Aimé Césaire, Winston Churchill, van Gogh, Matisse, the daughters of Soumam, Likouala-Mossaka, and Calvary. And so does Emmet Till. The place names that invade the poem as they invade the poet's consciousness are equally far-ranging: Paris, Europe, the Caribbean Islands, Kilimanjaro; South Africa's Durban, Pretoria, and New Bell; the Congo's Kin, Kinshasa, and Léopoldville; Madagascar's Antsirabé; and America's Harlem. Except for the first two, all are places where black men have long known oppression.

Though the label "poet of negritude" is one whose restrictions Tchicaya U Tam'si has sometimes objected to, Senghor feels he merits this title for having in his poems "assumed the Negro's mingled despair and hope, particularly his suffering, his passion in the ethnological sense of the word." Senghor might have spoken of the black man's passion in the etymological sense of the word as well, for *Epitome* is haunted not only by the martyrdom of Till but by an implied comparison between the "passion" of Lumumba's Congo in the early 1960s and that of Christ, His betrayal and suffering from His capture in the garden of Gethsemane until His death upon the Cross. One finds it in the very title and subtitle of U Tam'si's poem: *Epitome: Headline to Summarize a Passion.*

A poet profoundly concerned with good and evil, guilt and responsibility, despair and love, Tchicaya is perpetually self-questioning, exploring an inner world deeply identified with his homeland and its fate. *Epitome* and other of his poems must be understood as a kind of poetic examination of conscience, a confessional. The narrator's self-accusation reappears in different forms: "From horror at myself," "I win by cheating," "I console myself . . . in order to justify my unconcern," "I who know nothing/of the tree of my life,/my scandal was tricolored." These passages of nightmarish but dazzling word pictures, vignettes with marvelously allusive aural and visual effects, sometimes comic, sometimes profound, sometimes merely puzzling, translate well into English: and yet their ultimate personal meanings remain opaque. The poet's suffer-

* The poet is as often referred to by the name Tchicaya as by his other family name, U Tam'si. In signing his poems, he drops his first and middle names, Gérard and Félix.

ings are private. He speaks of them hermetically, in symbolic language, soothing his pain by the very act of transforming it into poems, "Since I have learned to make balm from my voice."

With the approach of independence in 1960, Tchicaya went back to Africa to edit a Léopoldville newspaper, *Le Congo*. He remained until his friend Patrice Lumumba, first president of the Congolese republic, was arrested in a *coup d'état*. The scandal referred to in *Epitome* directly concerns this abortive "return to his native land." Tchicaya had set out for Africa with the highest hopes, as if on a crusade, and his *Epitome* (1962) and *Le Ventre* (*The Belly*) (1965) are marked by this experience.

In *Epitome* the allusion to France, signaled in the poem by the blue, white, and red tricolor, suggests he may have been distrusted for being too French, or in any case too long out of touch with his homeland. Having returned to France, we gather, he "inhabited the palace of oblivion," attempting to forget the Congo. But newspaper stories are a constant reminder, like the withered flowers along with the letters from Africa in his mail box. "I console myself with being mortal here [in Paris] . . . in order to justify my unconcern." And then there is his reference to "the silence on the part of my conscience." By creating the poem the narrator seems to be performing a kind of penance for his failure to live up to his own expectations. Mockingly, he pictures himself as a Christlike figure "dirty . . . from being with the middle class," a "false Negro" who "sells [his] negritude four lines for a dollar."

Despite the fact that his poems reflect Congolese imagery and subject matter, Tchicaya U Tam'si appears very much the heir and practitioner of a highly sophisticated Western poetic tradition. One doubts that he will ever realize an earlier ambition, to compose his poems directly in the Lingala tongue rather than in French. U Tam'si seems destined to play out his life in the role of Congolese-poet-in-exile on a European stage.

Since his return from the Congo, U Tam'si has worked in Paris at UNESCO. He has written and produced radio plays for the French overseas radio, and edited a collection of African tales and legends for the French publisher Seghers. From time to time U Tam'si takes up the long novel he has been writing about a Congolese family, or publishes a short story. But he much prefers writing poetry to prose, which he finds limiting because it is "so much more riveted to reality."*

Here we offer, in new translations, short selections from three of his

---

* Conversation with the author in Paris, December 1970.

six books: *Bad Blood, Feu de brousse (Brush Fire),** and *L'Arc musical
(Bow Harp)*, concluding with long passages from *Epitome*, honored in
1962 by the Grand Prize for French-language poetry at the First World
Festival of Negro Arts at Dakar, in 1966. For a more extensive sampling
of all the Congolese poet's work, the reader is referred to *Selected Poems
of Tchicaya U Tam'si,* brilliantly presented by the English critic and
translator Gerald Moore.

A strange and intriguing figure, Tchicaya U Tam'si is no longer at
ease in his own land, and not entirely at home in Europe, either. His
stunning and remorselessly witty poetry transcends the particulars of an
African world and of a black world to become a meditation on the uni-
versal problems of living in our time.

* Translated by Sangodare Akanji (Ibadan, Nigeria: Mbari Press, 1964) and
distributed in the United States by Northwestern University Press.

F R O M   *Bad Blood*

Bad Blood

Tomorrow we'll be good
You believe me, don't you? Tomorrow
We will have a brand new
Destiny at the end of a journey

Yes yes we'll march
And in your hands so beautiful
Proud   faithful   I shall put
My joy: we'll sing

Full of forgetting without past
of what I've dreamed of
Your life   my life   life

Into its finished dream
Let us pour out our ciboriums
And our one night flower

TWO POEMS FROM *Brush Fire*

Brush Fire

the fire the river that is to say
the sea to drink following the sand
the feet the hands
within the heart to love
this river that lives in me repeoples me
only to you I said around the fire
my race
it flows here and there a river
the flames are the looks
of those who brood upon it
I said to you
my race
remembers
the taste of bronze drunk hot.

—Translated by Sangodare Akanji

A Mat to Weave

he had just surrendered the secret of the sun
and wanted to write the poem of his life

why the crystals in his blood
why the globules in his laughter

his soul was ripe
when someone shouted at him
dirty nigger

since what's left him is the suave act of his laughter
and the giant tree of a living wound
that used to be this land he lives in wildly
behind the beasts before behind the beasts

his river was the surest bowl
because it was of bronze
because it was his living flesh

it was then he told himself
no my life is not a poem

here's the tree, the river and the stones
beside this priesthood of what is to come

it is better to love wine
and get up in the morning
they advised him

but no more birds in the tenderness of mothers

dirty nigger
he is the younger brother of fire

here begins the jungle
and the sea no more now than the souvenir of sea gulls
standing upright beak to beak
against the foam in some deadly dance
the tree was the leafiest
the bark of the tree the tenderest

the jungle burned what more to say

why was there absinthe in the wine
why put back in hearts
and sea cows and canoers
and the flowing of the river

the grain of sand between two teeth
is it thus the world is pulverized
no
no
his river was the gentlest vessel
the safest
was his flesh the most alive

here begins the poem of his life
he was dragged into a school
he was hauled into a workshop
and he saw the roads planted with sphinxes

he is left with the suave arc of his laughter
then the tree then the water then the leaves

this is why you'll see him
the canoers on foot have once more seized
their cries
from the haulers of French cotton

this flight is a flying of doves

> the leeches did not know the bitterness
> of this blood
> in the soundest of vessels

> dirty nigger
> here is my Congolese head

> it's the sanest of vessels

SIX POEMS FROM *Epitome*

Headline to Summarize a Passion

> *The morning paper:*
> *Incident at Léopoldville—*
> *Three cards on my table*
> *expressing regrets*

I lend a deck of cards to someone passing by
more fertile in dialogues than the mute destiny
of my perishable heart
which no longer resists the road to Damascus that hugs
the bare belly of a shadowy hill . . .
To strip me at the epitome of my passion . . .

O my improbable genealogy!
From what tree do I descend? What flowers did it
wilt before the knell? Who tolled the knell?
Tolled it like an orphan girl weeping in the night!

A tree at the summit of a hill
raises candlelike a branch of blood,
bearing in its hand a green leaf

softly seen against the yellow light as flame.
The djinns are hooting at it!

There are trees I don't suspect
but where does such arborescent madness come from
that I take fleas from the woods
as the guide to my perdition?
From what tree shall I descend?
I give this improbable tree up as lost.
Is night truly my mourning time? . . .

I searched all the same pillaging the virgin forest,
my hands like blinkers searching,
when a rooster sneezed at the edge of a village
my voice at half-mast inclined its head,
a sun rose in the sky,
on earth a (mystic) dog gave absolution to a woman,
maundering his crazy hands above her bosom
painted with two solid moons.

Sleep takes night beneath the arm
and stumbles across the plain; a dog barks
as the passer-by goes by
telling fortunes to any taker
among the hibernating
. . . if they are asleep,
my obediently Negro brothers,
who knows of what death I am amiably dying?

· · · · · · · · · · · · · ·

> *The evening paper:*
> *There are dead and wounded—*
> *Retreat!*

In order to see my better world
amid this pus of things well done
I graft two orange blossoms to my retinas;
let them not be flame
let them be white to chill
the corpses in my sluggish conscience . . .

Reeking of this indolence, I win by cheating.
Let come a better cheat than I
pursuing me into this paradise where men
with knives in hand
endure most of their gangrene
in their slumber.
And that one,
will he raise the fire they extinguish
by pillaging the heart
whose scarce elucidated mystery
strips me, whips me, crucifies me
at the eptiome of my passion?

. . . .

Your eyes prophesy suffering,
said a nightingale to an owl,
at which the owl took fright.

They put out the fire whose scarce elucidated mystery
exhausts the astral tessitura of my soul
which they require to be flesh
and the error persists: two souls never made a couple.
The passer-by asked: what are two bodies doing
with two souls, facing the flames facing the fires?

I inhabited the soundless palace of oblivion
My heart in hand.
Wretched weather caused the building of a door
—my body—
a door with threshold open to all.
It was the threshold of the wind watched over by a woman
who spoiled an agile dream at a fetish's expense.
A thousand excrescences since have sprouted in my heart;
an executioner haggles with my fetishes for them
in exchange for gold rewards
—all my people live upon this commerce—
I inhabited the soundless palace of oblivion.

. . . .

False suffixes on the
roots of my tree give
me a dirty ending.

How could I rejoice
at being born entirely of flesh
which is no coat of mail
any more than is this wind that raps at each door
opened to each heart beating blue-sky white-sail red-blood?
I who know nothing
of the tree of my life,
my scandal was tricolored.

The passer-by said
yes yes reason to live reason to die.
In this sense it was I who was dreaming:
for a superhuman voice,
to count the contractions
of a sea in labor
on a worldly beach
in order for others to compose the prelude
of a tidal wave
on the savanna;
then came these flowers
in my letter box
from Kin.

It's too convincing,
false suffixes on the roots of my tree
give me a dirty ending,
I no longer know the essence of my soul,
all doors open on closed houses,
my hands already shrivel
like these wilted flowers.

.   .   .   .

*The silence on the part of my
conscience is understood: I
enjoy the king jabbering in
French*

I would speak if only I had memories.
Go on—don't tell me who I was like yesterday.
I console myself with being mortal here;
tomorrow very soon absence will come to my black brow,
the image of a woman and I shall have her fingernails,

the single tooth of her mouth attacking my heart
in order to justify my unconcern.

He who is worthy of love is worthy of slow death,
said the passer-by, the sea drove
the water-sprite back to the white wheel
knitting a coat of white foam on the lascivious waves
in summer.

The king jabbers: I rejoice
I am extensible like any honest heart.

. . . .

Viaticum

And the eyes without the hands
that hold them face to face
tear each other's hearts out . . .
the country brandished by its heart

You *are* from my country,
I see it by the tic
your soul has in the eyelids
and then you dance your sadness,
you really are from my land.

Go, time's on the lookout for us, if we're seduced by it
understand from this that the oil in your lamp
is still my blood brimming;
if it spills don't light your lamp,
we need a dark corner in the land
for our atavistic prayers.

All from the same umbilicus.
But who knows how we got such tough heads.

. . . .

On a mat of field grass
three flies drunk on absinthe

above the ancient destiny
disturb my nostrils
not to know
between life and death what my life was
and which way I am less nostalgic.

You too are surely from my country.
I can tell by your musty way of talking
you are baboons—go on be humble
in order to learn it from me,
who swallow flies at sunset.
But do make the effort of human memory.
Baboons—that's really it,
you have a megaphone-like mouth.
speak to the world tell them what we're like:
we dance our sadness.

.   .   .   .

What crime would I commit
tonight
if I desecrate the moon
in this water hole that's offered me?
They'll call it a poet's whim.
Play me a lullaby
with three horns and a hundred thousand cowbells.
The reddish-brown of certain recent household gods
persists in me on certain evenings
when the moths return.
Sleep has a thousand degradations
for the slanderous djinn
when night sucks the earth and the Congolese clay.
Go take my head
against what's left to me of night upon the soul.

.   .   .   .

We were people of the night
we had the destiny we had
congenitally

And I,
I forget to be Negro in order to forgive.
No longer will I see my blood upon their hands,
it's sworn.

A vertebrate soliloquy
(once upon a time, it was already mine),
a vertebrate soliloquy
doesn't make Christianity delirious.
Who is wrong for being crafty,
the vertebrate, Christianity, or I?

The farce continues to the next death;
let them burn my backbone.
Enough of this scandal on my life,
I'll no longer see my blood upon their hands.
I forget to be Negro to forgive the world for this.
I've said it, let them leave me peacefully to be Congolese.

.   .   .   .

These lines on my hand are harbinger signs.
Set a knife before my sleep
so the web of ancient destiny may cut its thread.
I want to be free of my destiny,
I give the dew back to the grass.
May the lines of my hand
open all the ways to me of this long river.

The Scorner

I drink to your glory, God,
You who have made me so sad,
You who have given me a people who distill not for themselves.
What wine shall I drink at your celebration
In this land which is no vineyard?
In this desert where all shrubs are cactus
Shall I take their yearly flowers

For the flames of the burning bush of your desire?
Tell me in what Egypt my people go with irons on their feet.

Christ, I mock your sadness,
O my sweet Christ,
Thorn for thorn,
We have a common crown of thorns.
I shall be converted for you tempt me.
Joseph comes to me,
I nurse already at your Virgin Mother's breast,
I count more than one Judas on my fingers besides you,
My eyes lie to my soul
Wherein the world is lamb your pascal lamb.
                    Christ,
I shall waltz to the sound of your indolent sadness.

Am I only your brother?
They've already killed me in your name.
Was I guilty of my death?
I had love-flowers all dark upon my eyes;
My hands played at night with palm fronds
Kissing your cross the blood reddened my mouth.

Was I not your brother?
I dance to your sadness.
Neither mother nor father do I take as witness for me
And yet my pain equals yours.
Sweet is the water of my river—go swallows go.
The rock loves the sea which beats it senseless.

You tempt me
And I rejoice,
I lose myself in the music of your soul
And yet it's not only the fish who sing out of tune.
And I, I dance death for the slow sadness.
The evils in my skin are the three iron nails
In your hands and your feet.
How dirty you are, Christ, from being with the middle class,
Their luxury is a golden calf around their bourgeois necks.

Walk where I limp, along my people's way.
You'll tell me in what Egypt my people are moaning.
My heart is not the desert; speak, O Christ, speak,
Is it you who put the living gold into my joyful wine?
Do I owe my two beginnings to you,
My heart and my soul?
Is it you who gave my heart two such tiny ventricles?
Tell me why I'd suffer from loving by rote?
A tree of dead life decked my oblivion with flowers.

You remain immobile.
The Congo is rent with pain.
Oh how dirty you are, Christ, from sticking with the middle class!
Christ, the Christ of my Saint Anne,
Say what wine I shall drink
To lie to my people;
My joy is too clairvoyant,
My sadness too filthy
To be brush fire.

Dogs pursued me
when I was a beggar.
For the Eucharist I begged
the wine, the salt, the leaven.
I was the Wandering Jew
To betray you who had betrayed me.
They've already killed me in your name,
Betrayed me, then sold me.

Night withered the roses
That used to shed their leaves in grief.

My own Mary Magdalene had Annie for a name
Less dirty than yours and therefore less absolvable.
I'll die then without her.
The bread of exile is unleavened
And I am Jew from pure madness.
my folly is the well of an oasis.
the oasis is not the wound in your left side

Christ, I spit on your joy.
The sun is black with suffering Negroes,
With dead Jews searching for the leaven for their bread.

What do you know of New Bell?
At Durban two thousand women,
At Pretoria two thousand,
At Kin as well two thousand,
And at Antsirabé two thousand more.
What do you know of Harlem?

The wine weighs on my heart and I hurt from rejoicing.
Christ, I hate your Christians.

I am empty of love to love all your cowards.
I spit on your joy
At having middle-class wives
To right and left.
I'm sick from having drunk too much.
Your temple has merchants who sell your cross, Christ.
I sell my negritude
Four lines for a dollar
And sail the galley
Toward the sold-out Indies.

Ah, what continent hasn't its false Negroes!
I've enough to sell,
Even Africa has hers,
The Congo has its false Negroes.
If they were Christian, would they be any less liable to caution?

Oh I die for your glory,
For you have tempted me
By making me so sad.

Sea Nocturne

The sea retreats as I advance;
the sea advances, I retreat;

thus we danced
one whole equinoctial night
according to a code,

and according to this code
five immobile continents
are drifting toward
each signature
a comet traces
in the sky that shields me
from the grip of waves
of too lascivious waves
at night in summer.

Fragile (excerpts)

.   .   .   .

I am no longer master of my tears,
master of these graynesses of time—
what flowers can I weave for Emmet Till
the child whose soul
in mine lies bleeding!

They killed him under water.
His mother caught her arms in fire
cooking him his midday meal.
At first the sun, miserable riot
of eunuch schoolboys
flying off in uproar
at his childish eyes' first ecstasy!
Then the strange martyrology—
Mother, I know!
The memory of another's flesh burns more
than the quick flame that caught your arms
neither for his midday nor his evening meal,
he whom death dissects with bootkicks in the kidneys
. . . the story was the child saluted her

a common woman in the crowd . . . that night
he walked along the bank to see the river pass
. . . his greeting meant to compliment this wicked
woman . . . that he greeted: they killed him
in the water
the way they baptize here
in a Christian manner
never in a mother's name!

.   .   .   .

I die alone from pride
I leave to Emmet Till his death
from horror at myself.

Who loves the sun enough
to throw both soul and body in it?

.   .   .   .

Here is the plain that I inhabit.
My hand is wide here on the door.
Take my share of fruit
though I do not know what tree it comes from,
take my share of tears
even though I know what heart it saps.
Don't be long,
already I am far from my beginnings.

Don't be long,
I can be useful.
I've already done my nails,
shaved my head;
I am ready for the night.

The Promenade

Here I am in Europe
without a cane in hand

effusive mouth held trumpet shape
more French than Joan of Arc.
Vipers mock my poisons;
eucalyptus makes me lewd.
I know, I know, say nothing of it
my brain is clay
pressed into headlines
that bawl my headaches into Braille;
head trampled on by boots,
boots knowingly studded with nails,
boots cleverly injurious;
my mind is clay,
I know, I know say nothing of it.
All streams meander to the sea.

I've seen my "France through young love's eyes"
and I tell myself again
all streams meander to the sea.

FROM *Bow Harp*

Communion II

When man becomes more faithful to man
woman more attentive to the moon
child docile to fond father's touch
my hands carbon-copying a dawn
life will reinvent my body
and my sudden silex memory
will no longer mold the clay of crime
on the back of any of my brothers

O light of the communion bread!
O warmth of the wine in this chalice!
all in the image of a blessèd belly!
my life no longer consumes me even now . . .

Time was when it was sad to be a man
every color of the body was a ghetto

one only left through the pores by sweating
wherever I was shadow whip cracked
even now my tongue clacks
at the bland taste nettle has
since I have learned to make balm from my voice.

Indian Ocean Poets in French

※ *Rabéarivelo*

※ *Rabémananjara*

※ *Ranaivo*

※ *Maunick*

MADAGASCAR (1901–1937)

Jean-Joseph Rabéarivelo

JEAN-JOSEPH RABÉARIVELO, WHO PUBLISHED HIS FIRST book in 1924, is the first modern African poet in French. He was born and lived his whole life in Madagascar, one of the world's largest islands, separated from the eastern coast of Africa by the Channel of Mozambique.

Rabéarivelo's homeland has an interesting history. From the sixteenth century onward, Madagascar often fell prey to pirates and adventurers. But for more than two hundred years its population of Malagasy tribes successfully resisted attempts, first by the Portuguese and later by the English, to found permanent settlements. Toward the end of the eighteenth century, kings of the Hova tribe, the largest Malagasy group, to which Rabéarivelo's family belongs, gained domination of the island and held it for about a century. During a crucial period from 1864 until 1895, an extremely clever Hova minister named Rainilaiarivony played off the British and the French against each other and managed to keep both from taking the island. By 1895, however, the French invaded. Madagascar became a French Overseas Territory, and remained such until 1960, when it was restored to independence.*

Rabéarivelo's family was of noble ancestry, but poor. He attended Catholic schools until the age of thirteen, losing his scholarship for some sort of insubordination. After a time at the Ecole Flacourt in Faravohitra, he worked as secretary and interpreter for a provincial chief, as a lace designer, and finally as a librarian at the Cercle de l'Union.

On his own, Rabéarivelo continued to perfect his French and to read widely, acquiring a European literary culture that would have been impressive even if he were not almost completely self-taught. Soon he began to write both poetry and prose in French. At first he needed help from French friends with his grammar, but little by little he mastered the

* For further details, see notes on Jacques Rabémananjara, pp. 239–42.

language, until eventually, as his countryman and literary executor Rabémananjara has written, "Rabéarivelo assimilated the French language so well that instead of his being its servant, it served him [particularly in *Presque Songes* (*Near Dreams*, 1934) and in *Traduit de la Nuit* (*Translated from the Night*, 1935)] as an extraordinarily docile and fertile divining rod, as an instrument of human achievement." Rabéarivelo also taught himself Spanish, in which he published a volume of poems, *Vientos de la mañana* (*Winds of the Morning*), in South America. "In the exercise of his art, Rabéarivelo used foreign elements only as one might use a dictionary," Senghor once said. "He acclimated to the Malagasy land, to its soul, ideas and words that came from elsewhere. It is he who created the new Malagasy poetry, whether or not its language is French."*

In 1930 and 1931 Rabéarivelo was co-editor of *Capricorne* (*Capricorn*), a small literary review that pioneered the development of a Malagasy literature in French. He contributed many articles and poems to newspapers and magazines in Madagascar itself; in Mauritius, the nearest Indian Ocean island with a French-speaking community; and in Vienna, Paris, and Belgium as well.

Craving communication with his literary peers in the outside world and the recognition that he never received in his own country, Rabéarivelo carried on a correspondence that was international. Yet his social and economic situation at home was never to match his literary accomplishments. To support the widowed mother, wife, and three children to whom he was devoted, he worked for thirteen years for a pittance as proofreader for a local printing company. He was often in debt and suffered constant petty humiliations. Despite the efforts of his friends he was never able to land a better job, one which would have permitted him to live decently and still give him the leisure to write. He was extremely emotional and given to various excesses, including an addiction to opium. These private difficulties were surely among the reasons narrow-minded colonial officials several times refused the poet permission to visit France —a lifelong ambition.

Rabéarivelo's first three books, *La Coupe de cendres* (*The Cup of Ashes*), 1924, *Sylves* (*Little Poems*), 1927, and *Volumes* (*Scrolls*), 1928, were published locally in Madagascar in very small editions. These collections of short poems are still imitative of the melancholy Baudelaire

---

* Senghor's address to L'Académie Malgache (1961) in *Liberty One: Negritude and Humanism*, p. 320.

and later minor French poets, the "Fantaisistes." One of these poets was a French colonial official, Pierre Camo, much older than Rabéarivelo, who became his great friend and literary mentor. Camo lived ten years in Madagascar, and his influence as a cultural leader extended to the French community on Mauritius as well. It was Camo's encouragement that gradually weaned Rabéarivelo from the "maudlin self-centeredness" of his early poetry to a mature style more strongly expressing his own inner world. The later volumes, *Near Dreams, Translated from the Night,* and *Chants pour Abéone (Songs for Abéone),* 1937, are considered by critics to contain the Malagasy poet's finest work. Here, abandoning imitative rhymes and meter in favor of free verse, Rabéarivelo had mastered a sense of form and created dreamlike poems of strange and compelling imagery, drawn from his own fantasies as well as from a Malagasy culture foreign to Western readers. Rabéarivelo's originality lies in the skillful blending of these elements. "Like his favorite French poet, Baudelaire," Ulli Beier writes, "Rabéarivelo had a disgust of reality. His poems destroy reality, building out of its fragments a new mythical world."

Vieilles chansons des pays d'Imerina (Old Songs of Imerina Land), published in 1939 after the poet's death, is quite different in form and language from Rabéarivelo's other work. These are French renderings of traditional Malagasy *hain-teny,* formal love poems which are sometimes dialogues, sometimes monologues. Rabéarivelo also wrote poems directly in Hova, and sometimes translated into that musical Malagasy tongue poems he had originally written in French.

Rabéarivelo stands apart from other African poets in this volume. There are no "negritude" themes in his work, nothing of the shared awareness of a larger racial past. He was not concerned with social or political themes. He was deeply enamored of French and other Western cultures and the links they provided to civilizations other than his own. Toward the end of his life, however, he became interested in exploring and preserving the Malagasy past. He began to conceive of this as his major artistic goal, although he did not live long enough to accomplish it.

Rabéarivelo was certainly a victim of the colonial situation as much as a beneficiary of it. The paradox was that the Western culture he had acquired with such effort and assimilated with such brilliance dazzled him with the riches of the wider world and at the same time continually denied him real access to its bounties, leaving him imprisoned on his island. He was a solitary, tormented person whose struggles with the real world were as much internal as external. In the end, they became overwhelming. The spectacular gesture of his suicide became both the poet's only way out and his most violent form of protest against endless poverty and humiliation. Rabéarivelo poisoned himself on June 22, 1937, leaving a number of unpublished manuscripts, among them a play on Malgagasy themes and an eighteen-hundred-page journal, *Les Calepins bleus* (*Blue Notebooks*), in which the last entry records his final moments of agony.

It is ironic that Rabéarivelo's increasing despair and sense of isolation should lead him finally to suicide in the same year that, unknown to him, Damas, Senghor, and Césaire were launching, with *L'Etudiant noir,* a new literary community that posthumously would include him. Within ten years of his death, he would rank as a leading poet in both the movement's key anthologies, Damas's and Senghor's.

Rabéarivelo merits more extended scholarly and critical study than he has yet received either in the French- or English-speaking world. Except for a preliminary selection of *Twenty-Four Poems,** a short (and still untranslated) book on the poet's life by Robert Boudry, and a handful of critical articles and appearances in anthologies, Rabéarivelo's work is scarcely known outside his island.

Our selections from Rabéarivelo's poems are in new translations from the French texts. "Reading" introduces the hidden world in which the poet lives. Books are for him "a forest humming with silence" into which he sees himself fleeing like a bird, who will be held captive by forest mysteries and "made to sing or weep." "Your Work" and selections 4, 5, and 7 from his *Translated from the Night* are cast as inner debates about the artist and his work. The motif of the poet as a bird occurs again in selection 4, with its allusions to three poets: the Indian, Rabindranath Tagore; the American, Walt Whitman; and the Frenchman, Francis Jammes, whom he wishes to emulate. These almost autobiographical poems, with their dream of being read and understood someday with the same intensity that Rabéarivelo himself had read his beloved Baudelaire, underline their author's wish for artistic immortality. They are completely unlike the selections from *Near Dawn* or numbers 1, 2, 3, and 6 of *Translated from the Night,* which are surrealistic visions of mysterious beauty, bits of a fantasy world created in the poet's imagination. These poems truly do "rustle with what is unreal/ unreal from being too real/

* Translated by Gerald Moore and Ulli Beier (Ibadan, Nigeria: Mbari Press, 1962). Distributed in the United States by Northwestern University Press.

like dreams." The unforgettable Rabéarivelo is he who writes of "Cactus" as a "multitude of melted hands," of "she whose eyes are the prisms of sleep," of the strange black spider which casts its webs across the sky, or the peculiar tree that emerges from mud, twisting its roots toward subterranean waters and its branches high, suddenly becoming a person who shares the poet's bed. As an ensemble these poems seem, like the image in the final selection, to be towers made of words, constructed in some nether world "beneath the wind" and above the water.

Finally, we offer two of Rabéarivelo's re-creations of *Old Songs of Imerina Land*.

FOUR POEMS FROM *Near Dawn*

Reading

Make no sound, do not speak:
   eyes, heart, mind, dreams
   are about to explore a forest.

A secret but tangible forest.

A forest humming with silence
   into which the bird to be ensnared
   has fled,
   the bird to be ensnared
   who will be made to sing
   or weep.

To whom will it make him sing,
For whom will it make him weep,
   the place in which he comes to life?

Forest. Bird.
   Bird hidden
   in your hands.

Three Dawns

Daybreak

Have you already seen the dawn
   poaching in night's orchard?
   Here she comes homeward from the East
   on pathways overgrown with iris;
   she's all stained with milk
   like those children of old raised by heifers;
   her hands, carrying a torch,
   are blue and black
   like the lips of a girl
   munching grapes.

One by one, the birds she has ensnared
   escape, and fly before her.

Another Daybreak

Whether the first call came
   from East or West no one knows;
   but now,
   from hills suffused with stars
   and shafts of darkness,
   roosters sound the roll,
   blowing into conch shells
   and echoing from everywhere
   until he-who-went-to-sleep-in-the-ocean
   returns, and the lark rises to meet him
   singing
   songs drenched in dew.

Another

Melted in the crucible of time
   then frozen in the sea
   the stars become a gem of many facets.
   The lapidary night, ever so reluctantly
   expiring, feels its millstones crumbling,

crumbling like ashes in the wind
as lovingly they carve the prism,

A luminous slab
the artist would set
above his invisible tomb.

Cactus

This multitude of melted hands
still offering flowers to the blue,
this multitude of hands without fingers
that the wind can't move:
hidden water rises in their seamless palms,
I'm told, to satisfy the thirst of
a thousand cattle
and the nomad tribes
that wander to the limits of the South.

Hands without fingers sprung from streams,
Melted hands that stand against the blue.

Here,
when the City's flanks were still as green
as moonlight leaping in the forests,
when goats still grazed the hills of Iarive,
it was on the steep forbidding rocks
they stood to guard their source,
these lepers decked in flowers.

Penetrate the grotto that they spring from
to know the sickness that afflicts them
—its origin more nebulous than night,
more distant than the dawn—
but you will know no more than I:
blood from the earth, sweat from the stone,
and sperm from the wind
have run together in these palms,
dissolved their fingers
and set golden flowers in their place.

I know a child
    a prince still in God's realm
    who'd add:
    "And Destiny, taking pity on these lepers
    told them to plant flowers
    and to keep their sources
    far from cruel men."

Your Work

"You have done nothing but listen to songs.
    You have done nothing but sing,
    you have not listened to other men speak
    nor have you spoken.
"What books have you read
    but those preserving female voices
    and things that are unreal?
"You have sung, but not spoken,
    you have not sought the heart of things
    and cannot know them,"
    say the orators and scribes
    who laugh to see you magnify
    the daily miracle of sea and sky.
But still you sing
    and wonder at the ship
    that finds a path unmarked
    on the slack water
    and travels toward some unknown bay.
You wonder at the bird your eyes trace
    across the desert of the sky
    who never strays but finds
    within the wind
    the pathway to his woodland home.
. . . The books you write
    will rustle with what's unreal,
    unreal from being too real
    like dreams.

SEVEN POEMS FROM *Translated from the Night*

1.

What invisible rat
come from the walls of night
gnaws at the milky cake of moon?
Tomorrow morning
when he's gone
there will be bleeding marks of teeth.
Tomorrow morning
those who spent the whole night drinking,
leaving chips and cards behind
to glimpse the moon
will mumble:
Whose coin is this
rolling on the gaming table?
Oh, one of them will answer,
it belongs to the fellow who lost everything
and killed himself!
Staggering, all of them will snicker
and fall.
The moon will be there no longer.
The rat will have pulled her into his hole.

2.

There you are
standing straight and bare!
You are mud and you remember it;
but truly you were born of the parturient darkness
that feasts on lunar lactogen;
slowly then the trunk in you took shape
above this little wall that dreams of flowers clear
and the scent of waning summer.

To feel, to think that roots sprout from your feet
and run and twist like thirsty serpents

toward some subterranean stream,
or fix themselves in sand
and bind you to it even now,
you, O living,
unknown, unassimilated tree,
who swell with fruits that you yourself will gather.

Your summit
of hair tousled by the wind
conceals a nest of insubstantial birds
and when you come to share my bed
and I recognize you, O my errant brother,
your touch, your breathing, and the odor of your skin
will rouse the sound of mystic wings
until we cross the border into sleep.

3.

Here is
she whose eyes are the prisms of sleep,
whose eyelids are heavy with dreams,
whose feet are sunk into the sea,
and whose sticky hands emerge
full of corals and blocks of sparkling salt.

She will put them into little piles
near a foggy bay
and dole them out to naked sailors
whose tongues have been cut out
until the rain begins to fall.

Then she will be visible no longer,
only her hair scattered by the wind
unwinding like a reel of seaweed
and perhaps as well some tasteless specks of salt.

4.

You delude yourself,
you who look like a little bird
lost in the snowy forest that reaches to
the chest of Tagore, Whitman, Jammes,
who take the place of Christ beside your bed.
For it is not the world's antiquity
nor that of the several times millennial day
here stroking his beard,
thick and white as oblivion,
as hope, and the mist of steamy mornings;
there, atop all mountains
an astrologer questioning the stars
and drawing on his earthen pipe;
it is the world's youth, my child,
its eternal youth:
metamorphosed
(thanks perhaps to the song of your
favorite poets
who create your religion
in this endless silence
inhabited by rivers and by pillars
by the living and the dead),
it is merely the shadow of all the past
listening only to the lonely present.

5.

One day some young poet
will make your impossible wish come true
by knowing your books,
books as rare as flowers underground,
written for a hundred friends,
not for one, nor for a thousand.

In the gulf of darkness where he reads you over
lighted only by his heart

in which yours beats once more
he will not believe
that you are in the peaceful surge
that always fills abysses without sunlight
or in the sand or the red earth
or underneath the lichen-covered rocks
that will stretch behind him
as far as the land of the living
blind and deaf since Genesis.
He will lift his head
and think it's in the blue
amid the stars and winds
your tomb must be.

6.

Slowly
like a crippled cow
or a powerful hamstrung bull
a fat black spider emerges from the earth,
creeps along the walls,
strenuously vaults above the trees,

tossing threads into the wind, rising,
weaving a cloth that touches the sky
spreading nets across the blue.

Where are the multicolored birds?
Where are the poets of the sun?
—The glimmers pulsing from eyes
dead with sleep in viny swings
echo and revive their dreams.
This evanescence of fireflies
becomes a host of stars
to counteract the cobweb trap
a leaping calf will sunder with his horns.

7.

You built yourself a tower in the wind,
then you crouched upon the water,
O faceless queen
whose pointed crown
challenges what-will-be-rain,
whose misty diamonds
are made of stars and naught but stars.

O beautiful soul of that-which-changes,
O sister and daughter in turn
of this moon new born
at the edge of an orchard,
you have built beneath the wind
and you live upon the water
like my dreams of wisdom!

What would it do to us,
the sudden fall of all that is our kingdom?

Like your tower, like mine,
like the traitress our feet trample,
this joy that makes our eyes sparkle—
if it soon must be extinguished
will it not return to us
in a new and different form?

FOUR POEMS FROM *Old Songs of Imerina Land*

Imaginary tremolo.
The daughter had come to meet me
When her parents took the notion to prevent it.
I spoke soft words to her.
She did not answer.
You will grow old there, you and remorse:
We and love
Shall go home to our house.

Thursdays for he-who-has-good-fortune,
Fridays for he-who-has-a-sweetheart.
Bring me strong tobacco
To chew as a digestive;
Bring me gentle sayings
That I may root my life in them.
Let come what may.
If my father and my mother must die
I must find an amulet to bring back life;
If my love and I must part
May the earth and sky be joined.

The wife of another, O my elder brother,
Is like a tree that grows by a ravine,
The more one shakes it, the more it takes root,
Take her at night, take her in the evening,
Only he who takes her
May have her altogether.

Poor blue water lilies:
All year long up to their neck in tears,
Blades of water grass,
Reeds, rushes, ponds dragged by canoes,
Give me sanctuary, I am so unfortunate!
Steal a bit of love for me: I am another's.
Delight in your wife.
He who has no pepper
Takes no delight in eating.
He who loses his fishing net
Will have nothing to fry.
And I, if I lose you
Will lose my nearest kinsman.

XVIII

Close by, to the north, there were two oranges: one was ripe, the other so beautiful it made one happy. I gave the ripe fruit to the Cherished One and the one-so-beautiful-as-to-bring-happiness to the Beloved. But I cherish the one and truly love the other in vain. If either had a passion to subdue me, I would not know what to do.

XLVII

—May I come in? May I come in?
—Who is there? Who is it?
—It is I, the first-born of my mother and my father.
—The first-born of his mother and his father. The one who wears brightly colored clothes and carries high his head? The one who hops into his shoes and goes to lie inside his litter? In that case, come in, young man: the calf is neatly tied, and my father and my mother are away. But if you're seeking robes as fine as wings of dragonfly or locust, look elsewhere. And if you come for short-lived love, I'd rather give you up before than after.

LVII

A wife is like a blade of grass: she stands upon her feet but is easily withered. A husband is like a clump of seaweed: he flourishes in water but is easily shredded.
—Young man, how many loves have you?
—I have hardly any, cousin, for they are only seven: the first, who cuts my fingernails; the second, who takes over for the one who stays at home when we go out; the third, who replaces the second in emergencies; the fourth, who follows me with longing eyes when I depart; the fifth, who comes to meet me when I return; the sixth, who nourishes my life as much as rice; the seventh, who doesn't mix with the crowd, and even if she does, always manages to make herself distinguished.

Rondo for the Poet's Children

What will our father bring to us
from his trip tomorrow?

—Solafo am I, therefore a new sprout,
a young shoot from the foot of a tree:
I wish for a new shoot of reeds
with thick honey inside.

—Sahondra am I, therefore a flower,
a flower taller than the grass:
I wish for flowers in a wreath
to set upon my hair.

—Vohangy am I, therefore, coral beads,
fat pearls of coral:
I wish for crimson coral
to string along the necklace of my name.

—Our father will bring a young shoot
rolled within coral-red clusters.

Jacques Rabémananjara

JACQUES RABÉMANANJARA PAID A HEAVY PERSONAL price for his country's freedom. He spent almost ten years in French colonial prisons, and later was exiled to France for his alleged role in a 1947 uprising in Madagascar. In the late 1950s, his personal cause and the vigor of the patriotic poems written from his prison cell excited such emotion on the part of black students in Paris that for a time Senghor, Césaire, and Rabémananjara (instead of Damas) were touted as negritude's major triumvirate. When the first public edition of Rabémananjara's *Antsa* (*Song*—a Malagasy word) appeared in France in 1956, it was a political more than a literary event. François Mauriac wrote in a preface, "This cry that love and pain have torn from a son of Madagascar [are testimony that] it is liberty and not oppression that nations learn from us, in spite of us." Mauriac's "brother in Christ," as he described Rabémananjara, was finally freed that year in a general amnesty for political prisoners, but exiled to Paris. Until his return to Madagascar in 1960, when he was named Minister of Economic Affairs (and more recently Foreign Minister) of the new Malagasy Republic, Rabémananjara worked with his Senegalese friend Alioune Diop at *Présence Africaine* and the Société Africaine de Culture.

Rabémananjara was born in 1913, in a town on the Bay of Antongil, legendary landing place of his Southeast Asian ancestors, the earliest known settlers of Madagascar. Until he was twelve, the boy had a traditional education directed by his maternal grandfather, who was of the Betsimisaraka tribe. Through him, Rabémananjara learned the cult of his ancestors, the history of his family and his people, and tales and legends extolling the exploits of *railovy,* the family's totem bird. Later he attended missionary schools.

After leaving school, Rabémananjara went to work as a clerk in the colonial service. He became an organizer of the first union of Malagasy civil servants, and in his early twenties became a co-founder of *La Revue des Jeunes de Madagascar* (*The Young People's Magazine of Madagascar*). The nationalist sentiments of this magazine were considered so daring, however, that soon no one would print it, and the young editors had to cease publication. Rabéarivelo took an interest in the young firebrand, who was twelve years his junior. When Rabéarivelo died, he named Rabémananjara his literary executor. "I pass the torch to you," he wrote. "Hold it very high!"

In 1939 Rabémananjara obtained a part-time job in Paris with a French cabinet minister, at the same time studying for a degree in literature at the Sorbonne. There he met and fell in love with the German poet and translator Erica de Bary. De Bary became the heroine of his *Rites millénaires* (*Thousand-Year Rites*), 1942, love poems written during his early years in France. It was Erica de Bary who, many years later, would translate Rabémananjara's *Song* and *Lamba* into German.

Before going to France, Rabémananjara already had completed several manuscripts of poems, including *Les Marches du soir* (*The Steps of Evening*), inspired by youthful romanticism and subjects of Malagasy history, published in Madagascar in 1940. He had finished an ambitious verse play, *Les Dieux Malgaches* (*The Malagasy Gods*), later published in Paris, which imitated the classical style of Racine. Caught in France by the advent of World War II, Rabémananjara remained to finish his studies. Before the war ended, he married a young Frenchwoman, to whom his cantata-like love poem, *Lyre à sept cordes* (*Seven-Stringed Lyre*) is dedicated.

It was during the war years in France that Rabémananjara became close to the negritude school, and particularly to Alioune Diop, whose family later offered great comfort and support to Rabémananjara's wife and eldest daughter while he was in prison. Rabémananjara is the only Malagasy writer and intellectual to have actively allied himself with negritude and, since his years in France, to have conceived his work as being connected with its ideas. Although he recognized that the racial and cultural origins of his people were far more Asian than African, Rabémananjara found natural affinities with the new movement. His countrymen were feeling the same desire for self-determination in government as any black West Indian or African. And, as darker-skinned colonial peoples, they met the same prejudices and had the same need to affirm and find acceptance for their own cultural identity. Certainly Rabémananjara felt too that the destiny of Madagascar would inevitably remain closer to that of continental Africa, particularly to the French-speaking nations, than to Asia.

Returning to Madagascar with his family soon after the war, Rabémananjara began organizing a group of young intellectuals to discuss and disseminate the new ideas. In 1946 the French government invited colonial territories to elect representatives to the French National Assembly. Rabémananjara led the formation of a new political party in his native land, campaigned vigorously, and in November 1946 won an election making him one of three Malagasy deputies to Paris.

Only a few months later, in March 1947, four hundred Malagasy revolutionaries attacked a French military installation, and in several towns, government buildings were set on fire. A hundred and fifty French citizens were killed. There is evidence that Rabémananjara's *Mouvement démocratique de Rénovation Malgache* party had nothing to do with the insurrection, and indeed had made efforts to prevent it, but he and his party were immediately implicated. A severe repression followed. According to official French figures, eighty thousand Madagascans were killed or wounded. The MDRM leaders, including the three new deputies, were summarily accused, arrested, and in some cases tortured. Like several other leading Madagascans, Rabémananjara was threatened with death. The French suspected that Rabémananjara himself had given the order of revolt. The new deputy was presented a piece of paper and asked if he would like to make his will. Protesting his innocence, he saved the paper, and later wrote on it a highly original kind of testament: the poem *Song.* Months later the manuscript was found beneath the mattress in his cell by a guard. Miraculously, he received permission to send it to friends in Paris, who circulated it privately. The "Malagasy affair" became a *cause célèbre.* Rabémananjara's friends did everything they could to save him from a miscarriage of justice. Nonetheless, he was tried, found guilty, and, in October 1948, sentenced to life imprisonment at hard labor.

Song, written in May 1947 during Rabémananjara's eighteen-month detention before his trial, is only the first of a steady stream of poems, plays, letters, and essays he was to write as an "antidote" to the poisonous atmosphere of his confinement.

In her study of Rabémananjara, Eliane de Schutter describes *Song* as "the pact that unites the hero with his people . . . a promise to his country . . . whose eroticism takes on legendary dimensions, uniting a poet-god with an island-woman." This vision of homeland as a passionately desired woman is not new with Rabémananjara, or in African poetry. Senghor's "Naked Woman, Black Woman" is another good example. But *Lamba,* a still untranslated meditation on Malagasy sources, written three years later and considered, with *Song,* as Rabémananjara's best work, has an even more pronounced eroticism, blending images of carnal and patriotic passion. *Lamba* was also published by *Présence Africaine* the year of Rabémananjara's release, while *Antidote,* collected shorter poems he wrote from prison, did not appear in print until 1961. Rabémananjara is also the author of two plays, *Les Boutriers de l'aurore* (*The Mariners of Dawn*), 1957, and *Agape des dieux: tragédie malgache* (*Feasts of the Gods, or Tritriva*), published in 1957 and 1962.

Today, in his sixties, Jacques Rabémananjara is foreign minister of an African republic whose population is close to five million. He has made eloquent contributions to several international conferences of black artists and writers, and written two studies of Madagascan affairs, *Témoignage malgache et colonialisme* (*Malagasy Experience and Colonialism*), 1956, and *Nationalisme et problèmes malgaches* (*Nationalism and Malagasy Problems*), 1958. As Rabéarivelo's literary executor, he provided a sensitive preface to new editions of *Near Dawn* and *Translated from the Night,* which were reissued in Madagascar in 1961.

FROM *Antidote*

Lament

Blue, so blue that eye of sky
   beyond the pane.
Life blooms between my lashes,
the whole sky within my lids,
blue so blue that eye of sky
   beyond the pane.

Gloom, such gloom in these four walls.
Death saturates this earth and stone
with an otherworldly dampness . . .
Fresh, so fresh the children shouting
   in the grass.

But who, bright innocence, will hear it?
   Your song, too pure,
   your voice, too gentle
in the tumult of the night.

The blind force of hell
   draws the sharp sound of agony
   with his whip.
Sensitive to pain, the skin
bleeds at the cord's hard kiss.

Stars die without a gasp.
What hand raised at the horizon
will tender the red offering to dawn,
to heroes' lips?

I have shed no blood,
I have sown no death,
my hands are pure as springtime,
my heart as new as the sacred Host.

But who, chaste warrior; will hear it?
   Your voice, too pure,
   your song, too sweet
In the croaking shadows.

Blue, so blue this eye of sky
   beyond the bars.
Fresh, so fresh the children shouting
   in the grass.

Life blooms between my lashes,
the whole sky within my lids,
innocence in the creases of my soul. . . .

FROM *Lamba* (excerpt)

   In hermetic enclosure
   cool clitoris of the corolla

knob hard and velvet from caresses
lavished before the ecstasy
by mysterious seraphic fingers
by hurricane hands
with artful strategy
encircling refusal's last refuge
the unicolor fortress
where the flag of pride
snaps in the night wind.

Nosy Lava Prison
September 1950

Song (excerpts)

Isle!
Island of the syllables of flame!
Never was your name
dearer to my soul!
Island
never sweeter to my heart!
Island of the syllables of flame,
Madagascar!

. . . .

I shall stretch myself
upon your breast
with the heat of your most ardent
and most faithful lover,
Madagascar!

. . . .

They
who spit in my face,
who dragged your royal name and mine
in the mud and excrement of their tongue,
my innocence will burst their skulls
with the violence and the rolling fire

of penultimate thunder
at the summit of Mangabe!

. . . .

I salute you, Island!
In the confines of my torment,
I adore you!

My right hand
brandishes your beauty
to the stars,
Madagascar!

. . . .

From the summit of the mountains
the blind shadow of the Lie
falls and spreads across the plain.

Curse the iniquitous idol
whose impetuosity has
destroyed the young and growing things,
the yellowing of corn!

. . . .

Weep, Madagascar, weep!
Grief has stuck its dagger
in the bosom of our race!

. . . .

The anguish will pass
as the storms of the millennia have passed
that gnawed upon the eight bones
of your birth,
noble offspring of the waters.

Your grace is daughter to the storms.
Your strength is sister to the hurricanes.
Your totem, the eagle, friend of the lightning,
Madagascar!

Island,
you will endure,
your sleep scarce interrupted,

your goddess-like sleep,
calmly
stretched against the arm of time
in your bed of seaweed and of sea spray.

. . . .

Your destiny
foreseen since the beginning
will spring forth from the darkness,
Madagascar!

. . . .

O magnificent rebirth of Dawn,
whose eyes will countenance your splendors?
who will sing your nameless glory?

. . . .

One word, Island,
Island of the syllables of flame!

This word, Island,
and you tremble,
this word, Ocean,
and you leap!

Word of our desires,
word of our imprisonment,
of our lamentation,
shining
in the tears of widows,
in the eyes of mothers
and proud orphans,
taking seed
in the flowers of the tombs,
in the insomnias and the unyielding pride of captives!

Island of my Ancestors,
This word is my salvation.
This word is my message,
sounding in the wind from the highest height.

One word:
from the zenith of its flight a rapturous

Papanga dives
Whistling to the ears of the four dimensions:
Freedom! Freedom! Freedom! Freedom!

Antanimora Prison
Tananarive, Madagascar
May 1947

MADAGASCAR (1914–)

Flavien Ranaivo

FLAVIEN RANAIVO, A THIRD CONTEMPORARY MADAGAScan poet, is Minister of Information in the Malagasy government. He has published three books of poems: *L'Ombre et le vent* (*The Darkness and the Wind*), 1947, *Mes Chansons de toujours* (*My Songs of Forever*), 1955, and *Le Retour au bercail* (*Return to the Fold*), the last with a preface by Léopold Senghor.

While composed in French, Ranaivo's poems are always close to the native Malagasy *hain-teny* already briefly described in the notes on Rabéarivelo (page 225). This folk poetry, in the form of dialogues or disputations, has its own traditional rules and style in the Malagasy languages. Léopold Senghor has written of Ranaivo that he "enlarges rather than breaks the confines of the *hain-teny*. He introduces drama, above all his own drama, to the heart of his poems." Essentially a love poet, Ranaivo, Senghor says, conserves the characteristic melancholy of the Malagasy people, building his poems with "image-symbols that have mysterious correspondences" while omitting, as much as possible, "the useless ornament of such wordy tools as articles, pronouns, conjunctions." From this, Senghor observes, comes the "density" of Ranaivo's style, which is "sprinkled with antitheses, parallelisms, asymmetries, transpositions, ellipses and syllepses: a thrifty, vivid style, full of surprises."

Like Rabéarivelo, Ranaivo works independently of West Indian and African influences outside of Malagasy culture. Nor is there any trace of European literary influence in his poems.

Ranaivo's originality, Lilyan Kesteloot points out, is to have turned his back on French literature and "made himself a pupil of the popular poets of his land." What talent it must take, writes Professor Kesteloot, to translate into French the genius of a language and a culture as distant from Descartes and Racine as it is possible to be. She notes, too, that Ranaivo's poetry reveals how much closer Malagasy culture is to Asia than to Africa.

FOUR POEMS FROM *Return to the Fold*

Carry Me

Carry me
O these feet of mine,
Carry me there
To where the road meets
The road that's overhung
With leaves both thick and moving:
It is a long time since I have seen
My father and my mother.

The Humped Ox

His lips move ceaselessly
But they neither swell nor wear out;
His teeth are two handsome rows of coral;
His horns form a circle
That never closes;
His eyes: immense pearls that gleam in the night;
His hump is a mountain of abundance;
His tail strikes the air
But is only half a fly-whisk;
His body is a well-filled coffer
Held up by four withered stalks.

Choice

—Who is she whose-feet-go-clattering-the-hard-ground?
—The daughter of the new chief-of-thousand.
—If it is the daughter of the chief-of-thousand

tell her soon the night will fall
and that I will exchange love red as coral
for a hint of friendship.

—Who is she-who-comes-from-the-north?
—The sister of the widow-with-the-jamerose-perfume.
—Tell her to come in without delay,
I will prepare her something good to eat.
—She will not taste it, if I know her:
she takes only rice water
not because she is thirsty
but capricious about you.

Distress

—Ohé, long-haired beauty!

—Who goes there?

—I am the one cursed by my father, cursed by
my mother; though small I'm dressed in silk;
though taciturn, my thinking is profound; though
easily chilled I am amber from the sun; being
sensitive, I am sentimental all the more;
a wanderer, though supple is my gait.

—The water cowrie is tiny too, young man;
but many oxen are its victims.
Silent is a glance and yet how eloquent.
As for me I like a bronze skin best,
it gives more warmth.
Nostalgia has a sweetness too
but not from he-who-rubs-his-nose-in-it.
So sink, young man, collapse!
Go founder in your dreams.
Tomorrow's sunrise will be rather late
for I and pining
will be gone
tonight.

TWO POEMS FROM *The Darkness and the Wind*

The Common Lover's Song

Do not love me, cousin,
like a shadow
for shadows vanish with the evening
and I would keep you with me
all night long;
or like pepper
which makes the belly hot
for then I couldn't
satisfy my hunger;
or like a pillow
for then we'd be together
while we're sleeping
but hardly see each other
once it's day;
or like rice
for once swallowed
you think no more of it:
or like sweet words
for they evaporate;
or like honey
sweet enough but all too common.
Love me like a lovely dream,
your life at night,
my hope by day;
like the silver coin
I keep close on earth
and on the great voyage,
a faithful companion;
like a calabash,
intact, for drawing water
in pieces, bridges for my lute.

Old Merina Theme

Plants grow
driven by their roots
and driven by my love I come to you.

At the top of the great trees, my dear,
the bird completes his flight.
My journeys are not done until I'm close to you.

The cascades of Farahantsana tumble, tumble.
They fall, they fall but do not break.

My love for you, my dear,
like water on the sand.
I wait for it to sink, it rises.

Two loves sprang up together
like two twins.
Misfortune to the first who is untrue.

Farewell, my dear, farewell,
careless love may fool the eye,
uncertain love brings madness.

Uncertain love, my dear,
like mist upon the pond.
There's much of it, but not to hold,
for mist upon the pond, my dear,
flirts and then is gone
while avoko flowers
settle 'round the fields.

A chicken snatched by the papango, dear,
and carried high grows lonely
far, far from his love.

Morning memories benumb,
daytime memories tire,
evening memories are delicious,
don't you think, my darling?

The two of us, my dear:
a speck of sand caught in the eye
a tiny thing, but dazing!

The two of us, my dear:
clay accumulating bit by bit
that grows into a house of brick.

Hurry, hurry then
my love,
or night will overtake you.

My limbs will break,
my eyes see dimly,
tell them I can do no more.

Let twilight cover up the earth—
my heart is in eternal moonlight.
Come then to my side.

> They'll scold at home.
> my elder sister says I mustn't go with you,
> but I don't mind her.

> I love, but can do nothing.
> I love, but am afraid.
> I'll come, but you come with me, dear.

> The door is closed, my dear,
> you come too late, my love,
> they'll scold me.

Open up, I'll tell you secrets—
open up, so we can talk,
open up, I love you!

> The door is closed, my darling,
> but my heart is open.
> so do come in: I love you, cousin.

Is the door not made of reeds, my love,
that you close it with a key?
Open up to me, I'm tired of waiting.

Edouard J. Maunick

EDOUARD MAUNICK COMES FROM A VOLCANIC DOT 720 miles square that lies west of Madagascar, midway between Africa and India. Settled early in the eighteenth century by the French, who established its importance in sugar production with the aid of slaves imported from the East African mainland, Mauritius, like Madagascar, was a haunt of pirates who preyed on the European trade routes to Asia. In 1810 the British occupied the island, making it a naval base. By 1834, with the Negro slave trade outlawed, Indian laborers were recruited to work the plantations. Mauritius remained a British colony until independence in 1967. For more than two hundred years, however, within its population of half a million it has kept a large community whose strongest ties of language and culture are to metropolitan France.

Edouard Maunick is a mixture of the French, African, and Indian strains that make up his island homeland. He was related to a prominent French family, but illegitimately. Neither his schoolmates nor his professors let him forget either this fact, or that of his color.

Maunick taught school for several years after graduating from the lycée, and before leaving the island published a book of verse, *Ces Oiseaux de sang* (*These Birds of Blood*), probably around 1955. He saved for years to pay his passage to France. Once there, his charm, good looks, and speaking voice landed him a job with the French Overseas Radio Service, where he is now a producer. Also on the staff was a young Frenchwoman, Jacqueline, who became Maunick's wife and who figures under the name of Neige (Snow) in all the poems he has written since.

Settling in Paris when he was in his late twenties, Maunick was drawn to the by now long-established circle of black West Indian and African intellectuals whose hub was *Présence Africaine*. Like so many others before him, Maunick found a good friend in Alioune Diop. He got to know Césaire, Senghor, and the other leading black writers in

Paris. It seems doubtful that Maunick had known a great deal about this group before moving to Paris. He recalls, for example, that when *Présence* put out his highly praised poems *Les Manèges de la mer* (*Carrousels of the Sea*) in 1964, with its manifesto-like declaration *"J'ai choisi d'être nègre"* ("I have chosen to be black"), his relatives in Mauritius wrote him in surprise, "Since when are you black?"

Several years later, Maunick was named among the ten best "new French poets of the 1960s" by a leading Parisian literary supplement. As the only poet of foreign extraction, it was his turn to chuckle. "So now I'm a *French* poet!" He remembers all too well being but rarely graced with the "purity" of that national distinction in his colonial homeland. To carry the irony further, Maunick, as a Mauritian, for a long time was actually a British subject. Though from a French-speaking community, he traveled, until independence, on a British passport.

Unlike most of the African poets in this volume, and unlike his Madagascan neighbors, Edouard Maunick did not have a childhood steeped in some ancient ethnic culture, preserving its own language, religion, or oral traditions. He has not been preoccupied with striking a balance between two different ways of life or making a synthesis of opposing cultures. Maunick has been obsessed with a search for roots, with a need to discover who he is, where he belongs. As a poet he is heir to no Imerina Land, no Edenic childhood, no ancestral tales told nightly by the fire. Rather, as Pierre Emmanuel puts it, Maunick "has been nourished on the sap of all our modern poetry, from symbolism to surrealism, as well as on the . . . often bitter sap peculiar to our time."

Two books of poems have established Maunick's reputation, *Carrousels of the Sea* and *Mascaret, ou Le Livre de la mer et de la mort* (*Tidal Wave, or The Book of Death and the Sea*), 1966. As the French poet and critic Pierre Emmanuel writes in a preface to the former, "The fact of having mixed blood, which the poet analyzes first for himself and thereby for us . . . is not only a question of color, but of the mind and the soul. One must read this poem as an enigma. . . . If it does not deliver itself easily, this is because its ambivalence is sometimes so painful as to make the poet himself hesitate." We are fortunate in being able to reprint from *Poetry* magazine Carolyn Kizer's translation of "Seven Sides and Seven Syllables." Although the phonic quality of the English version is very different from the French—the original verses have a musical sonority peculiar to French—Miss Kizer accomplishes the difficult technical feat of duplicating the seven-syllable lines with which Maunick composed his poem. His powerful imagery is intact, along with the challenging syntax. Pierre Emmanuel wrote that the love story between Maunick and the language of his poem duplicates an actual love story, that of a man in search of his race, and of a man discovering the woman he will love. The themes are continued in Maunick's *Tidal Wave,* from which we include "This Strange Calculation of Roots," in Teo Savory's translation from the *Unicorn Journal,* Spring, 1968.

"As Far as Yoruba Land," which appeared in *Présence Africaine* (No. 55, 1965), is Maunick's prose-and-poetry account of a visit he had made in Nigeria with Wole Soyinka and Ulli Beier to the sacred place of the Yoruba goddess Oshun. Our version is a new translation and abridgment of the French text.

The experience of a high holy place of African religion had a profound effect on Maunick. Face to face with an ancient African culture, he felt as much moved as a Christian might at the holy places of Jerusalem. He knows that Ofatedo, like Gethsemane, the prehistoric caves of Lascaux, or the ruins at Stonehenge, is among the holy places of all mankind. Having been there, having "made the gestures of the sacred place," the poet finds he can "clothe the Bible now with [his] whole self," instead of just with part of it.

The final poem has never before appeared in print. It was written by Maunick for an American friend after a curious incident at the Dakar Festival, in April 1966. His friend had been getting acquainted with another American woman and her little boy at the tourist market. The boy, a beautiful child of about five or six, had been playing tiger, and growling, "Watch out! Watch out! I'm gonna eat you up!" Maunick's friend, who was white, answered in surprise, "Hey, that's what the tiger said to Sambo! And he said, 'Oh, please, Mister Tiger, don't eat me up, and I'll give you my fine green umbrella! . . .'" Suddenly the boy's mother, who was black, turned on the other woman and gave her a furious tongue-lashing. Hearing the word "Sambo," she thought the stranger had meant to insult her child.

Maunick's friend was stunned. There was nothing she could do or say to stop the woman's onslaught, no way to explain she had only been recalling the story of a small brave boy who outwits four ferocious tigers. Retreating as fast as she could and finding her husband and Maunick, she burst into uncontrollable sobs trying to explain what had happened. Maunick was much moved. The following evening he gave her the poem that concludes this volume.

FROM *Carrousels of the Sea*

Seven Sides and Seven Syllables

for Aimé Césaire and Pierre Emmanuel

I

happen you come on your own
to this contradicted place
recelebrate ebony
the original metal

> happen you essay the dream
> before you outlive yourself
> before the blood surges back
> before your father expires

this land once was a mirror
which was silvered by the sea
in the sweat of oars, islands
with keys girded up their loins

> good fortune surrounded us
> in no way surprising us
> if we wager on the sea
> for the last possible time

but what can be the last time
for the deracinated?
again, those who oppose him
share the flesh of the poet

> unaware, he keeps going
> not heeding all the mad ways
> all countries merge dizzily
> in this country of his own

II

my love is improbable
let the saliva well up

neutrality, its token
skimming the garden of birth

> here the roses are roses
> sword-lilies prohibited
> a man who speaks standing up
> has his eyes bandaged with rain

we all take powerful root
on assassination day
with the garden's iron pickets
stained bright by the equinox

> here a man who speaks standing
> is submerged in the symbol:
> I say rose and it means hope
> but who will live by this game?

who will take up sword-lilies
in their form of machetes
to knot up with blood once more
what survives as a mongrel?

> the whole world I name garden
> I leave no place unbaptized
> who will plant garden fences
> if not I, or my kinfolk?

I, the child of all races
soul of India, Europe,
my identity branded
in the cry of Mozambique

III

> thus I am anonymous
> while holding the heritage
> of your ancestral truncheons
> and your black man's evasions

I could accept your labels
and stay unidentified

be tattooed by your numbers
while remaining uncounted

       command all your battlements
       cloak myself in your panic
       recognizing the thunder
       and recognizing the wind

know the substance of exile:
on the sea, wind and thunder
recognizing all roots
of the tree that rejects me

       recognizing all the roots
       tongue-ties me with bereavement
       on the shores of denial
       I will choose to be Negro

I've read Senghor and Césaire
and Guillén and Richard Wright
but Lorca and St. John Perse
Dylan Thomas and Cadou

       Paul Eluard, vertical
       all reinvent memory
       you step out of the mirror
       to marry morning with night

IV

rising in me, the promise:
my mouth will spit bitterness
to crack the rejecting rock
at the end of all stanzas

       utterance moves toward a place
       where snow, thunder cohabit
       of words fouled by long weeping
       of visions searing the skin

with desires pure and bitter
tumultuous silences
I here spell out my poem
releasing my love of you

withholding what must be said
dividing my blood from blood
inhabiting somewhere else
than the habitable space

exile is no easy thing
despite obscure boundaries
open doors and living hands
no, it is never easy!

to accept is to refuse
refusal reveals anger
fling open your registers!
bring your mortal crucifix!

I swear to understand flesh
transparent as lake water
I shall murder ancient seas
set fire to their slave cargoes

V

CHRIST, but the odor of chains
and this rattling of metal
against the defeated bones
these quincunxes of ropes!

I can force my eyes to see
but the sight is too tragic:
dogs trained to attack the blacks
and their spirituals stabbed

yes, to watch the capsizing
of woman and child voices
whose offense is vertical
because they refuse to crawl

is this Christmas and manger?
are these our poems pure white?
are these our poems deep black?
this the summation of poems?

VI

what right have I to denounce
while shooting with your own guns?
or healing with your own hands?
I freeze and starve for us all

if I could find a kingdom
between midday and midnight
I would go forth and proclaim
my mixed blood to the core

for I choose the you-in-me
without color or passport
they say we all long for God
and we are all forgiven

VII

happen you come on your own
to this contradicted place
to embrace the bitter dream
of the solar boundaries

discover the point of light
which is the true equator
having no need of the sea
to conceal your departures

happen you come without wrath
to this place of denial
open your eyes to the rain
lave the body till it splits

at last, for a final time
adjust your steps to the steps
of the sole presence in you:
a man the size of a man

my love may only exist
when endorsed by your absence
I no longer need the past
to stand up in the present

the carrousels of the sea
are not mad carrousels now
I had to silence my fate
with this, my derisive voice.

—Translated by Carolyn Kizer

As Far as Yoruba Land (excerpts)

Where does this poem come from?

Nigeria, the town of Oshogbo, toward noon, or shortly afterward. I had driven there at breakneck speed with Wole Soyinka. It was he who taught me the meaning of Ofatedo, which we had crossed coming from Ibadan; "The place where bow and arrow rest," he uttered between two steps on the gas. I jotted it down on the corner of an envelope. Was I already persuaded Ofatedo would nourish a poem? Perhaps!

Reaching Oshogbo, Ulli Beier did the honors of the place. He took me to the temple of Oshun, which had had a real restoration because of a revival of the local people's faith. They had learned to mold cement. Using and abusing forms, colors, and above all their faith, to bring the sacred serpent back to life, once more they had succeeded at envisioning an invisible God.

Ulli Beier kept talking: he was explaining every ikon, every pattern in the wall that protected the temple. He was initiating me into the secrets of Oshun's worship. She had promised the victorious warrior from Ibokin to watch over the kingdom of Oshogbo if he would agree to build his palace not where the shrine is, but a little farther away on the hillside. She also persuaded him to come feed the fish of the river nearby once every year. He had held out his hands to receive the first fish, and his name was born: Ataoja. I listened, astonished. The silence of dead leaves, the vertical trees, the bareness of their roots, the water stark and stiff under the weight of branches sleeping between life and death, the statues and the patterns "strange as belief in God," the wall, paradoxically enlarging the sacred space, and Ulli Beier, the Westerner who had altered his identity, all this took me far away. Very far, to my native island, Mauritius (*stella clavisque meris indici*), to the Black River there, kingdom of the African *mestizos*, "the Mozambiques" as they are called, fishermen who live close to the fish, accomplices of the sea and dancers of the Sega. It carried me back to when I was baptized, "my Christian name uttered against time, my head bowed over bowl of stone, unexpected Jordan." And further still, to Gethsemane, to the other garden. My head began to swim. I yielded to the warning vertigo. The poem was shooting its first bullets. . . .

Now that it is written, peace is back . . . the reverse of "the brutal game of knowledge and of doubt." I am from everywhere, from the rational and Christian West, from India contemplative and igneous, from Africa animistic and louder than a judgment voice: I have written this poem.

My birth has traced me all the way to Yoruba Land, challenging the world beyond to the point of trial: I yielded to temptation but did not fall.

Where does this poem come from and when?

From deep within me, the vulnerable noontime of a man in search of a love he dreams of giving others in order to live himself a little: "I am not *of* the game, I *am* the game."

As far as Yoruba Land, my contradiction, my wealth.

I.

Point no scornful finger at Yoruba Land
just call the stranger to the witness stand
he set out upon the journey
anxiously
his testimony interacts with memory
for Oshogbo liberates the past
like a woman sowing seeds with her right hand.

Oshogbo town
a nowhere place
without the place of Oshun
Goddess-line-of-Life.

III.

I have mentioned it by name
Oshun's place
its kneeling river
—did you know the water breathes
because it's fed on branches

aged by many deaths?—
I have named the place of Oshun
its wall that contradicts all walls
—I entered saying sesames
as simple as surprise—
I have mentioned it by name
Oshun's place
but not its cryptogramic trees
whose genesis is lost.

IV.

This is where the warrior from Ibokun came
oh do not speak of war
for life comes after weapons
when the entrails are exhausted
from hammering against the night
do not speak of war.

I have seized the bows
filling the quivers with images and proverbs
this is where the king stretched out his hands
to receive the fish
this is where they named him
Ataoja
the one who came from Ibokun.

V.

The trees were forbidden me
because they'd lost their genesis
—doubtless they were high priests
who installed Oshun before the solitude,
before the sacramental time—
their bark retains the secret
perhaps they were watchmen, forgotten
fulfilled, who looked on Oshun
before the ikon
before the dancing
was it to teach me of the blood?

VI.

For there is an African virtue of the tree
that Strangers share by way of baptism
—this time it seemed familiar
another noon but known already—
a poem copied over
a brand new spouting
how old then is the traveler
not as ancient as his name
but as old as all the gods he's not
the temples
the initiations
and all the faces in the crowd.

VII.

I made the motions of the sacred place
the visible baptism
and was touched by the touchable water
one day you may imitate the gesture
proclaim a name
as living as green leaf
at the edge of an earth
equally made flesh
equally as promised
I had rushed the season
by some thirty years, yes, thirty-three
had we all been battered by the selfsame storm?

VIII.

Accept from me not silence
or the tom-tom talk you like
to say this name I'll pilfer all my proverbs
a way of being Negro with no accent
in words that scorch the skin
carrying the gangrene
the very ancient theme
whose undertow

describes the estuary
this place expected me to make a new beginning
I crossed Ofatedo
the town where bow and arrow rest.

IX.

Ofatedo
seek it out upon the skin of Africa
find it glued there on the belly of the world
see it on the face of man
expand his hugeness into poetry
his first reality, his fortune
Ofatedo is well worth Elsinore
and all words swollen with temptation
in Ofatedo at least the silence of the weapons.

X.

I am from everywhere
I had to be from Oshogbo
and all the kingdoms dead or living
this wall makes boundaries boundless
it bears the trace of men
as strange as man's belief in God

I've understood nothing
I have lived through everything
I speak of this dark share
that continued to survive
of this survival equal to the oracles
I visited Oshun
and found my piety adulterous.

XIV.

Speaking of Gethsemane in Yoruba Land
is to go beyond the difficult
I sent my memory back through the forbidden trees

to the other garden
without the noisy throng
my eyes on Oshun
came without anger
to unravel quest on quest
I was free to walk
neither back nor forward
but with the action of a blade
to clothe the Bible now with my whole self.

XVI.

I have understood nothing
I have lived everything
and it is difficult to relate
but I hunger so to speak
will the word come at the end of the line?
will the psalm be sung in good voice?
will the poem be able to cheat
in me, among you, royally cheat?
The answer lies here between Oshun and me
between me and my baptism
a bastard, of mixed blood, to the very end;
I dare pronounce the hard hard word.

XVIII.

And I have chosen the sea as no man's land
but see how every shore every land
is a fidelity to try
I say I am not *of* the game I *am* the game
how is the weather with you
who do not know my alterations
my seasons my danced prayers
what weight of bread will you place on the table
what weight of rice what weight of water
for I shall eat among you and I shall be thirsty
send for the sorcerer
and let him show our blood is brotherly.

XIX.

Enter in the circle
I've a hand to spare for each of you
the mask is dead from having waited
point no scornful finger at Yoruba Land
I'm the only witness on the witness stand
I journeyed there in anguish
in search of lost beginnings
Oshun stood upon my path
I made the motions of her sacred place
my entrails are still throbbing
from holding off too long from the prayer that is a dance
enter in the circle
let us begin the trial again.

FROM *Tidal Wave, or The Book of Death and the Sea*

This Strange Calculation of Roots

just as fear never kills
but keeps death alive
and becomes fear of dying
like fear I am threatening
from my deep vigilance of life

and making poetry more watchful than ever

writing point-blank
without playing dead
polishing words that they may not age
returning from exile
all that can sing
unsealing the darkness
without mercy

the voyage is the dream in reverse
it is enough to lay hands on the blood
(the soul's twin accomplice)
that has hunted us down in our flesh

enough to watch without blinking
the work of unrest

living is also speaking
I hold my voice in reserve
so that I need not be wounded
more than my share
grief is an old story

identity is proof of the grandeur of man
today I shall break the mirror of race
I shall bury my graves
and pack up my sea gear

it is up to you now to carry my dead
to escort my ships
to aggravate the silence
I have grown tired of turning back

.   .   .   .

I shall go elsewhere to find myself
here is the snow over Bethlehem
                    the rain over Timbuktu

you say host
I say hostage
transhumance
replies to transsubstance

passion is long
and knows no end

this evening I stand
facing all wars

I waited for you in this place
performing your gestures
using abusing your sky

now it is my epidermis
I have chased your angels
with blows of *séga*

49. The *séga*: Danced in Mauritius by the African population.

I dance my prayers
my loins speak for me

I abandon none of my signs
you have torn them away before me
but my age is greater than yours

I am the age of exodus
my belly's fear
is millenary
my flowers my fetishes
throw shadows on your jewels

let the ring fall
it has an ancient resonance
I am lost between crozier and stave

when is the moment for the exact division of our goods

I am hurrying to take back my images
to carve me a madness
stronger than despair
this is believing
and this is earning

if you need a likeness
for denouncing the ruler
it will not be gold
or stone
or mud
or wood
but the likeness of man
who breathes and bleeds

I do not know how the star was lit
in deep snow over Bethlehem
I do not know nor wish to know
already the hour strikes inside my flesh
as if grace had changed her plans
that I might
desert myself

after putting myself to the sack
I wanted her to come toward me

the game of fear begins again for me
more terrible than the game of death
I had washed the fate-lines
from my hands
here they are captured by solitude
cold now no longer belonging
to the perhaps the possible the probable
will I be able to be the witness I must be

what have I made of living
but to reach for life

my riches are here
speak among you the word of connivance
heaping word upon word
announcing the celebration

I come from overseas
my language is equal to the voyage
it rejects shipwreck
declares itself incendiary
dreams of beating you in open dialogue

my poem is sand in the hourglass
it falls before falling
understanding nothing knowing nothing
otherwise magic makes magic

it dies from time
as we die in the end
but in magic itself is the durable fire
defying me to say NO
I sail toward you
my words the riding lights

it is empty to say
I have chosen this sorcery
to cross out the sign of fear
I am sailing toward you
in spite of your scuttled moorings

death will have no key to my city
just because you refuse to hear
time listens for you
it knows I am naked
it knows I am rich
it knows that it knows

I know that someone will turn over the hourglass

—*Translated by Teo Savory*

Letter to Ellen Conroy Kennedy

There is the weight of the word
the bilingual semantic
the sea opened my mouth
on a certain morning immemorial
and here I stand
to shred my birth certificate
and laugh the negro laugh
over name and passport.

But sometimes I remember
and accept
the vocabulary game
the endless trial of black and white
where is my shore
the rightful place
   to land
   to stand
to christen my bastard *manèges*
now that I have burnt the letters of wrath
and made of violence the prayer
and no more the cry
sea is the sole navel
the only possible race. . . .

You spoke of Sambo
to the black boy

and his mother was caught
in the web of ancient insult
and you wept red tears
red as the rods now rusted
but still flogging
and you were flogged in the mother's pain

The byword is despair
sign and symbol of
a terrible divide
the war of words
the war of roots and branches
lies heavy in a stranger's mouth
despite her uncontrary mind
the sea has landed
with bitterness its baggage
and because you marched on Washington
you wept and wept
in Africa. . . .

And because I know why you wept
I write you in the middle of another night
of my intimate dispute
my belief and my doubt
my wish to pay the debt
of blood and skin
my pariah's memory of the future

Your tears began a ritual
a baptismal rite
like blows that once were rained on me
and still ache
even as I stroll along the Seine
in the true white land
even as I laugh the negro laugh
Do not wipe your eyes
the salt must survive
to keep us living with a love for all.

Detect the vigilance in what I say
not the reason spare the instinct

remember that you walked in Washington
forget the dagger of birth through the entrails
and let the cradle rock
the child Sambo
is still the right weapon
a weapon like a tree
it will live it will grow it will last.

Dakar, 1966

Notes on the Translators

SAMUEL ALLEN, the frequently anthologized black poet and essayist, is the editor of a new book, *Poems from Africa. Ivory Tusks,* a book of his early poems, was translated into German by Janheinz Jahn. As an undergraduate at Fisk, Allen studied writing under the late James Weldon Johnson. Later, in Paris, he came to know Richard Wright, Alioune Diop, and the *Présence Africaine* group. Samuel Allen is also a Harvard-trained lawyer, and before retiring several years ago to teach and write, he held high posts in Washington with the United States Information Agency and the Department of Justice. He travels and lectures widely, and taught African and Afro-American literature at Tuskegee, Duke, and Wesleyan, before settling in Massachusetts to teach at Boston University.

JOHN PEALE BISHOP (1892–1944) was born in the South, attended Princeton University, lived in Paris among the American literary expatriates during the 1920s, and later settled in Connecticut. Bishop's "poems, fiction, and essays often reflect the conflict between his Southern background and the larger work in which he lived," writes Hayden Carruth. Bishop's translation of a poem by the Haitian Emile Roumer first appeared in Dudley Fitts's anthology of Latin-American poets. His *Collected Poems* was edited by Allen Tate in 1948.

CLAYTON ESHLEMAN, born and educated in Indiana, has lived in Mexico, Japan, and Peru. He began editing and publishing his own quarterly, *Caterpillar,* in New York in 1967. Prose and poetry from the first four years were collected in *A Caterpillar Anthology* in 1971, before his move to Sherman Oaks, California, where Mr. Eshleman continues to publish his magazine. He teaches at the new California Institute of the Arts. His books of poems are *Bearings* (Santa Barbara; Capricorn Press, 1971) and *Altars* (Black Sparrow Press, Los Angeles, 1971). He has translated works by Pablo Neruda, César Vallejo, and Antonin Artaud, as well as Aimé Césaire.

JESSIE REDMOND FAUSET was literary and managing editor of the NAACP magazine, *The Crisis,* for a number of years when W. E. B. DuBois was editor. She came from a prominent New York Negro family and taught high-school French. In the late 1920s and early 1930s she published four novels that dealt primly and genteelly with middle-class Negro life. Yet Mrs. Fauset personally championed writers of the Harlem Renaissance such as Hughes and McKay, whose literary tastes were rather distant from her own.

LANGSTON HUGHES (1902–1967), whose reputation continues to grow, was a much-loved poet, novelist, humorist, essayist, anthologist, and writer of children's books. His poems, *The Weary Blues* (1926), were only the first step in the longest, most sustained, varied, and prolific writing career of any author of the Harlem Renaissance/New Negro generation. In 1966, the year before his death, Hughes was an honored guest and participant at the First World Festival of Negro Arts in Dakar.

DENIS KELLY teaches at St. Mary's College in Moraga, California. He became interested in Aimé Césaire in the early 1960s while a student at the Sorbonne, and only later began to collaborate with Clayton Eshleman on "a few" translations. Césaire "was such an interesting, difficult, exciting and at times exasperating poet," he writes, "that we kept on until we finished a book."

CAROLYN KIZER has long been interested in the art of literary translation, and has rendered poems from the Chinese as well as from the French. As founder and for seven years editor of *Poetry Northwest,* she offered an annual prize in translation. In 1964–1965 she was Poet-in-Residence in Pakistan under the auspices of the Department of State. On her return home, she moved from Seattle to Washington, D.C., to become the first director of literary programs for the newly established National Endowment of the Arts. She has written three books of poetry: *Knock upon Silence, The Ungrateful Garden,* and *Midnight Was My Cry.* She now lives in Chapel Hill, North Carolina.

PAULETTE J. TROUT, co-translator and selector of many African poems in this volume, is the author of a study of Stendhal published in France. She has contributed articles and reviews on African authors to *Africa Report* and *Journal of the New Africa Literature and the Arts,* and wrote a preface to the American edition of Senghor's *Nocturnes.* Mrs. Trout has taught at Yale and Columbia universities and now lives in Cambridge, Massachusetts.

TEO SAVORY lives in Santa Barbara, California, where she edits *The Unicorn Journal,* a quarterly. She has been a television scriptwriter, a play-editor for ANTA, has published four novels and two volumes of poetry, and has translated the French poets Corbière, Jammes, Prévert, Superville, Guillevic, and Michaux as well as the Indian Ocean poet Edouard Maunick.

EDNA WORTHLEY UNDERWOOD edited and translated a book entitled *The Poets of Haiti 1792–1934,* published by the Mosher Press of Portland, Maine. Earlier, she had collected and translated poems from Russian and other Slavic languages.

Bibliography

In the fresh perspective of the 1970s, with "black studies" rapidly developing —and implicitly international, multi-lingual and polycultural in scope—writings by black authors in French are increasingly translated into English. In literature, for the present, the need is to retrieve important and long-neglected works rather more than to keep up to date on new authors and new works. Many writers long out of print in French are reappearing in new editions, Jacques Roumain for one. Landmark works like Senghor's *Anthologie de la nouvelle poésie nègre et malgache* (1948), Damas's *Pigments* (1937), and Césaire's *Les Armes miraculeuses* (1946) have recently been reprinted. For libraries and researchers, the German scholar Janheinz Jahn is collecting and bringing back into print several of the rare and often unobtainable little magazines that played so vital a role in black cultural life.

Though always haphazardly, translations follow not far behind. René Maran's *Batouala* has just appeared in a new American edition (Rockville, Md.: Black Orpheus Press, 1972), its third translation since the novel's Goncourt Prize in 1921. Likewise, Aimé Césaire's *Cahier d'un retour au pays natal* is currently in print in two English translations, to which our new abridged version adds a third. Notable gaps still exist, but one hopes enterprising publishers will soon be filling them. A serious history and criticism of this literature is developing, too, and these factors combine to make any bibliography dated almost upon publication.

Still, some kind of reader's guide to further exploration of the negritude poets, related works, and authors seems a necessity. The present list is offered as a summary. Titles mentioned earlier in the volume are not necessarily repeated, since our focus here is primarily on poetry and criticism currently available in English and in translations. While space prohibits a survey of articles in periodicals, we do list the major specialized journals that regularly publish, translate, or review black French-language writings. All poets whose work is available to date in individual translated editions are listed, as well as the anthologies that include negritude poets, when possible with a descriptive note. A section of literary history and criticism covers the major offerings in

277

English at this writing. Finally, a short bibliography of bibliographies should be useful to those seeking access to the poetry in the original French editions, to a fuller listing of creative and critical work in genres other than poetry, to articles in periodicals, and to literatures of the Negro diaspora in English, Spanish, and Portuguese, as well as French.

ENGLISH TRANSLATIONS OF BLACK POETRY IN FRENCH

INDIVIDUAL WORKS

Césaire, Aimé. *Cadastre.* Bilingual edition. Poems translated by Emile Snyder and Sanford Upson. New York: The Third Press, 1973. 141 pages.

———. *Cahier d'un retour au pays natal (Memorandum on My Martinique).* Bilingual edition, French and English on facing pages, preceded by "Un grand poète noir" by André Breton, with translations by Lionel Abel and Ivan Goll. New York: Brentano's, 1947. 158 pages.

———. *Return to My Native Land (Cahier d'un retour au pays natal).* First bilingual edition of definitive text as established in revised edition of 1956. Reprinted 1960. English version adapted by Emile Snyder from 1947 translation by Ivan Goll and Lionel Abel. Paris: Présence Africaine, 1968. 141 pages.

———. *Return to My Native Land.* Translated by John Berger and Anna Bostock, with introduction by Mazisi Kunene. Baltimore, Md.: Penguin Books, 1969. 95 pages.

———. *State of the Union.* Translated from the French by Clayton Eshleman and Denis Kelly. Bloomington, Indiana: Caterpillar, 1966. 39 pages (mimeographed) from *Les Armes Miraculeuses, Cadastre,* and *Ferrements.*

Diop, David. "Ten Poems," in new translations by Paulette J. Trout and Ellen Conroy Kennedy. Bilingual. *Journal of the New African Literature and the Arts,* Stanford, California, Spring and Fall 1968, pp. 28–49.

Rabéarivelo, Jean-Joseph. *Twenty-Four Poems* (translated from the French). Ibadan: Mbari, 1962. Distributed by Northwestern University Press.

Senghor, Léopold Sédar. *Nocturnes.* Translated by John Reed and Clive Wake, with introduction by Paulette J. Trout. New York: The Third Press, 1971. 60 pages.

———. *Prose and Poetry.* Edited and translated by John Reed and Clive Wake. New York: Oxford University Press (a Three Crowns Book), 1965. 182 pages.

———. *Selected Poems.* Translated and introduced by John Reed and Clive Wake. New York: Atheneum, 1964. 99 pages.

U Tam'si, Tchicaya. *Brush Fire* (translated from the French). Ibadan, Mbari: 1962. Distributed by Northwestern University Press.

———. *Selected Poems*. Introduced and translated by Gerald Moore. London: Heinemann Educational Books, 1970. 143 pages. Distributed by Humanities Press, New York.

ANTHOLOGIES:

Allen, Samuel W., ed. *Poems from Africa*. New York: Thomas Y. Crowell, 1973.

Bassir, Olumbe, ed. *An Anthology of West African Verse*. Ibadan: Ibadan University Press, 1957. 68 pages. Includes four poems by David Diop, one poem by Birago Diop, and four by Léopold Senghor in translations by Bassir and Margaret Peatman.

Collins, Marie, ed. *Black Poets in French: a Collection of Caribbean and African Poets*. New York: Scribners, 1972.

Fitts, Dudley. *Anthology of Contemporary Latin-American Poetry*. Norfolk, Conn.: New Directions, 1942. Includes translations of several Haitian poets; Pressoir, Roumain, Roumer, presented bilingually on facing pages.

Hughes, Langston. *Poems from Black Africa*. Bloomington, Ind.: Indiana University Press, 1963. 160 pages. Includes fifteen poems by six French-language African poets: Rabéarivelo, Ranaivo, U Tam'si, Lumumba, Senghor, David Diop, in translations by Hughes, Miriam Koshland, Ulli Beier, E. S. Yntema.

Lomax, Alan, and Raoul Abdul, eds. *Three Thousand Years of Black Poetry*. New York: Dodd, Mead and Co., 1970. 261 pages. Includes twenty-six poems by eighteen black French-language poets, mostly in familiar translations reprinted from other sources.

Moore, Gerald, and Ulli Beier, eds. *Modern Poetry from Africa*. Baltimore, Md: Penguin Books, 1963. Revised edition 1968. 268 pages. Excellent introduction by the editors. The 1968 edition includes translations of poems by thirteen French-language African poets.

Reed, John, and Clive Wake, eds. *A Book of African Verse*. With introduction and notes. London: Heinemann Educational Books, 1964. 119 pages. Includes twenty-seven poems by eight French-language African poets: Dadié, David Diop, Birago Diop, Rabéarivelo, Rabémananjara, Roumain, Senghor, Sinda in translations by the editors.

———. *French African Verse: An Anthology from French-speaking Africa*. With translations. London: Heinemann Educational Books, 1972.

Shapiro, Norman R., ed. *Négritude: Black Poetry from Africa and the Caribbean*. In French with English translation, introduced by Wilfred Cartey. New York: October House, 1970.

Underwood, Edna Worthley, ed. *The Poets of Haiti 1792–1934*. Portland, Me.: The Mosher Press, 1934. An anthology in poor-to-fair English translations, one hundred thirty selections by forty-eight poets, now nearly forty years out of date.

Wake, Clive, ed. *An Anthology of African and Malagasy Poetry in French*. New York: Oxford University Press (A Three Crowns Book), 1965. 182 pages. Notes and introduction in English, poems in French text only.

Wolitz, Seth L. *Black Poetry of the French Antilles: Haiti, Martinique, Guadeloupe, Guiana*. In English translation. Berkeley, Calif. Fybate Lecture Notes, 1968.

HISTORY AND CRITICISM OF BLACK POETRY IN FRENCH

Africa Seen by American Negro Scholars. Paris: Présence Africaine, 1958; second edition, 1963. Distributed by American Society of African Culture, New York City. 418 pages.

Includes essays by Samuel W. Allen and Mercer Cook.

Ba, Sylvia Washington. *The Concept of Negritude in the Poetry of Léopold Sédar Senghor*. Princeton, N.J.: Princeton University Press, 1973.

Baldwin, James. *Nobody Knows My Name*. New York: Dell, 1961.

Especially "Princes and Powers," pages 24–54, a lively and penetrating report on the Conference of Negro-African Writers and Artists, September 1956, in Paris.

Beier, Ulli, ed. *Introduction to African Literature: An Anthology of Critical Writings from* Black Orpheus. Evanston, Ill.: Northwestern University Press, 1967.

Important articles from the Nigerian magazine on the poetry of Césaire, Rabéarivelo, Senghor, U Tam'si, among others.

Bigsby, C. W. E., ed. *The Black American Writer*. Volume I: Fiction, and Volume II: Poetry and Drama. Baltimore, Md.: Penguin Books, 1971.

Of special note in Volume II are J. P. Sartre's "Black Orpheus" and Gerald Moore's "Poetry of the Harlem Renaissance," the latter discussing influence on negritude poets and the new black American poets.

Cartey, Wilfred. *Black Images*, New York: Teachers' College Press, 1970. 186 pages.

A critical study of contemporary black poetry and the black man in white poetry from the 1920s to the 1950s, covering the United States, the Caribbean, and West Africa, with special emphasis on French- and Spanish-language writers.

———. *Whispers from a Continent: The Literature of Contemporary Black*

Africa. New York: Random House, 1969; Vintage edition, 1970. 397 pages.
  A critical survey, organized by theme, of contemporary novels and poetry
  by black writers in English and French from the Caribbean and West
  and Southern Africa. Needs an index.

Cook, Mercer. "African Voices of Protest." In Mercer Cook and Stephen E.
  Henderson, *The Militant Black Writer in Africa and the United States.*
  Madison, Wis.: University of Wisconsin Press, 1969.

———. *Five French Negro Authors.* Washington, D.C.: The Associates Pub-
  lishers, Inc., 1943. 164 pages. Indexed.
  See fine chapter on René Maran. Julien Raimond, Cyrille Bisette,
  Alexandre Dumas père, and Auguste Lacaussade, nineteenth-century
  writers from Haiti, Martinique, France, and Ile Réunion, are the other
  French-language writers whose lives and literary careers are reviewed in
  this book.

Drachler, Jacob, ed. *African Heritage: Intimate Views of Black Africans.*
  Preface by Melville Herskovitz. New York: Collier Books, 1964. 283 pages.
  A rich paperback anthology, including fine though sparse samplings in
  translation of prose and poetry by B. Diop, D. Diop, Maran, Dadie,
  Césaire, Senghor, and Camara Faye. Also Samuel Allen's "The Black
  Poet's Search for Identity."

Fanon, Frantz. *Black Skin, White Masks.* Translated by Charles Lam Mark-
  mann. New York: Grove Press, 1969. 232 pages.
  Fanon's first book, a psychological analysis of being black in the French
  world, includes perceptive discussion of the poetry, novels, and essays of
  Senghor, Césaire, Maran, and other black intellectuals of French culture.

Garret, Naomi M. *The Renaissance of Haitian Poetry.* Paris: Présence
  Africaine, 1963. 257 pages.
  The indispensable study of Haitian poetry, published several years after
  its acceptance as a doctoral dissertation at Columbia University. Helpful
  background material and good discussions of Durand, Coicou, Roumain,
  early Depestre, and other Haitian writers. Excellent bibliographies.

Jahn, Janheinz. *Muntu, The New African Culture.* Translated by Marjorie
  Greene. New York: Grove Press, 1961. 269 pages. Illustrated.
  Chapters 2, 7, and 8, on Haitian Voodoo, Literary History, and Conflict
  of Cultures are highly recommended, as are Jahn's illustrations. Excellent
  bibliography. The sweeping mystical and philosophical theories of African
  culture projected in the remainder of *Muntu,* however, are controversial
  and should be treated with caution.

———. *Neo-African Literature: A History of Black Writing.* Translated from
  the German by Oliver Coburn and Ursula Lehrburger. New York: Grove
  Press, 1968. 301 pages.
  This German scholar of the black literatures of Africa and the Americas

is the first to trace and to survey black or Negro literatures on a world-wide comparative basis. Chapters 11–16 are especially recommended.

Kesteloot, Lilyan. *Black Writers in French: A Literary History of Negritude.* Translated and with an introduction by Ellen Conroy Kennedy. Bibliography. Index. Illustrations. Philadelphia: Temple University Press, 1974. The pioneering historical and critical study of black poets in French covers the period to 1960, with special emphasis on origins of negritude, and discussion of early poetry of Damas, Césaire, and Senghor. Includes 1966 article "Problems of the literary critic in Africa."

———. *Intellectual Origins of the African Revolution.* Rockville, Md.: Black Orpheus Press, 1972. 128 pages.
This short book by the noted Belgian scholar, omitted in first draft from her longer pioneering work (see above), reviews and analyzes the role black poetry in French played over a thirty-year period in forging the new black awareness that led to African independence and decolonization. It is a translation of *Négritude et Situation Coloniale.*

Moore, Gerald, ed. *African Literature and the Universities.* Introduction by the editor. Ibadan: Ibadan University Press, 1965. 148 pages.
Well-edited transcript of papers and discussions at African writers' conferences in Dakar, Senegal, and Freetown, Sierra Leone, in the spring of 1963. Includes several fine papers (Moore on U Tam'si, Jahn on Rhythm and Style in African poetry, etc). The chapter "The Writers Speak" preserves the heat of the actual confrontation between writers of pro- and anti-negritude persuasion. Ends with remarks by Davidson Nicol.

———. *Seven African Writers.* London: Oxford University Press. 1962; reprinted, corrected and extended bibliography, 1966. 108 pages.
Good introduction, essays on Senghor, David Diop, and others.

Mphalele, Ezekiel. *The African Image.* New York: Praeger, 1962.
Discussions of negritude, black French-language poets, and black American writers are threaded through the early chapters of this partly autobiographical work of literary criticism by the noted black South African writer.

Pieterse, Cosmo, and Donald Munro. *Protest and Conflict in African Literature.* New York: Africana Publishing Co., 1969. 127 pages.
Articles by Moore, Wake, on black poetry in French.

Wauthier, Claude. *The Literature and Thought of Modern Africa: a Survey.* Translated by Shirley Kay. New York: Praeger, 1967. 323 pages. Indexed. Sweeping and impressive consideration of some 150 modern African authors from throughout the continent, first published in 1963. Though discussion of negritude poetry and thought has an important place, Wauthier covers economists, sociologists, historians, and ethnologists as well as creative writers.

PERIODICALS

Abbia, the Cameroon Cultural Review. B. P. 808, Yaounde, Cameroon. Published by the Minister of National Education, since 1963. Appears irregularly, several issues a year; articles in French and English.

African Arts/Arts d'Afrique. African Studies Center, University of California, Los Angeles. Four issues a year of which one is primarily devoted to literature. Articles in English and French.

African Forum (1965–1968), 401 Broadway, New York 10013. Quarterly review published by American Society of African Culture. Several issues were devoted primarily to literature.

African Literature Today: A Journal of Explanatory Criticism. Editor, Eldred Jones. Heinemann's Educational Books, 48 Charles St., London W.I. Since 1967. Formerly two issues yearly, now annual hardcover edition. Critical and interpretive articles. Edited in Freetown, Sierra Leone.

L'Afrique actuelle. Published by Olympe Bhêly-Quenum, 23, rue Barbet-de-Jouy, Paris 2^8. Monthly, bilingual.

L'Afrique littéraire et artistique. Société africaine d'edition, 32 rue de l'Echiquier, Paris 10^8. Creative work and criticism.

Black Orpheus. Editor, Abiola Irele. Mbari Publications, Ibadan, Nigeria. Published since 1957, with interruption during Biafra War. The oldest English-language literary magazine in Africa, it frequently publishes translations and/or reviews of black French-language authors.

Black World (formerly *Negro Digest*). Editor, Hoyt Fuller. Johnson Publications, Chicago, Illinois. Monthly.

Jeune Afrique. 51, Avenue des Ternes, Paris 17^8. Weekly.

Journal of the New African Literature and the Arts. Editor Joseph Okpaku, Third Press, 444 Central Park West, New York City. Biannually since 1966. Literature and criticism in English and French.

Légitime Défense. Single issue only, Paris, June 1931.

Présence Africaine, Cultural Review of the Black World. Since 1947. Editor, Alioune Diop, 25 bis, rue des Ecoles, Paris 5^8. Quarterly. A French-language journal which for a time printed separate English and French editions of each issue. Now has articles in French and English.

Présence Francophone, Sherbrooke, Quebec. Biannual. All French literatures. Started in 1970.

Research in African Literature. Editor, Bernth Lindfors. African and Afro-American Research Institute, University of Texas, Austin, Texas. Biannual. Since 1969.

Tropiques, Revue culturelle. Fort-de-France, Martinique. Nos. 1–9, April 1941–October 1943.

BIBLIOGRAPHIES

Amosu, M. *A Preliminary Bibliography of Creative African Writing in the European Languages*. Ibadan: Institute of African Studies, University of Ibadan, 1964.

Baratte, Thérèse. *Bibliographie des auteurs africains et malgaches de langue française*. 2nd edition. Paris: OCORA, 1968.

Cameron, J. M. *Pan Africanism and Négritude: A Bibliography*. Ibadan: Institute of African Studies, University of Ibadan, 1964.

Jahn, Janheinz. *A Bibliography of Neo-African Literature from Africa, America and the Caribbean*. New York: Praeger, 1965.

Jahn, Janheinz, and Claus Peter Dressler. *Bibliography of Creative African Writing*. Lichtenstein: Nendeln, 1971.

Lindfors, Bernth. "Additions and Corrections to Janheinz Jahn's *Bibliography of Neo-African Literature* (1965)" in *African Studies Bulletin*, Vol. II, No. 2, September 1968.

MacGaffey, Janet. "Selected Bibliography," an independent contribution to Kesteloot, *Black Writers in French*. Philadelphia: Temple University Press, 1974. Pages 367–89.

Mercier, R. "Bibliographie africaine et malgache." *Revue de littérature comparée*, Vol. 37, 1963.

Paricsy, Pal. "Selected International Bibliography of Negritude: 1960–1969." *Studies in Black Literature 1*, No. 1 (1970).

Ramsaran, J. *New Approaches to African Literature: A Guide to Negro-African Writing and Related Studies*. Ibadan: Ibadan University Press, 1965.

Zell, Hans, and Helene Silver, eds. *A Reader's Guide to African Literature*. New York: Africana Publishing Co., 1971.